"The sheriff says you don't exist."

Ellen's offhand comment zinged like a cattle prod. Kevin's jaw tightened. "I'm real enough. You checked my references."

"They only go back a few years. What did you do before?"

This was the time. All he had to do was open his mouth and let the truth spill out. *I'm Kyle. I've come to pay back my debt to you.*

But the truth would sting. So he turned away, peered into the night.

"I was in an accident," he started. The words stuck in his throat. "I spent a couple of years recovering."

"Why did you change your identity?"

Did she know? He glanced at her over his shoulder. Her gaze studied him. Did she see through his scars, through his deception? What would she do if he ran a finger along the curve of her cheek? Would she recognize the taste of his kiss?

Dear Harlequin Intrigue Reader,

We've got another explosive lineup of four thrilling titles for you this month. Like you'd expect anything less of Harlequin Intrigue—*the* line for breathtaking romantic suspense.

Sylvie Kurtz returns to east Texas in *Red Thunder Reckoning* to conclude her emotional story of the Makepeace brothers in her two-book FLESH AND BLOOD series. Dani Sinclair takes *Scarlet Vows* in the third title of our modern Gothic continuity, MORIAH'S LANDING. Next month you can catch Joanna Wayne's exciting series resolution in *Behind the Veil*.

The agents at Debra Webb's COLBY AGENCY are taking appointments this month—fortunately for one woman who's in serious jeopardy. But with a heartthrob Latino bodyguard for protection, it's uncertain who poses the most danger—the killer *or* her *Personal Protector*.

Finally, in a truly innovative story, Rita Herron brings us to NIGHTHAWK ISLAND. When one woman's hearing is restored by an experimental surgery, she's awakened to the sound of murder in *Silent Surrender*. But only one hardened detective believes her. And only he can guard her from certain death.

So don't forget to pick up all four for a complete reading experience. Enjoy!

Sincerely,

Denise O'Sullivan
Associate Senior Editor
Harlequin Intrigue

RED THUNDER
RECKONING
SYLVIE KURTZ

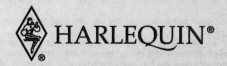

HARLEQUIN®

TORONTO • NEW YORK • LONDON
AMSTERDAM • PARIS • SYDNEY • HAMBURG
STOCKHOLM • ATHENS • TOKYO • MILAN • MADRID
PRAGUE • WARSAW • BUDAPEST • AUCKLAND

For Marci—
For all the phone calls, the emergency road service and
brainstorming—but mostly for the friendship.

ISBN 0-373-22657-8

RED THUNDER RECKONING

Copyright © 2002 by Sylvie L. Kurtz

ABOUT THE AUTHOR

Flying an eight-hour solo cross-country in a Piper Arrow with only the airplane's crackling radio and a large bag of M&M's for company, Sylvie Kurtz realized a pilot's life wasn't for her. The stories zooming in and out of her mind proved more entertaining than the flight itself. Not a quitter, she finished her pilot's course and earned her commercial license and instrument rating.

Since then, she has traded in her wings for a keyboard, where she lets her imagination soar to create fictional adventures that explore the power of love and the thrill of suspense. When not writing, she enjoys the outdoors with her husband and two children, quilt making, photography and reading whatever catches her interest.

You can write to Sylvie at P.O. Box 702, Milford, NH 03055. And visit her Web site at www.sylviekurtz.com.

Books by Sylvie Kurtz

HARLEQUIN INTRIGUE
527—ONE TEXAS NIGHT
575—BLACKMAILED BRIDE
600—ALYSSA AGAIN
653—REMEMBERING RED THUNDER*
657—RED THUNDER RECKONING*

*Flesh and Blood

All underlined places are fictitious.

CAST OF CHARACTERS

Kevin Ransom—He needs to make things right, not worse, so to help the woman he once loved earn a piece of her dream, he comes to her assistance pretending to be a stranger.

Ellen Paxton—To heal, she needs to be the voice of the broken horses who have come to her from a highway wreck. But when a drifter with a scarred face comes into her life, will she let him heal her heart?

Nina Rainwater—Kevin's "grandmother" gave him a second chance at life. Now her dying wish is for the son of her heart to find peace.

Chance Conover—He'll see that no one hurts Ellen again, especially not a drifter cowboy who reminds her of the past.

Taryn Conover—Ellen's friend sees through the scars both visible and invisible.

Garth Ramsey—Even behind bars, he seems to know just how to find Ellen's most tender scar.

Bradley Bancroft—He's used to winning and doesn't take no for an answer very well.

Tessa Bancroft—The trophy wife talks of protocol and data, but doesn't fit the part of horsewoman she seems to desire.

Dr. Silas Warner—He sold his soul years ago. What does he have to lose?

Dr. Lillian Harmon—Her discovery has unexpected side effects.

Vance Dalton—The judge holds the power over the horses Ellen hopes to save.

ELLEN'S EASY SPAGHETTI SAUCE

1 onion, diced
1 green pepper, seeded and diced
1 celery stalk, diced
1 garlic clove, minced
1 tbsp olive oil
1 28-oz can of crushed tomatoes
1 15-oz can of tomato sauce
1 14.5-oz can of diced tomatoes
1 6-oz can of tomato paste
2 tsp Italian seasoning
1/2 tsp crushed red pepper

Sauté vegetables and garlic in olive oil until onions are soft and transparent. Add crushed tomatoes, tomato sauce, diced tomatoes, tomato paste, Italian seasonings and crushed red pepper. Bring to boil, lower heat and simmer for twenty minutes.

This sauce can also be placed in a crockpot and slow cooked all day for an easy dinner after a long day at work. Leftovers freeze well.

Variation: Add one pound of browned hamburger, meatballs or a bag of soy crumbles to sauce, then simmer.

Prologue

"Not bad." Tessa Bancroft clicked the stopwatch as the black colt crossed the six-furlong mark. From beneath the protection of the covered stand her giddy delight galloped in time to the thunder of hooves making mud fly. Neither rain, nor mud, nor wind could slow him down. *Nothing.*

He was the one. Come November he would win the Texas Breeders' Cup championship for two-year-old colts. She had no doubt. The first true test was in less than a month—the Texas Stars Derby. He would make a splash.

And so would she.

Then next year she would go national. She could practically taste the mint juleps now.

"Best I've ever seen," said the trainer as he mopped rain from his face with a faded bandanna. "He's got heart, soul and guts. Come inside. I'll show you the training schedule for next week. I wish you'd reconsider and let me work him in the morning with the others."

"No, I don't want him seen until I'm ready." She wanted to take all those highbrow blue bloods by surprise. Teresa Vega was born in the gutter, but Tessa Bancroft belonged among the cream. When they saw him, when he won...

Sharp trumpets of terror blared from the television set

on the corner of the desk in the cramped barn office. The trainer reached for the knob. With a hand clawed around his wrist Tessa stopped him.

Spreading pools of blood, drumming spikes of rain and the fitful windmill of trapped equine legs filled the screen. Then the camera zoomed in on a pair of firemen opening the side of a trailer like a sardine can. A woman's hand soothed one of the horses jammed inside. The animal's eyes were wide with panic. Rain slicked its red mane against its neck. Blood ran in rivulets tracing pink worms on the white blaze on its face.

Horror crawled down her spine as she recognized the beast.

"On the outskirts of the small town of Gabenburg, northeast of Beaumont," a reporter said, "a horse-transport van overturned on the slick roads caused by to-day's torrential downpour and the near hurricane-strength winds blowing through the Gulf Coast region." The reporter's yellow slicker flapped in the wind, sending her careful hairdo into frenzied flight. Her eyes narrowed against the onslaught of rain and her grip tightened around the microphone. "The six horses trapped inside are still alive. Sheriff Conover, can you tell us how the rescue operation is going?"

Tessa swore and flicked down the volume. She didn't need this. Not so close to reaching her goal. No one could know about the project.

Without asking, she snagged the phone off its cradle and dialed. "Have you seen the news?"

"No," the voice hedged.

"Turn on your set. Now." She waited until she heard the report buzzing in the background. "Get out there and take care of that mess."

"I can't leave—"

"How *is* your dear Lillian?" She let the threat hang.

The time to call on ethics was long past. The good doctor had made his choice years ago. He could blame his choice on youth. He could blame it on mistaken idealism. But that did not alter the fact he was responsible for making the decision in the first place. No one had held a gun to his head. At least not then.

Now, well, sometimes people needed a reminder of their goals. She would use every weapon at her disposal to ensure he saw the project he'd started to its perfect completion—even his dying wife's welfare. "I want them back at the clinic *tonight*."

Chapter One

"What is this?" Nina Rainwater asked in disgust, flipping through channels and landing on the only one showing news. "A million channels and this is what I get? I'm in Colorado, how come I've got to listen to weather from Beaumont, Texas?"

"Satellite dish, Grandmother," Kevin Ransom said as he entered the hospice room. Nina looked out of place in the pink frill of the room. He'd always associated her with blue skies and green pastures, with the scent of sweet hay and the smoke of a wood fire—with undying energy.

She didn't look well this evening. Strands of hair, dull as a rainy November sky, poked out of her usually neat braid. Her brown eyes were listless and her breathing seemed more labored in spite of the tubes feeding her oxygen through her nose.

The mock disgust was for his benefit. She didn't want him to worry about her. But he couldn't help himself. She'd given him his life back after he'd thrown it away. He owed her more than gratitude, and now, when she needed him most, he was helpless again. "Sometimes you can't get local news with a satellite dish."

"Pah!" She pitched the remote and looked longingly at the sun starting to set outside her window. The bearberry flowers, pussytoes and columbines in the rock garden bordering the property swayed in the breeze.

"Want me to turn off the TV?" Kevin asked.

She shrugged.

Kevin reached for the remote—a mere five inches from where she'd launched it—and aimed the gadget at the television set on the roll cart at the foot of Nina's bed. He was about to press the power button when the image on the screen jumped straight out of his nightmare. It rose like a ghost from his past and laughed at him with satanic glee.

You can run as fast and as far as you want from trouble, but it will never let you forget.

He dreaded evenings when his mind had time to catch up with his body, prompting the assault of all he longed to forget. For sixteen years he'd lived a lie, trying to erase the mental picture of his brother's lifeless body ripped from his grasp on the Red Thunder's flood-swollen waters.

Like some punishment cursed upon him by a Greek god, Kent, Ellen and the accident on that awful evening visited him nightly, torturing him with all he'd lost.

The television screen showed a transport van filled with racehorses toppled on a rain-slicked highway outside a small East Texas town. As much as his life revolved around horses, it wasn't his equine brothers that held him entranced but the man swaddled in a black slicker trying to save them. Watching the sheriff on the screen was as if he were viewing his own face, had the rocks in the Red Thunder River not altered it all those years ago.

He couldn't breathe. He couldn't move. Blood roared in his ears. Thoughts tumbled through his mind like debris on a storm-tossed sea. It's the rain, he tried to convince himself. It made him think of the river, of that night.

It's not him. It can't be. Look, the name's different. Con-

*over, not Makepeace. And Beaumont is at least a hundred
miles from Ashbrook.*

Downriver, he reminded himself. The sharp cheekbones.
The hard eyes. The mantle of responsibility square on his
shoulders. Familiar. Could Kent have survived such a long
trek down the raging Red Thunder?

The face on the screen joined the haunted memories
preying on his mind, overlapping, morphing one into the
other, mocking him. Kent, Ellen, anger, so much anger.

"Pajackok? What's wrong?"

When Nina had found him his broken jaw had made
him unable to talk. She'd renamed him Pajackok, the Al-
gonquian word for thunder. She'd told him he was all
thunder and no lightning. Told him she'd help him find
his spark. He'd done his best to discourage her care but
she'd ignored him.

She still didn't know about Ellen, about his brother,
about the damage he'd done with one raw burst of anger.

Pajackok...Kevin Ransom. Both lies.

If he'd changed his name, maybe Kent had, too, and
given himself a second chance. Kent hadn't been happy in
Ashbrook but he'd been the responsible one, and those
self-imposed responsibilities had weighed him down and
cemented him into place. Would he have welcomed the
chance at freedom?

Could it be? Could Kevin have avoided all of this torture
if he'd just had the courage to face the consequences of
his actions? Was Kent alive?

"Pajackok?"

To reassure Nina, Kevin strained to find a smile. The
gesture was shallow and didn't linger long on his lips. The
spot of warmth on his heart for his adoptive grandmother
grew cold in the shade of guilt and shame from his mem-

ories. For Nina's sake he swallowed them back and forced another smile. "Nothing, Grandmother."

Despite her shortness of breath she laughed, shaking a finger at him. "Nothing translates to everything when you say it that way."

"Sometimes, I wish you weren't so good at reading my mind."

"Not your mind, Pajackok, your face."

He ran a hand over the scars that landscaped his cheeks like a dropped puzzle. The ugliness was his due.

"Are you going to tell me or am I going to have to guess?" she insisted on a wheeze.

"I'm worried about you."

She nodded and looked away. "I'm going home to-night."

"No, don't say that." Sitting on the edge of the bed he took her frail hand in his.

"It's time." Her eyes implored understanding. "This robe no longer fits. It's so heavy."

He didn't want to hear this, didn't want to lose her.

Her gaze once again sought the flowers swaying in the breeze, then searched the hills fading into darkness. "Take me to the ranch. I want to see the stars rising over the mountains."

"Grandmother…"

She tugged at the tubes dangling from her nose, then swept the room with a hand. "This is not my wish."

Dying, a stranger among strangers. He couldn't blame her. She'd wandered all of her life, picking up bits and pieces of Native American philosophy along the way. He wasn't sure what kind or if she even had any Indian blood. All he knew was that because of Nina he'd learned to make peace with most of his demons and had found a noble purpose in life. If she wanted to "shed her robe" watching the evening stars rise over the mountains, who was he to deny her her final wish?

"It's those damn cigarettes of yours." Gritting back a flash of anger, he strode to the closet and yanked her purple jacket off the hanger.

"Pah! Cigarettes, whiskey, demons. They all get you in the end. I've had a long walk on the good Red Road. I have no regrets. It's just the start of another circle, Pajackok."

"I know." She'd told him enough stories about life and circles and connections. Hanging on to her when she was in such pain was selfish. But he still needed her wisdom, still needed her friendship…still needed her love.

He supported her as they walked down the corridor, wheeling the oxygen bottle behind them. She greeted everyone with a smile. Despite his silent plea, no one tried to stop her. In his truck, he tucked a clean horse rug around her knees and switched the heat to high to keep her warm.

On the hill overlooking the grazing horses she'd raised, a peace he hadn't seen for months came over her face. In the moonlight the horses were nothing more than dark shapes, moving slowly to the rhythm of their hunger. She sat and motioned for him to join her.

"This is a good place," Nina said.

"You should have bought your own ranch years ago." He tucked the blanket around her knees and lifted the hood of her coat onto her head.

"I didn't feel the need." She stared at the sky as if it were a gazing ball. "Do the demons still visit you at night?"

Her question took him by surprise and he found the denial strangling in his throat. How could she possibly know about the demons?

"Honor me, son of my heart, by having the courage to

go back to your roots and heal your past. Only in that way will you find your peace.''

She was pulling all the strings she'd carefully lain over the years. Honor, discipline, connection, respect. They were the touchstones of her life, her guiding principles, and she'd quietly instilled them in him. He would give his own lungs to see her live, but he couldn't go back to Texas. Not with the memories of Kent and Ellen tearing him up inside. What could he say to either of them to make them understand the depth of his regret?

He shook his head. ''Grandmother, I honor you, b—''

''Good, I'm glad that's settled. I didn't want to go home until I was certain you would follow the right path.''

''The horses—''

''Stanley Black Bear will take care of them until you're ready to let go. When you do, he's promised to give you a good price for the ranch.''

''I couldn't sell this place.''

''Not today, but soon.''

He said nothing. Arguing with her was useless. She was too damn stubborn.

''I'm not leaving you.'' She placed a gnarled hand against her heart, then covered his own with it. A pulse of energy passed between them. ''Soon you will be my heart. I will be with you always in your heartbeat, in your son's heartbeat, in your daughter's heartbeat.''

She was wrong. For him there would be no son, no daughter. Once he'd shared dreams of a family with Ellen. They'd mapped out a whole future filled with horses and children…and love. But those dreams had died on the river sixteen years ago. The void stirred an eddy of sorrow in his heart.

Nina dug into the worn leather pouch she carried at her

waist and brought out what looked like a piece of bone. "This is for you."

He took the bone and saw Nina had carved and painted it into an eagle feather. On the upper right side she'd emblazoned a medicine wheel. "Protection from your demons until you can let them go."

"Grandmother..." He gazed at the feather-shaped stone in the palm of his hand and fought the burning itch scratching the back of his eyes. The feelings wound so tight inside him wouldn't form into thought, into words.

"Oh, look, Pajackok, the midnight star is here. Do you hear its song?"

He realized then that he didn't need to say anything. She already knew his heart better than he did. He sat by her and held her close. With her he watched the midnight star until she shed her robe.

Then, not knowing quite where the consciousness to do so had come from, he sang her spirit home.

THREE DAYS LATER, to honor Nina and all she'd done for him, Kevin headed south and east.

His brother was alive. He had to find him. He had to humble himself and ask for forgiveness. Only then could he stop working so hard at trying to forget the brother he thought he'd killed and the woman he'd loved too much.

"HE CAN'T DO THIS!" Ellen Paxton steamed her way to the sheriff's desk and slapped the letter down on the blotter. Black spots danced in front of her eyes, colors faded, shapes blurred. She blinked madly, trying to control the body doing its damnedest to remind her of her weakened state. "There wasn't even a hearing. I didn't get to speak for the horses."

And speaking for the horses had become her obsession.

She was shaking so badly that, when Chance eased her down into a chair, she couldn't fight him.

"Now take a deep breath," he said, "and start from the beginning."

Hanging on to the collar of Chance's tan uniform shirt she dragged in a breath and blew it out. Chance was the law in Gabenburg but he was also her friend. If he could help her, he would. "This guy shows up with a trailer and gives me this letter and insists on taking the horses back. They're nowhere near ready to leave."

Mentally and physically scarred, the half-dozen horses she'd rescued from the highway wreck were in no shape to travel anywhere. She'd used up a day's worth of energy sending Bancroft's errand boy on his way, but she wasn't stupid enough to think that would end the situation. The weight of that exhaustion finally caught up with her. Her hands fell back onto her lap. "What was the judge thinking?"

"Let me take a look," Chance said. He leaned his backside against the desk and read the letter.

A ceiling fan stirred the air-conditioned air, keeping the sheriff's office cool in spite of the June heat blazing outside. Fluorescent light poured from an overhead fixture, drenching the room in white. The muted sounds of radio chatter crackled from a unit behind Chance's desk. A wanted poster, along with half a dozen notices, were tacked on a corkboard above a bank of black file cabinets. Wire baskets and folders kept everything on the desk contained and neat.

The only thing in the room that added a touch of personality was the portrait of Chance's family. His wife, Taryn, and his daughter, Shauna, smiled at him from a quilt spread on the grass behind their home.

A pinch of jealousy tweaked at her heart but she brushed it aside. Chance deserved his happiness.

She'd once dreamed of raising horses and babies with her high-school sweetheart, but Kyle was dead, and she was relearning to live. Rubbing the heel of her hand on her chest, she erased the edge of sadness creeping around her heart. Her body's betrayal made babies unlikely. Besides, the horses were almost more than she could handle.

She glanced at her watch. She flipped her braid behind her back. She rubbed a hand on the thigh of her jeans. Chance's care was a quality she admired but today his slow reading of the judge's writ was driving her crazy.

"You're holding the man's property," Chance said finally, letting the letter fall to the desktop. "He wants it back."

"The horses are too weak to travel." Her hackles were going up. They did so much too easily since she'd come back to herself. Impatience, not temper. So much wasted time. She couldn't abide to squander a minute more than she had to.

"Judge Dalton seems to think they're strong enough."

Chance's keen dark eyes were studying her. Irritation twitched her foot into a jittery dance. "But he didn't give me a chance to show him they aren't. How can this happen?"

Chance gave a slow shake of his head. "Influence."

Her stomach churned. Influence had kept her a prisoner in a nursing home for fifteen years. Influence had nearly cost Chance and Taryn their lives a year ago. All because of one man's greed. Now someone else's greed was willing to sacrifice six horses who'd gone through hell just for the sake of convenience.

The unfairness of it all was enough to make her want

to roar. She swallowed back her outrage. "How can I fight this?"

"Let it go, Ellen."

Her mouth gaped open. "After all you've been through, I thought you'd understand. I thought I could count on you."

"Ellen—"

"I can't let it go." Her voice cracked and her vision was blurring again. "They deserve a voice." Just as she had.

Chance pushed himself off the desk, scrubbed a hand through his hair, then faced her once again. "I know they mean a lot to you, but they're not yours. I can't do anything but follow the law."

"They've been abused."

"There's no way to prove that."

"All it would take is one visit by the judge to see how bad off they are."

Like a soldier about to face a firing squad, Chance stood ramrod straight. "There's the other side, Ellen."

"What other side?"

He hesitated.

"Just spit it out, Chance. I've wasted too much time already to worry about couching words because you're afraid I'm not strong enough to handle them."

He nodded. "You've come a long way in a year—"

"But."

"But you're still weak. After fifteen years of near vegetation, you're expecting too much of yourself. You're still going to physical therapy. You can't operate at one hundred percent."

She gaped at him. "You don't think I can handle taking care of the horses?"

"You've got three of your own, plus these six—"

Fisting her hands by her side, she jumped up. "Wait a min—"

"Now let me finish." He held up a hand. "All of these horses have special needs. I think that's a load too heavy for anybody, let alone for someone in your position."

Her mind reeled at the possibility of losing the horses due to her own weakness. "So what, you expect me to just let them go and say, hey, sorry I can't take care of you, so goodbye and good luck? I've been taking care of them for nearly a week. I'm *handling* the work just fine."

He cocked his head, a dead-serious look on his face. "You asked me to shoot straight."

"And you did," she acknowledged, bracing herself for the next attack.

"You spend half your life in the sunshine and you look as pale as the moon. You don't just look tired, you look downright exhausted. You've lost weight when you should be gaining. If you don't start taking care of yourself, none of these horses will be able to count on you."

With that, he'd hit her rawest nerve. She stumbled back a step, losing all her fury. He was right. If she did run herself ragged, the horses would have no one to give them voice.

"There's also the question of space," Chance said. "You've got eight stalls and nine horses."

"That's okay, I've got two that won't come inside. I've got enough pasture for them all. I've got two corrals, a ring and I'm working on a round pen—"

"You're not digging holes and lugging lumber on your own, are you?"

She jutted her chin, straightened her stance. "I'm doing what I have to do."

"Ellen…"

He reached for her shoulders. She shrugged off his hold.

"So, how do I resolve this? I'm not going to let the horses go. Not while they still need care."

Chance blew out a long breath and squeezed the nape of his neck. "Tell you what, you hire yourself a hand and I'll talk Judge Dalton into taking a look-see at your operation."

The pinprick of escalating panic stampeded through her. Shaking her head, she said, "Chance, you know how I feel about the ranch."

"It's non-negotiable. You want my help, you've got to give me something to work with." He offered her his hand. "Deal?"

This wasn't going to work. She couldn't have anybody looking, watching…reporting. She couldn't do it. Not after having no choice in the matter for fifteen years.

But if you don't, she reminded herself, *you'll lose the horses and they need you.*

"This way, you'll at least get the chance to convince the judge you can handle the load."

For fifteen years she was forced into silence, drugged against her will, kept a prisoner in her own body by a man who cared nothing about her. She'd had no voice, no one to fight for her. Stuck in the prison of her mind all she'd had for company was the nightmarish image of Kent and Kyle drowning in the river, of her dreams dying with them. Only in the collection of crystal horses catching rainbows of light on the dresser had she found a ray of hope. Horses had kept her fighting for her life.

She *had* to keep fighting for the horses. They were voiceless. They needed her. Not Bancroft. Not Chance. Not the judge. No one would stop her from seeing them healthy again. She couldn't let them down.

She took Chance's hand and reluctantly shook it hard once. "Deal."

The phone rang. She spun on her heels and strode to the door. Rubbing the wrist that held her watch she cursed Garth Ramsey for marrying her when she couldn't object, for stealing nearly half her life. She cursed Brad Bancroft for his careless disregard for his animals' needs. She cursed her body for betraying her when she needed it most.

But all the cursing in the world wasn't going to change the facts. It hadn't saved Kyle. It hadn't brought him back to life. And over the past year if she'd learned anything, it was to face the facts before her no matter how unpleasant they were.

"Well, shoot," she muttered as she plowed through the sheriff's office door.

For the horses she was going to have to hire help. And having someone trespass on her sanctuary was going to feel like being under glass all over again.

Chapter Two

The hum hit him first, deep in his gut. Recognition slapped him next. Shock rooted him.

"Ellen," Kevin whispered.

Of all the things he'd expected to find in Gabenburg, she had never even entered his mind. If he hadn't been holding on to the doorknob to the sheriff's office, the blow of seeing her standing there might have knocked him over.

What was she doing so far from home? Her roots were planted so deeply in Ashbrook that she hadn't understood his need to catch a ride on the wind before settling. What had caused her to leave the land where she'd seeded her dreams?

He swallowed hard and stared at her narrow back. The hum in his gut whirred until it burned, then spread until he was wound so tight his fingers dented the wood on the doorjamb.

She still wore her hair in a loose French braid that tickled the bottom of her shoulder blades. Light still played with the gold, making it shimmer with her every move. Errant strands still framed her face with corkscrews of curls. His index finger twitched with an ache to wrap itself around one of those golden curls.

When she turned, her gray-green eyes reflected every

emotion coursing through her. A sharp gnaw of hunger champed through him as he remembered the sizzle of energy her emotion-filled body could transmit.

Even after all those years, she still had the power to knock him off balance just by being there.

He'd prepared himself to handle his brother. He'd prepared himself to take whatever punishment was his due. But seeing Ellen scrambled his mind, undid his purpose.

He needed to think. But he couldn't drag his gaze from the woman he'd once wanted with such a fierce passion he hadn't been able to see straight.

A flood of regret, of need, of pain surged through him in a tidal wave. Anger and desire roiled like the Red Thunder's water, churning forgotten silt to the surface. The part of his memory he hadn't dared to look at in years whirled through his mind like a ruthless hurricane. Then longing settled over him and sank, drowning him in a pool of sorrow so deep he could barely breathe.

He remembered her laughter, brook bubbly and wind-chime light. He remembered her tears, salty and warm. He remembered her love, tender and sweet. Worst of all, he remembered the way he'd refused to listen to her fears about his leaving for the summer, believing that if he did, they'd cage him.

Through the swell of his memories, the conversation between Ellen and the sheriff floated up. What he heard made his stomach curdle.

Before Kevin could quite recover his mental balance, Ellen spun on her heels, wobbled and strode toward the door. As he started to retreat, the door blew open. The edge caught his shoulder, loosing an *oomph* of discomfort from him. The Australian cattle dog at his side cowered against the outside wall. Muttering under her breath, Ellen plowed past them without a glance.

Shifting his gaze from Ellen to his brother, Kevin was torn. Should he face Kent or go after Ellen?

With the sheriff busy answering a call, Kevin slipped away before anyone noticed him. He needed time to think.

Cap bill pulled down low, chin bent nearly to his chest, hands thrust deep into his jeans pockets, he started walking. The dog, Blue, slanted him a worried glance, but kept pace.

There wasn't much to Gabenburg. The town was neat and compact and held an old-fashioned appeal. The bakery, the general store, the feed store all bore the pride of ownership. No litter dirtied the main street. Pots of geraniums, planters of impatiens and borders of red-veined caladium splashed the storefronts with color. Judging by the friendly hellos bouncing back and forth, everyone knew everybody.

Ellen, she was here.

An unexpected tightness banded his chest. He shrugged it off as uneasiness. Not caused by Ellen. He'd made peace with his undying desire for her long ago. Cities, towns, even villages, had a way of making him feel hemmed in. That was it. He longed for Nina's ranch, for the mountains of Colorado with their green pastures and crisp air.

Spotting the river, Kevin veered toward it. He needed space, he decided, and time to revise his plan. Blue dutifully followed him.

Far from being the gift of absolution Kevin had imagined, his visit to Gabenburg was plunging him back in the thick of his nightmare. Ellen, Kent, anger, so much anger. He palmed the bone feather Nina had given him and worried the carved ridges with his thumb.

All he'd wanted to do was fulfill his promise to Nina. A day, maybe two, then he'd get back to training the horses waiting for him. He wasn't expecting Kent to receive him with open arms or to forgive him. More likely his brother would just send him packing—and have every right to.

But Ellen complicated things.

He closed his eyes against the picture forming in his mind. The last time he'd seen her, he'd hauled her out of the Red Thunder. A gash had scored her temple, winding threads of blood through her hair, leaving her rag-doll limp in his arms. More than anything, he'd wanted to stay with her. But Kent couldn't swim. He'd had no choice. He'd had to go after his brother.

Fifteen years of near vegetation. How could one small cut have caused so much damage?

His thoughts jumbled into a snarl of anger so potent, he could feel his blood start to boil. He dragged in a breath and forced himself to focus on the heat of the noontime sun beating down on him.

Summer wouldn't arrive for another two weeks, but already sweltering heat hung like a weight and seemed to suck the very breath out of him. The furious sounds of the swollen river pounded his determination as he walked along the bank. The mud beneath his boots appeared intent on keeping him from reaching his goal. Moving each foot forward required a Herculean effort.

The memories of Ellen and Kent and that awful evening by the Red Thunder he'd tried so hard to forget leeched into him. He'd need more than a lifetime to repay his debt to both of them.

I've really messed things up, Grandmother.

Then it's time to rewrap the prayer stick, Pajackok.

To the rhythm of the relentless race of the river, he tried to order his thoughts. Blue gave a hoarse whine. Kevin dismissed the worry with a motion of his hand.

Ellen. She was here.

Kevin stopped and faced the river. *Fifteen years of near vegetation.* "I didn't know how badly she was hurt."

Blue cocked his head.

"I know," Kevin said, squinting at the sun glimmering off the water. "Ignorance doesn't make it right."

He'd understood her desperation that evening. He'd even understood her tactic of trying to incite jealousy. But the jumble of love and fear and anger inside him had known no logic. And when she'd turned her attention to Kent to try to win *him* back, he'd chosen the wrong way to express the feelings storming inside him.

"I was seventeen," he tried to rationalize.

Blue batted a paw at Kevin's jean-clad leg.

"I know. That's no excuse either."

His feelings had run too deep, too fast. He'd pushed Kent into the river and everything had gone to hell.

Fifteen years of near-vegetation.

His flash of temper had changed all of their lives. It had altered the course of Kent's. It had turned Ellen's into a living nightmare.

"Nina was right," he told the dog. "I have debts that need paying."

Blue bumped at Kevin's hand with his nose.

His brother deserved an apology—and would get one—but if Kent chose to run him out of town, Kevin could never repay Ellen.

He kicked a stone. Blue chased it through the rough grass, but skidded to a halt at the bank. The stone sank hard and fast into the water. Blue boomeranged back to Kevin's side.

Kevin scraped a hand along his jaw, over his cheek. Time and the river had changed his face. "My own twin probably couldn't recognize me."

Blue cocked his head, offered a paw.

"No one else in Gabenburg knows me."

His main concern was helping Ellen. Someone was trying to steal another dream from her. He couldn't let that happen. She'd lost too much already. He had to do everything in his power to see her hang on to it—even if it meant he had to hire himself out as her ranch hand.

He'd deal with his debt to Kent later.

"If I show up on her front door and say I'm Kyle Makepeace, do you think she'd even hear me out?" The pain of the imagined rejection squeezed him hard.

Blue licked his hand.

"No," Kevin said, scratching Blue behind the ear. "She's better off thinking of me as Kevin Ransom rather than the boy who's responsible for those fifteen years of near vegetation."

Hunching his shoulders, he turned away from the river. He motioned to Blue and headed for his truck.

First he needed more information. Then he needed a plan.

The truth could wait until he'd repaired a bit of the damage he'd created.

TESSA BANCROFT PEERED inside the empty trailer, waiting for her eyes to adjust to the dim interior. The stale stink of horse manure and hay assaulted her nostrils and made her sneeze. Her voice bounced against the metal walls. "Where are the horses?"

"She no let me load them," the burly Mexican said.

Gilberto Ramirez didn't even have to nerve to look her in the eye when he told her of his failure. The poor excuse of a man gazed at his well-worn boots and held his battered straw hat in both hands. Deportation, she suddenly realized, held more fear for him than her wrath.

"*She* could not tell you no. Don't you understand that?"

Tessa could barely control the impatience rattling through her. First the good doctor had failed in his mission. He'd actually sided with the Paxton woman and agreed the horses were too hurt to transport. Now this. She thrust out a hand. "Give me the writ."

Gilberto's forehead wrinkled in confusion.

"The piece of paper," she said, swallowing back the half-dozen epithets on the tip of her tongue.

"I give to her—like you say."

She wanted to tear her hair out by the roots. Throwing up her hands, she pounded down the ramp. "I'm surrounded by incompetent fools!"

Her step faltered. Ellen Paxton was a woman alone. How much would it take to prove *her* incompetent? Tessa swallowed a smile. Incompetence. That was the answer to protecting the project.

"You," she said to Gilberto, "come with me. Let's see if you can do something right for a change."

She marched to the high-tech barn that served as the project's headquarters. Barging into an office, she startled the mousy technician entering data into the computer. "Get me Judge Dalton on the phone."

When the girl simply blinked at her, Tessa plunked the Rolodex in front of her. "Now."

What was the point of influence if you couldn't exploit it?

ELLEN HAD BARELY started the evening feed when she heard a truck chugging up the road. Instantly wary, she put the grain bucket down in the middle of the concrete aisle and went to the barn door. Few people came this way unless she invited them. Bancroft's attempt to retrieve the horses was still fresh in her mind. Her body stiffened, ready for another battle. Shading her eyes against the sun, she watched the truck's approach.

Pudge, the Shetland pony with the foundered feet, had never missed a meal and didn't plan on making this a first. He made his displeasure at the wait known with a series of snorts and the thumping of his well-padded rump against the stall wall.

"In a minute," she said, distracted. At least it wasn't a trailer. The white truck looked too plain to belong to the flashy Double B outfit. But if it wasn't one of Bancroft's minions, who was it?

The truck stopped at the electric gate. A man and a dog exited. When he couldn't find a latch, he crawled through the metal bars and hiked up her driveway.

Despite the sun's heat, a shiver skated through her. Backlit by the sun, with the wind stirring dirt around his feet, he made her think of an opening scene in a spaghetti western. Hero lighting, Kyle had called it. The man walked over the uneven grade with the power and grace of a sure-footed horse, but something about him also made her want to run for cover. Maybe it was the black T-shirt on such a hot day. Maybe it was the way his black baseball cap shaded his features. Maybe it was the air of menace around his canine companion.

The dog, with its tan-patched throat and legs, and gray-flecked coat, reminded her of a hyena. Even the blue bandanna wrapped around its neck couldn't soften the feral air of the beast. Its eyes sported a worried and tentative look—almost as if *she* was the one who needed fearing.

"Ms. Paxton." The man extended a hand toward her. The tanned fingers and work-roughened palm hung in mid-air.

How did he know her name? She took a step back, careful to keep plenty of room between them.

"My name's Kevin Ransom." He let his hand fall back to his side. "I heard you're looking to hire a ranch hand."

With his black hair and his keen dark eyes, he wasn't the hero of this show. He could easily have played the villain in one of those old-time westerns Kyle had liked to watch. There was something unsettling about the coarse chiseling of his features and the way the scars veined his skin like the wrong side of a crooked seam. From the raspy sound of his drawl, she guessed he'd suffered some sort of damage to his vocal chords.

His appearance was enough to make even the most genial person leery. But it was his penetrating gaze that sent another frisson of warning down her spine.

There was something a little too timely about his arrival. And she'd never liked coincidences. Was Bancroft planting a mole because she'd refused him access to the horses this morning? If so, why had he sent someone who would frighten her? Was this "ranch hand" meant as an intimidation tactic?

A glance to the side showed her a pitchfork leaning against a post. Not much of a weapon, but she could reach it in two steps—if she didn't trip over her own feet first. Tension still affected her ability to move in spite of the weekly physical therapy sessions.

Why hadn't she thought to get a rifle? Or a guard dog? Or an alarm system of some sort? But she didn't have anything worth stealing—not even her ragged band of horses would interest a normal thief. Until today, she'd felt safe in her little corner of the world. "Who told you I was hiring?"

"Ms. Conover down at the Bread and Butter bakery. I've got experience with horses."

Taryn had sent him? Ellen could check that fact easily enough.

He ran a hand over his scarred face. "I know I don't look like much, but I'm harmless." He smiled and the gesture added an odd gentleness to his features. "Ask Blue here, he'll tell you." As if on cue, the dog licked the tips of his master's fingers. "I've got references. I'd be glad to have you call them."

He thought she was judging him by his looks. For heaven's sake, taking care of broken creatures was her business. Horrified at having given him the wrong impression, she fumbled to reassure him. "No, no, it's not your face."

No, the reason for her reticence was pure fear. In the past year, she'd worked hard to make every decision her own. Running this ranch had gone a long way to speed her recovery. She didn't want to hire anyone. She needed to be alone. She had to prove to herself that she could control her own destiny.

"It's just that I've already promised the job to the son of a friend," she lied, unable to pin down why this man set her nerves so on edge. The narrowing of his eyes told her he didn't believe her. How many times had people turned him away because of his unfortunate looks? She shrugged, feeling more awkward by the minute. "You know how that goes."

"Sure." He nodded once, then jerked his chin in the direction of the grain bucket behind her. "Tell you what, since he isn't here now, and you're in the middle of feeding, why don't I help you out?"

Why the persistence? "That's not necessary. I can handle it."

"All I'll charge is some water for me and my friend." He patted the dog's head. The dog looked up at him adoringly.

Talk about feeling lower than a snake. Here she was

ready to assign evil motives to him just because Bancroft had wanted his horses back. All Kevin Ransom was doing was trying to earn some food. He looked lean enough to have skipped a few meals, but not totally desperate.

"I can spare you a meal," she said. Then she'd send him and his dog on their way. She didn't need the kind of tension this stranger—any stranger—in her home could spark. "But I really don't need the help."

Something in the pasture caught the dog's interest. A low, rusty growl issued from his throat. He shifted. The movement strained the bandanna at his neck, exposing a hairless necklace of shiny red skin. She gasped. Without thinking, she knelt by the animal. The dog promptly hid behind the man's legs. "What happened to your dog?"

The man shrugged and looked away. "Some drunk ya-hoo had him tied with a rope in the back of his pickup and turned a corner too sharply. Blue here went over the side, but the jerk didn't notice. Took me a mile to get his attention. I thought for sure the dog was dead." He smiled crookedly, but his eyes were cold and hard. The look warned you didn't want to get on *this* man's wrong side. "I convinced his owner he didn't want him anymore. Other than the fact he can't bark, Blue's as healthy as can be."

When the man reached down to help her up, she realized how close he was…how isolated the ranch was…how vulnerable she was. She shot up too fast. Dizzy, she lost her balance. He caught her elbow. She snatched it out of his grasp and stumbled a few paces back, landing on her butt.

He lifted both his hands in surrender. "I'm sorry. I'm not going to hurt you."

She was making things worse by the minute. He thought it was his looks that were scaring her, but her action was pure instinct. She couldn't stand anyone touching her. Not after fifteen years of being poked and prodded against her will. Bancroft and his threats this morning had made her tenser than usual.

This time, she got up slowly and dusted off the seat of her jeans while she rounded up her scattered thoughts.

"I just lost my balance is all. I'm sorry." She puffed out a long breath. "Look, why don't I—"

A whinny of terror rent the air.

The dog shot forward to respond. A motion of the man's hand stopped him cold. Crouched low on his haunches, muscles shaking, Blue waited for permission to herd.

Without thinking, Ellen raced toward the pasture behind the barn. Her leg muscles protested. She ignored their complaint. Her vision couldn't adjust to the rapid change of focus and began to blur. She shook her head. *Not now!*

A thunder of hooves stampeded her way from the far end of the main pasture. What had set the horses off? Luci veered right as the fence approached. C.C. swerved left. But head high in the air, Apollo kept running straight.

"No, Apollo, no!" She blinked madly to refocus. "You can't jump. Not with that leg."

Trying to stop him, Ellen flagged her arms. But he was wild with panic and paid her no heed. She could do nothing to stop him.

The chestnut horse tried in vain to jump. Somehow, he caught his right front leg between the top and the second rail as he crashed into the fence. Wood cracked as his full weight barreled into the rails, but held. His panic doubled. He fought and lunged and skidded in the mud with his hind feet, but remained stuck.

Ellen stopped in her tracks. "Whoa, Apollo, whoa. It's okay, boy." Slowly, knowing that a fast approach could alarm him even more, she talked to him in a soothing voice. "Well, you've got yourself in quite a fix. How are we going to get you out of there?"

The mad scrambling to free himself only got worse.

"Back away," the man behind her said in a low, assertive voice.

"I can't leave him like this. He'll hurt himself more."

"In his mind, he's in a life-and-death situation. His leg's caught and he's got a predator rushing at him."

"I'm not a predator. He knows I won't harm him." But did he? Was a week long enough to trust someone with your life when you'd suffered abuse?

"He's in a panic. He's not thinking." The voice stroked her as surely as a caress. She shivered. "He's reacting with nature's programmed response for survival. Flight. To calm him enough to free his leg, you're going to have to make him think the threat is moving away."

In a twisted way, what he said made sense. But she couldn't just leave Apollo like this. He needed help. He needed it now. She took a step forward. Apollo's head whipped from side to side, looking for escape. He pulled on his trapped leg, scraping skin and jamming the limb in tighter. One back foot skidded from under him and thwacked against a post. She stopped.

"Apollo." Her heart wrenched with helplessness. "Let me help you."

"Back away," the man said. There was something compelling, seductive almost, about the sandy scrape of his voice.

Suddenly, she was back in the nursing home, strapped to a bed, fighting for her life. Just like Apollo. Garth's drawling voice had tried to control her and she'd had to battle it with every ounce of her will. Now, the need to move away from the danger this man presented made her muscles twitch. What she wanted, what she had to do, dueled inside her.

Reluctantly, she took a step back, moving closer to the stranger with the gritty voice, giving Apollo the relief she herself had not found.

She kept her gaze fixed on the struggling chestnut horse, ready to rush in should the situation change.

Slowly, the panic in his eyes ebbed. His breathing slowed. His ears flicked back and forth. Then he stood still. With a groan and a puff, Apollo pulled his leg free. Unbalanced, he scampered backward, fell on his hip, then rolled onto his side. Almost immediately, he was back on his feet and running with a jagged gait toward the shed. There he stopped. Huffing and puffing, he scanned the area, then bellowed.

Luci, the dappled gray mare covered by a crust of mud, answered, and ambled toward the frightened horse. Her presence seemed to calm him. He glued himself to her side. C.C., the Appaloosa, grazed his way closer to them, but kept his distance.

"I need to look at his leg," Ellen said, hitching a foot on the lower rail of the fence.

A hand on her elbow held her back. "Give him a minute to calm down, then I'll go fetch him for you."

She twisted, turning away from the touch that shot through her like a firecracker. "That'll make things worse. Luci'll freak when you get close and that'll send Apollo into another panic."

"What's her story?"

Ellen glanced at the mare grazing peacefully. "She's a track reject. She was beaten over the poll by a male trainer because she was afraid of the starting gate." She snorted. "Like that was going to help. I can't wear a hat around her. She doesn't let a man get within ten feet of her."

The silence beside her was midnight deep. Ellen had to fight the urge to look back at the man with the damaged face and seductive voice. But she felt him—almost as intimately as if he were a lover. His presence pressed against her with a magnetic force that felt oddly familiar and had her holding her breath, waiting for something. What, she wasn't sure.

"If I can get past her and bring in Apollo, will you reconsider me for the job?"

"Why do you want to work where you're not wanted?"

"Your friend said you'd had some trouble and could use a hand."

Taryn had said that? To a stranger? Why? Bancroft had the influence to cause her trouble, but he wouldn't resort to a physical attack. Would he? "Nothing I can't handle."

"This stampede wasn't natural."

She shrugged, hating that he echoed her own fear. She'd seen the look of pure panic on all the horses' faces. How far *would* Bancroft go to get these horses back? "Anything could have caused them to run. A deer. A skunk. A snake in the grass."

He nodded.

"I can handle it," she said.

"I didn't say you couldn't. I'm just offering a helping hand."

She looked at Apollo. If he were human, he'd be the type to wake up in the middle of the night, sweating from the terror of reliving his trailer ordeal. Since the accident, he'd refused to bed down in a stall. Just getting him inside the barn's wide center aisle to doctor his cut back leg took an infinite reserve of patience.

She looked at Luci. The pain the mare had suffered had altered her permanently. The mere sight of a saddle, any weight on her back, glazed her eyes and sent her into a shocked stupor. Even six months of care and patience hadn't convinced her it was safe to wear a halter.

Then forearms leaning on the top rail, she looked over her shoulder at the man and his canine companion. He wasn't Garth Ramsey come back to haunt her. He wasn't Bancroft threatening to take the horses by force. He was just a ranch hand. The only thing he wanted from her was the dignity of working for his supper.

Like her horses, he was broken. Being judged by his scars rather than his skills was more than likely an every-day battle. The haunted look in his dark eyes was one she'd seen in every horse in her care. One meal. What would it hurt? "Every horse here has suffered either phys-ical or mental abuse, most often both. I won't stand for any strong-arm tactics."

"I don't believe in violence." A ghost of pain shadowed his eyes, making her wonder what curve life had thrown him.

"If you can get past Luci and bring Apollo in without using force or violence, I'll look at your references."

He nodded. "Fair enough."

ELLEN HAD NEVER KNOWN anyone with such an instinctual understanding of horses. Phone in hand, she stared at Kevin through her kitchen window. Out in the pasture, a silent conversation was taking place between Luci and Apollo and the man. He balanced approaching and retreat-ing with the horses' curiosity and fear. There was a race-horse-like ripple of power to his muscles when he moved that warmed her with unwanted pleasure.

"What's going on?" Taryn asked on the other end of the line.

"I'm not sure." She gave Taryn a blow-by-blow ac-count of the slow developments.

Kevin was standing head to chest, shoulders rounded and motionless, waiting for the horses to make the next move. He'd removed his baseball cap, and his jet-black hair seemed to absorb the early-evening light. Luci was the first to give in to curiosity. She took three steps toward Kevin. Then she took another. Ever so slowly, she approached until she stood a few feet from him. Another few steps and she was standing next to him, head low. Five minutes later, he was touching her. In another ten, she was following him back to the pen behind the barn as if mesmerized.

Ellen gasped.

"What?" Taryn asked. "What happened?"

"Luci's following him like a puppy."

"Wow!"

"It took me a week to get her to let me touch her. A month to get her to follow me."

Taryn chuckled. "I'm sensing a bit of jealousy."

"Of course not." She wasn't jealous, was she? Luci was finally starting to trust. That was good. *I'm cheering her progress. I'm not jealous.* Frowning, she turned to the stove and stirred the spaghetti sauce she'd thrown together for dinner. "Why'd you send him out here?"

"Chance said you needed some help."

"But why him?"

Ellen heard Taryn take in a long breath. "I don't like the idea of you being out there alone with Bancroft making trouble for you. Kevin looks more than capable."

Too capable. "I can handle Bancroft."

"But can you afford to? Remember the talk-show host he sued last year for disparaging beef? He dug out every bit of dirt possible on her and flung it all over the air. She's still trying to do damage control."

"Having a man around the ranch isn't going to solve

that type of attack.'' Ellen blew out a breath. "He's a stranger, Taryn. I can't have him stay here.''

The sounds of Chance and Shauna playing filtered through the line. The baby laughed wholeheartedly at Chance's baby talk, tugging a reluctant smile from Ellen.

"I know,'' Taryn said. "But I like him.''

"Didn't his face throw you off?'' Ellen frowned at the pot and stirred the thick red sauce.

"You know, after a couple of minutes, I didn't even see his scars. He's got a great laugh. In a way, he sort of reminds me of Chance.''

Ellen's frown deepened. When she thought of Kevin, it wasn't his face that came to mind either. Since feeding time, it was his hands. He had the most beautiful hands she'd ever seen on a man. The horses seemed to love his touch. Some ancient-Greek sculptor would have paid a small fortune for the privilege of immortalizing them in bronze or marble. Then there was the voice. She shook her head and turned down the heat under the sauce.

"Still,'' Ellen said, not quite knowing what it was she wanted from Taryn.

"You checked out his references.''

Oh, yeah, she'd checked. Staring at the spice shelf, she couldn't remember what she'd wanted. Everyone had spoken of Kevin Ransom in glowing terms. The praise had sounded genuine, the pleasure in his skill heartfelt. They'd made a Ransom-raised horse sound like a true prize. She'd heard enough stories of the horses he'd helped to fill a book. "Yes, but...''

"But what? You need help and he's obviously qualified. How can Judge Dalton use your rehabilitation against you when you've got Kevin around?''

Oregano in hand, Ellen turned to the window. If anything, Kevin was overqualified to work as a mere ranch hand. Something wasn't right. But what? Letting Apollo set the pace, Kevin was luring him into the net of his spell. A shiver danced across her shoulders.

That was it, she decided. Kevin could cast a spell.

He'd done so with his dog, with Taryn, with the horses. And she was afraid that, in her weakened state, she could easily fall prey to it, too, and lose the ground she'd fought for in the past year. The way he moved made her uncomfortably aware that he was a virile man. His voice made her shiver even in the heat. The keenness of his gaze made her feel a peculiar combination of desire and fear. Reacting so intensely to a man she didn't know was insane.

The last thing she needed right now was another con man around. She needed to be by herself. She needed to concentrate on the horses. She needed to know her own mind, her own strength, before she allowed another man to touch her life. "I've got to go."

"Ellen?"

He had to leave. Tonight. Bancroft and his manipulations were giving her enough to worry about without adding a man like Kevin to the mix. "He's got Apollo in the barn. I need to go check on his legs."

"Sure." Taryn hesitated. "Ellen?"

"What?"

"You can't judge every man by what Garth did to you."

"I know that." She jerked the pantry door open and snatched a box of spaghetti from the shelf. Horses, dogs and otherwise smart women trusted him. "He's not Garth. I can see that with my own eyes."

"But can you see it with your heart?"

She slapped the box of pasta onto the counter. "Of course."

Taryn sighed. "That's what I thought."

Ellen muttered a curse. "All right, I'm going to prove you wrong. I'm going to let him stay."

Where had that come from? Was she so easily influenced that she could change her mind in the space of a second? Shaking, she turned to the window. Her gaze scouted through the encroaching darkness. Kevin's bent silhouette walked the pasture as if he was searching for something.

She'd forgotten about the trigger. What had started the mad stampede? Apollo was still too hurt to run for the sheer pleasure of it. Where was her mind? Why hadn't *she* thought to look for the cause? Was her memory affected as well as her balance and her ability to focus her eyes?

The shroud of evening tightened around the ranch. Shadows lengthened and stretched across the yard like the bars of a cage.

"That's a good start," Taryn said. "But don't do it for me."

"For the horses." *I'm healthy. I'm strong. I can take care of myself. I can handle having a simple ranch hand doing chores around the ranch.*

"Of course." Taryn sounded amused.

Ellen rolled her eyes. Why was it that married folks were in such a hurry to have you join in their misery? "Go back to your husband and baby. I've got a pair of legs to go doctor."

"Let it never be said I stood in the way of a good vetting." Taryn's voice warbled with laughter.

"Tell me again why I called you."

"For my unbiased opinion about your stubbornness."

"Right. Remind me not to do that again."

"It's a question of balance, Ellen."

"I know." And right now, she was on the wrong side of the fulcrum.

Chapter Three

In the pasture, Kevin crouched beside an old feed bag. Blue sat at his side. Stuck in a clump of grass at the edge of the field, the paper wrapping crinkled with each puff of breeze. With a finger, Kevin widened the scrunched opening. A rusty piece of barbed wire fell from the tangle of junk inside.

He followed the line of fence at the back of the field. Blue dogged his every step. Two more bags rolled through the pasture like noisy tumbleweeds. Blue sniffed at the trash inside them—bits of wire, jumbles of old rope, dried horsetail weed. All potential dangers to the horses.

Ellen had set up her grazing fields well. Two were in use. Well-maintained fences with rounded corners kept the horses safe and enclosed. Posts waiting for rails outlined a future third pasture. A dirt road formed a T, providing easy access to all three fields. Each had a hedge of mesquite and oak at one end to provide a windbreak and shade. Each contained an open shed for shelter from the rain. This field had a watering trough. The other had a pond fed by a brook.

Everything was neat, ordered, well kept…safe.

The garbage-filled bags were out of place.

From where he and Ellen had stood in the yard, a small

rise of land in the middle of this pasture had hidden the horses resting in the shade out of sight.

Whoever had set the bags free had done a good job. He'd started the stampede out of sight with means that would startle the horses without attracting Ellen's attention to what had frightened them—at least not right away. Someone had known the horses would be her first concern.

The question was why?

The answer's there if you ask the right question, Nina's voice echoed in his head.

Kevin rose. Stuffing his hands in his jeans pockets, he studied the pasture again. "The hard part is knowing the right question to ask."

What if a horse had tangled a leg in a piece of wire or rope from the bag? Had someone meant to hurt the horses? Or just scare them?

Again, why?

Kevin piled the bags out of harm's way and signaled to Blue. "Let's go."

One thing was sure, he decided as he made his way to the barn, someone had deliberately induced the panic.

He glanced at Luci, Apollo and C.C. huddled by the manger at the end of the field closest to the barn. Why would anyone want to hurt these horses? Hurting the horses would hurt Ellen. Why would anyone want to hurt her?

He'd failed to protect her sixteen years ago. This time he'd get it right. Somehow he had to convince her he had to stay.

Time, patience and understanding the other's point of view, that's how it goes, Nina's voice reminded him.

He was short on all three.

ELLEN SAW to Apollo's legs. Despite his wild thrashing, he'd only skinned his foreleg. The back leg simply required the usual icing, massage and change of bandage. She fussed over him, then turned him back out with C.C. She groomed Luci—for all the good that would do—then turned her out with the others. Because of her sensitive skin, Luci rolled in dirt as soon as she was released.

Kevin and Blue were still stalking the pasture. What was taking him so long? Her mouth went dry. Her palms itched. She rubbed her wrist with the fingers of her opposite hand. What had he found?

She'd fallen in love with this piece of land the moment she'd seen it. The little house with its sunny rooms and open spaces had reminded her of the one she and Kyle had drawn on the ground one night under the stars—right down to its porch and beds of moss roses. All that was missing was the two rockers on the porch to enjoy the view of their spread after a long day's work. The barn, the pastures had seemed just right to breed a horse or two and give training a try. Nothing fancy. All she wanted to do was make dependable saddle horses for girls with dreams of riding.

Then Luci had come along. Then C.C. Then Pudge. They'd needed her, and it seemed she'd needed them, too. Watching them heal gave her a sense of purpose she'd almost given up finding.

Now, she reflected as she headed out of the barn, a slight tarnish marred her simple joy. The spiked shadows of the barn, fences and trees creeping black over the pens and pasture seemed to snap at her boots like greedy vampires wanting to suck her energy. Something wasn't right and she wanted nothing more than to head for the house and hide in its cozy light. Instead, she crawled through the gate and headed toward Kevin and Blue coming her way.

"Got a wheelbarrow?" he asked.

She nodded. "What did you find?"

"I'll show you." From the barn he retrieved the wheel-barrow, then led her to the far corner near the windbreak of trees. There, he lifted a feed bag. "Someone wanted to scare your horses."

Suddenly shaky, she crouched to examine the contents of the bag.

"Barbed wire," he said. "Old rope and horsetail."

Rusty wire, frayed rope, poisonous weeds. She'd sent Bancroft's minion away. Had he wanted to punish her for defying him by harming Luci or C.C.? "Maybe the bags blew out of one of the neighbors' Dumpster."

Kevin gestured for her to follow him. On the other side of the fence, he showed her tire tracks. They led from the road to the fence, then back again. "They look like they were made by an ATV. And here…" He pointed to tracks in the mud. "Boot prints. Man's size ten or eleven."

It didn't make any sense. As much as she hated to admit it, the law was on Bancroft's side. All that stood between him and getting his horses back was time. Why would he resort to dumping trash in her pasture?

But if not Bancroft, then who would do such a cruel thing? "I didn't see any cars or anyone prowling around."

Kevin straightened and hooked his thumbs into his jeans pockets. "Who owns the land behind your pasture?"

"Mike Stockman. He runs a few head of cattle. It's mostly a hobby, though. He runs some sort of computer-support company."

"Do you know him? What about your other neighbors? Have you had any problems with them?"

She'd barely said hello to any of her neighbors. They minded their business and she minded hers. Eyebrows knit, she shook her head. "I don't see why any of them would want to scare the horses. They're all small-time ranchers, just like me. They all love their animals.''

''No water-rights feud or access disputes?''

''No.''

''How long have you lived here?''

''I bought the ranch nine months ago.'' She'd bought it with the out-of-court settlement from her suit against Garth and the nursing home. She could have gotten more if the case had gone to trial, but she didn't have the energy and she'd wasted too much time to scatter another couple of years in court. Getting on with her life had seemed more important. ''I moved in six months ago and Luci arrived a week later.''

''Ever have any problems before?'' Kevin piled the three bags into the wheelbarrow.

''None.''

He jerked his chin toward Luci and C.C. grazing the grass in the middle of the field, swishing their tails in slow arcs against the bugs. ''What's the story with your horses?''

''Luci, Pudge and Chocolate Chip, also known as C.C., are mine.'' She wasn't about to tell him she'd heard about Luci from a jockey at one of her weekly physical therapy sessions. ''Luci came by way of a friend. The humane society contacted me about C.C. and my vet sent me Pudge. No one else wanted them.''

''What about the Thoroughbreds?''

She looked at Apollo, standing on three legs, resting. If she closed her eyes, she could still see the panicked look in his eyes, the blood mixed with the rain, hear his trumpet of fear. ''There was a wreck last week. Where my road meets the highway. It was horrible. I'm taking care of them until they can travel again.''

''How badly does the owner want his horses back?''

Her heart thumped hard once. That was the question of the day. "They're all hurt. I can't see what use they are to him. Some might race again, but most probably won't."

"Breeding?"

She snorted. "Four geldings won't get him too far."

"Then why doesn't he wait until they can travel again?"

The helpless feeling wrapping around her was suddenly turning her ranch into just another cage. "I don't know."

Kevin picked up the wheelbarrow handle. "I think you should call the sheriff."

She looked at him long and hard, then nodded and headed for the house. She didn't know what to make of Kevin Ransom yet, but at least he had his priorities right.

The horses came first.

WHILE SHE WAITED for water to boil to make spaghetti for the sauce she started earlier, Ellen fought the urge to run a brush through her hair and change her shirt.

"Because I've been out all day and I'm hot and sweaty," she told her reflection on the microwave's black door. "Certainly not for a ranch hand."

Her image called her a liar. She stuck her tongue out at it, then plunged dry noodles into the boiling water. What did she care what he thought? He was a temporary necessity. That was all. Having a hand around might just make the difference in convincing the judge she could handle the workload these special horses required. Nothing more.

Chance had promised to come out in the morning to look at the tracks and the evidence Kevin had collected from the pasture. Until then, worrying would do her no good.

As she drained the noodles, the hot water steamed the window over the sink, erasing her view of the barn. She sensed Kevin's return to the kitchen before she saw him.

Having him here, even if he was simply washing up and sharing a meal, was changing the balance she'd set up for herself. Her awareness of him with its heavy imprint had the hair on the back of her neck standing at attention. Who was he? What was he doing here? Why would someone with such talent with horses have to work for his meals?

"Anything I can do to help?" he asked.

His gaze stroked the length of her disheveled braid, making her self-conscious of her untidy appearance. She nearly dropped the pot she was holding. "No. Sit. Everything'll be ready in a minute."

Blue, who was lying next to the boot bench by the door, sprang to his feet. When his wagging tail knocked one of her riding boots over, he jumped sideways and glanced at her with a crestfallen look.

"It's all right," she told the dog as she took a plate from one of the glass-fronted cabinets. "I don't bite."

Blue looked up at Kevin as if to ask his opinion.

"It's going to take more than a boot to work up her temper." He smiled and petted the dog's head. Blue relaxed. The tension in her gut twisted up another notch.

"He doesn't seem to be aware of how ferocious he looks," she said.

"He's absolutely clueless." Chuckling, Kevin pulled out a chair. The rush seat creaked as he sat.

"How long have you had him?" She piled spaghetti onto the plate, ladled on sauce, took one look at Kevin's lean body and added extra meatballs.

"A couple of months. We're still getting used to each other."

Used to each other? Hadn't he noticed the dog's total adoration?

To her horror, she seemed to turn all thumbs while serving him. Her hand cramped. The plate started wobbling.

The whole serving of noodles listed to one side. She slanted the plate up, but not before a meatball rolled off. It plopped against his T-shirt and rolled onto his lap.

"I'm sorry." Face on fire, she started toward him, then thought better of it. Was she ever going to have full control over her body again? What had possessed her to invite a stranger into her home? This was her sanctuary, her haven—the one place in the world where she could be herself without anyone judging her. Silently cursing, she plucked napkins from the holder and handed them to him. "I'm really sorry."

"Don't worry about it." He took the whole thing in stride, as if things like this happened to him every day. His mouth quirked up on one side.

Something about the gesture ruffled her inside. Another time, another face came to mind. She shook her head and turned to fill a plate for herself. *Kyle is dead. Stop thinking about him.* How was she going to get this man out of her kitchen without being rude?

"It's not funny," she said. "If you give me your shirt, I'll add it to the laundry tomorrow. Not now, I mean, after dinner. I mean, when you change." Her jerky movements flung strands of spaghetti across the counter.

"I make you nervous." Kevin tossed the offending meatball resting in his lap to Blue who gobbled it in one bite.

As Kevin dabbed at the tomato sauce staining his T-shirt, his gaze followed her every move. The insistent tracking enhanced the stiffening of her muscles. She seemed to grow ten thumbs and her feet seemed to work backward. Was he studying her? Looking for weakness? She might be down, but she wasn't out. "Did Bancroft send you?"

"I don't know anyone named Bancroft."

"He owns the Thoroughbreds."

Kevin got up and filled a glass of water at the sink. His shoulder zinged against hers, more breeze than touch, making her stiffen even more.

"I've got iced tea, if you like." She jigged sideways to put distance between them. Why did her chest squeeze so hard when he was close?

He raised the glass. "This is fine."

"Judge Dalton, then?" She suddenly feared finding the garbage-filled bags would become a black mark on her scorecard. *See, Judge Dalton, she can't take care of these horses. They could have gotten cut on the wire or tangled with the rope. And if they'd eaten any of that horsetail, they could have hurt themselves staggering like drunks. No, sir, Mr. Judge, this woman can't handle such expensive animals, especially in their delicate state.*

"Like I said, I found out about the job from Ms. Conover."

She set her plate on the table and forgot why she went to the fridge. "I have some Parmesan cheese, I think."

"I'm fine."

She returned to her chair and shook cheese she didn't want onto her spaghetti.

The refrigerator hummed. The air conditioner fanned cool air. The ice in her glass shifted and clunked.

He ate with reverence as if he was giving thanks for every bite. Blue tracked his master's fork, hoping for a little something to fall his way, although she'd seen Kevin feed him a bowl of kibble at the truck earlier.

The scent of garlic and oregano added a sense of warmth and comfort to the room. And the night shrank the world to the pool of yellow light brimming from the fixture overhead. Too cozy.

Though she hadn't eaten anything since breakfast, she

couldn't seem to work up an appetite. She twirled her fork into the pasta.

"You seem to get around," she said, breaking a meatball in half. "Oklahoma, Montana, Colorado."

"You checked my references."

The piercing intensity of his dark eyes made her want to push her chair back. She forced herself to eat a bite of meatball. "Of course."

He nodded.

Concentrating on her plate, she tried to eat more. She didn't want to feel anything toward him. Not sympathy. Not curiosity. Not even hatred. Any of those would require emotional investment. What she wanted was disinterest, detachment, indifference. There was no point creating ties only to break them. Especially with someone who seemed to burrow under her skin as easily as chiggers.

But try as she might, she couldn't keep the questions from bubbling until they spilled. "Who taught you...?"

He looked up from his plate, met her gaze and didn't flinch. His eyes were impossibly dark. Like a starless night, she thought. The vastness of the depth brought out a sudden sense of agoraphobia, of panic, whose grip was almost impossible to bear.

"Taught me what?"

"What you did with Luci and Apollo. I've never seen anything like it."

He took a long swallow of water, then set the glass down. When he looked at her once more, warmth swam in his eyes, bringing the sting of tears to her own eyes and a longing she didn't understand to her heart.

"My grandmother believed that everything is connected. Every human, every animal, every rock and tree. The horse isn't lower than the dog. The human isn't king above all. She believed that we're all equal, but different.

We all have a purpose. She taught me to treat the horse with respect.''

Ellen sipped her tea. "It took me a long time to gain Luci's trust. How could you reach through her fears so fast?"

"If you want to communicate with a horse, you listen to him talk, then respond to him in his language."

"You didn't say anything." Not that she could have heard him from inside the kitchen.

"The horse's instinct is honed to survive. He's programmed to run away, to protect himself from anything that scares him. To earn his trust, you need patience, a soft hand. You need to ask yourself how he feels in any given situation. Nothing magic about it."

She rose. Snatching her plate off the table, she headed toward the sink. It suddenly occurred to her that Kevin was using that very tactic on her. Patience. He'd stayed far longer than she'd wanted him to, hadn't he? A soft hand. He'd chosen to show her that skill through her horses. What did he see when he put himself in her shoes? Her isolation? Her weakness? "Why are you here?"

"I need a job."

"You could have a stable of your own. With the way you have with horses, you could put on clinics and make a ton of money. Why work hand to mouth?"

"I don't work for Bancroft. I don't work for Judge Dalton. I don't work for anyone but myself."

Independence. She could understand that. It was what she wanted for herself. Someone like him probably had to learn to depend on only himself to survive. She scraped the uneaten food into a container. Still…he had a talent that could easily overcome his looks. Why waste it on a rescue ranch that would never turn a profit?

"You want to work for me."

"Only for a while."

Then he'd move on. She didn't know why that should bother her so much. The need for change, Kyle had had it, too. Why did this man keep resurrecting Kyle when she was trying so hard to forget him? Of course with Chance a part of her life again, Kyle was never really far away from her thoughts.

"I like what you're trying to do here."

She looked at Kevin over her shoulder. The tenderness in his eyes caught her off guard. He quickly turned away, finishing the last bite on his plate. For a second, she wondered if her imagination had played a trick on her.

"And I don't like the fact someone's trying to get in your way."

She laughed softly as she stowed the food containers in the fridge. Her life was turning into a B-grade western right in front of her eyes. The cowboy had come riding into town. Okay, so he'd ridden a white truck instead of a white steed and worn a baseball cap instead of a Stetson. But if he was planning to play the strong hero to her weak damsel before riding into the sunset, he'd be sorely disappointed.

"If you're going to stick around," she said, "let's get one thing straight."

He gave her a quizzical look.

"Around here, I give the orders."

"YES, MA'AM." Kevin fought the urge to grin as he got up to leave.

At the kitchen door, they stood eye to eye. He'd liked that about Ellen. They'd been partners from their first date. It had taken a horse and a mighty fine display of horsemanship for him to notice her, but once he had, she'd owned his heart. And he'd owned hers—until one stupid outburst of temper, of insecurity, destroyed the best thing in his life.

"You can take a shower in the house, but you'll have to bunk down in the barn."

"Yes, ma'am." She wasn't going to let him get away with anything. Nothing had changed in that respect.

"And Mr. Ransom—"

"Kevin."

"The same as for the horses goes for me."

"You've been abused?" Would she admit it?

A spark of shock flashed through her eyes before she hid the pain with ice. "I won't stand for strong-arm tactics. If you can't follow orders, you might as well leave now."

"You need a hand. I'm here to help."

"I'm not as helpless as you might think."

"I never thought for a minute you were helpless."

She might look as if a good wind would blow her over, but he'd never made the mistake of thinking of her as weak. She had a spine of steel and titanium nerves. How she could still have a heart of gold after all she'd gone through was a mystery.

"I have a gun and I know how to use it."

Her eye contact slipped. Her body stiffened. Her fingers folded toward her palms. She was lying. He *had* made her nervous.

"I won't give you cause to use it."

He retrieved his gear from the truck, returned to the house, then let the water in the shower sluice over his tired body. Heat steamed into his knotted muscles, relaxing them a notch.

He didn't like lying to Ellen, but after all she'd gone through, she wouldn't welcome him here. And what he'd seen in her pasture tonight made the threat to her safety real enough. Bancroft wanted his horses back and his actions said he'd use any means to reach his goal. Kevin figured his presence here evened the odds.

But being near her without touching her, kissing her, holding her was a torture he hadn't anticipated. The hum he'd always felt when she was close sang through him in sweet agony. Walking that fine line between protecting her and hurting her would require all of Nina's lessons. Already, he was falling short. The anger he'd learned to tamp down with Nina's example was seeping out of its locked box and poisoning his blood.

Never lie to a horse.

"It can't be helped. Besides, she's not a horse. I'm just here to watch her back."

Never lie to yourself.

He brushed away the ping to his conscience. A bottle of pink shower gel, resting in a caddie beneath the showerhead, caught his attention. He reached for it. As he sniffed, the subtle scent he'd noticed on Ellen's skin filled him. He turned the bottle over and read the ingredients. "Essence of moonflower."

That suited her. She, too, had managed to bloom where there was no light. He'd always admired that quality in her. Her resilience had attracted him more than her beauty, more than her gentleness, more than her skill as a rider. And that quality had also made it easier to abandon her.

When he'd woken up in a torture of pain from his fractured bones, when he'd realized he was responsible for his own brother's death, he'd thought she'd be better off without him. *She'll survive the heartache,* he'd told himself as he'd glimpsed his broken face in the mirror. She'd go on to become the horse doctor she'd dreamed of becoming. She'd find someone else to love her and have the family she'd always wanted.

Fifteen years of near vegetation. The horror of it wouldn't stop haunting him.

Sharply, he cut off the stream of water. He dried off, dressed and hurried back to the barn.

From the door he watched Ellen as she readied her charges for the night. She inspected every horse, giving each a kind word. She made sure each was safe.

An orange cat perched on a stall door groomed itself. Blue seemed to have overcome his shyness and followed Ellen from horse to horse, head cocked toward the sound of her voice.

The sweetness of her smile notched at his heart. He relished the tenderness in her voice. He ached for the soft touch of her hands.

Then she noticed him and the soothing vision transformed into the picture of wariness.

''There's a cot and some linens.'' She pointed toward the tack room. ''The hayloft might be too hot, but there's an empty stall. Or the tack room, but the window's stuck. I'll be here at six for the morning feed.''

No doubt meaning his sorry butt better be ready to work by then. That was all right. He knew he had to prove himself to her.

She brushed by him, giving him one last whiff of exotic moonflowers. He saw her lock the doors to her house, latch every window and check them twice. Air-conditioning would come in handy in a house closed so tight.

He shifted uneasily.

If she never knew, then his lie couldn't hurt her. He'd laid the facts straight out. When the job was done, he'd leave.

Her trials had put a hard edge in her eyes, fear in her bones. She'd survived only to have her new dream tested.

Was it a wonder she softened, lit up and let down her guard only for the horses?

Love, not fear, should be her nightly companion. But it wasn't his place to show her. He'd lost that chance sixteen years ago when he'd let his temper rule his actions.

Blue danced around him. The dog crouched with his front legs extended, rear up. The soft noise in his throat said, "Let's play." When he got no response, he sat in front of Kevin with one paw slightly raised. Absently, Kevin petted the dog's head.

Troubled, he turned away from the snug little house and the woman for which he had no right to care.

His duty now was to keep Ellen safe. Nothing more.

THROUGH THE BLINDS' SLATS, Ellen sensed her new ranch hand's attention. Kevin's rugged silhouette against the light in the barn stirred something inside her. The sensation fascinated her and frightened her.

After Kyle's death, after the horror of being nearly killed by Garth, she never thought she'd be interested in another man.

She tugged the rope, snapping the slats into place, and erased her view of the barn. "Not that I'm interested."

But as she showered, she couldn't help wondering just how gentle the touch of his hands was, how warm his lips would feel, how seductive his whispers would be. The scars should distract from his appeal, but somehow they didn't.

Get a grip, Ellen. You heard him. He's a drifter. No fencing him in. He works for himself. He doesn't stay long in any one place. You need another cowboy in your life like you need a hole in the head. And the hole would probably do you more good. At least the memories of Kyle could finally drain away.

Luci had trusted Kevin with an ease she rarely showed the human race. She'd eaten oats out of his hands as if he were a long-lost friend. While they fed, shy Calliope had demanded her share of attention when he'd spent too much time with Pandora. Even gruff Titan had minded his manners. Hercules had allowed him to change his bandage without the usual half hour of coaxing. And Perseus had let him handle his ears without much of a fuss.

He was gentle yet firm. He was open with the horses in a way she sensed he wasn't with her. He confused her and she didn't like that. Shaking her head, she slipped into bed.

Sleep would not come. The soft *tick tick* of the clock on her bedside table failed to lull her into dreams. The slip of ocean tides on the soothing melody of a cello playing Pachelbel's *Canon* fell short of their usual relaxation effect. The complete darkness didn't trick her brain into slumber. She spent the night restlessly shifting to the imagined sound of Kevin's tantalizing whispers.

Then the whispers turned into threats as snakes of barbed wire and frayed rope wrapped around her wrists and ankles, tying her down. She staggered through the dark, spitting out the horsetail stuffed in her mouth. The horses' desperate whinnies echoed all around her. She tried to yell. She tried to fight. One by one the horses were led by her and into a black hole where their cries died unanswered.

Her heart pounded and pounded until finally her muddled mind realized the noise was coming not from inside her chest but from the kitchen door.

Blinking madly, she sprang out of bed and fell to one knee. Something was wrong. The horses. She had to get to the horses. Swearing, she reached for clothes and hobbled into them as she made her way across the room.

Kevin stood on the other side of the kitchen door.

"Who's hurt?" she asked breathlessly.

"The horses are fine."

The brightness of the day hit her like a slap. "What time is it?"

"Almost nine."

"Nine!" She'd slept in? She never slept in. After losing so many years, sleep seemed like such a waste. She rarely got more than five hours of rest on any given night. "My God, the horses were expecting food at six!"

She tried to push past him, but he stopped her. His fingers were warm and strong against her wrist. The molten effect to her blood shot up her arm. She backed out of his hold.

"I fed them." Shoving his hands into his jeans pockets, he jerked his chin toward the front gate. "There's a blue van, a truck and a sheriff's car at the gate wanting to come in."

She walked to the edge of the porch and craned her neck around the corner. A hand over her mouth, she gasped. "It's Bancroft and Chance."

Bancroft was going to take her horses away and Chance was going to let him. She'd trusted Chance. How could he betray her like that? For half a minute, she was glad Kevin was on her side. Then one look at the painful frown on his face and her heart sank anchor-heavy to her heels. Could she trust him? Could she trust anybody?

Bancroft leaned on the horn impatiently.

"Want me to let them in?"

"No," she said, and turned back to the house. She wasn't going to let them see how shaken she was. She'd brush her hair, get her boots on and meet them face-to-face. If they thought they'd be able to just walk over her, they were in for a surprise. The horses might not be able to speak, but she would give them voice. She wasn't letting these horses go—not until they were healed. "Let them get their boots muddy."

Chapter Four

Before going out to meet her enemies, Ellen made a quick call to her vet, Dr. Lamar Parnell. At least she was certain *he'd* put the horses' welfare above influence.

By the time she got back outside, Kevin had vanished. Four men and one woman were making their way to the top of the driveway. Bancroft had brought a lot of support this time. Her insides quivered. She felt eggshell fragile, but she'd have to be diamond tough for the horses. She straightened her spine and faced them head-on.

The horses depended on her.

She was ready.

She recognized Chance at the head of the pack. The uniform made this an official visit and she wasn't sure how she felt about his betrayal. She glanced away before their gazes could meet and studied the rest of the posse closing in on her.

She silently sneered. All that was missing was the dire music, the side arm and the high-noon sun, and she would be in the middle of a bad western.

The man holding the vet bag looked ill. His drawn features were painful to watch. He appeared to be in his early forties, but walked as if he were three times that old and twice as tired. His shoulders bowed under some invisible weight. His dark hair lacked a healthy luster. His blue eyes reflected no light. The khaki pants and double B logo-branded polo shirt he wore were clean but wrinkled.

Double B bought and paid for. No impartiality there.

The other man carried a leather portfolio. His study of her ranch measured and weighed. Did he find anything lacking? His silver hair, silver eyes and silver mustache lent him a dignified air. His bearing was that of a man accustomed to having his words heard and obeyed. Yet he had the loose-limbed gait of a walker. Golf perhaps?

How many deals had the judge sealed on the back nine of some country-club course?

She'd never met Bancroft, but anyone who lived around these parts knew who he was. At fifty, he looked like the beef that was his main business—a square, well-fed body on a heavy frame and a gait that seemed to shake the ground as he walked. Gold adorned his belt buckle, the cuffs of his starched white shirt and his wrist in the form of a dazzling watch that winked in the sun.

He didn't look pleased at the inconvenience of transporting his own weight.

The woman hanging on to his arm was the trophy wife personified. She was twenty years her escort's junior—at least. Looking at her, the first word that came to mind was *pampered*. Her makeup was china-doll faultless. Her features were soft and exotic. Not one hair was out of place in her sleek espresso-colored ponytail. Her choice of clothing exposed a vast amount of toned and tanned flesh. And there was something just as hard about her dark eyes. Only the garish locket at her throat marred the image of total perfection.

"What's going on?" Ellen asked Chance when they all came to a halt.

Before he could answer, Bancroft shuffled forward.

"I've come to collect what's mine." He shot one thumb toward the woman. "This here's my wife, Tessa. She raised these horses and knows them inside out. She knows what's best for them."

Raised the horses? Ellen silently scoffed. No horse-woman in her right mind would have worn open-toed sandals, a white skirt and a silk camisole to a stable. She was willing to bet Tessa Bancroft had never sat a horse in her life. Or touched one, for that matter. More likely she gave the orders and someone else did the dirty work.

"Naturally, Bradley wants what's best for the horses, so we've brought our vet along to examine them." Her voice had a musical lilt. Her smile was wide and warm, but failed to engage her eyes. "If you'll show us to them…"

Chance stepped in. "The way it works is that Dr. Warner will examine the horses and give his oral report to Judge Dalton."

Ellen crossed her arms in front of her. "That seems a bit biased."

"Judge Dalton has the final say and he's a fair man," Chance assured her.

"Fine." At least Chance had kept his promise and brought the judge. She couldn't keep the proceeding from happening, but she could keep it on an even footing. "Then let's give Judge Dalton a rounded view. Dr. Parnell is on his way."

Before any of them could speak, she spun on her heels and headed toward the barn. Blinking madly, she willed her eyes to focus. She wouldn't let the horses go without a fight.

Kevin had anticipated the need to catch Apollo. She saw him heading toward the back of the pasture with a halter and a lead rope. He was doing his best to fade into the background, yet his brief appearances seemed to make the point to her visitors that she wasn't alone to bear the burden of running the ranch.

Just as Chance had predicted.

Kevin had put Blue in the last stall and the dog didn't seem too happy about it. His rusty attempts at barking were pitiful. For once, she wished Kevin wasn't so efficient. She had a feeling Blue would have enjoyed getting a taste of the backside of Bancroft's perfectly pressed trousers.

"The ligaments in Titan's stifle were damaged in the accident," Ellen said as the group reached the first stall. "He can't bend the joint due to the inflammation. He can't walk. I've been giving him daily massages along with the anti-inflammatory medicine, but he may still require surgery."

"Why don't we let the doctor tell us what we need to know, little lady?"

Bancroft's condescending smile had her aching to wipe it off his face. Her hands fisted. Keeping them at her side took a great deal of restraint. Black spots danced in front of her eyes. She blinked them away.

"I'll allow the care keeper's opinion," the judge said as he slid glasses onto his nose.

Well, the judge may be unbiased after all. A touch of relief melted part of her tension.

Dr. Warner went from horse to horse, making monotone pronouncements. Bancroft and his wife followed, downplaying each injury. Judge Dalton took notes and asked surprisingly insightful questions.

Chance sidled up to Ellen, who was keeping close enough to the group to come to the horses' aid and make the occasional comment.

"Who's the hired hand?" he asked.

"You wanted me to hire someone, so I did." She kept her gaze fixed on Dr. Warner. Grudgingly, she had to admit he handled the horses, if not with genuine care then at least with respect toward their injuries.

"I meant someone local."

"Someone you could trust?" She was drawing the line at how much control Chance—or anyone—could exert over her affairs.

He ignored the question. "Where'd you find him?"

"Taryn sent him."

"Taryn?" Chance asked.

"She didn't mention him?" Now that was interesting. These two rarely kept anything from each other.

He shook his head.

"She said he reminded her of you." Ellen slanted him a sidelong glance.

"She did?" His forehead wrinkled. "So what do you know about him?"

"His references check out." She reached into the back pocket of her jeans and extracted the references Kevin had given her. "Kevin Ransom. He's from Colorado."

Chance grunted and took the sheet of paper from her.

"He's good with horses."

Chance's gaze tracked Kevin as he reappeared with Apollo. "I don't like seeing you out here all alone with a stranger."

Ellen shrugged. "It was your idea."

"I'll check him out."

She almost smiled. She felt sorry for Taryn. Her friend would undoubtedly undergo an interrogation over lunch. "You won't find anything."

"How can you be so sure?"

She couldn't, of course, but there was something about Kevin that spoke of quiet strength and integrity. The horses trusted him. The dog trusted him. Taryn trusted him. Either he was solid or the best con man that ever lived.

She looked at Kevin's firm back as he held Apollo for the vet. His T-shirt outlined powerful muscles. He could easily bully a horse into submission, but he always asked for willing cooperation—and got it, as well as trust. Without saying a word, he held Apollo's attention, distracting the horse from the vet's examination. When he gently drew his knuckles across the horse's muzzle, a warm shiver snaked down to her belly. She shrugged away the feeling of déjà vu and shifted her attention to Chance.

"Because the horses come first."

Chance looked at Kevin, then back at her. He refolded the sheet and put it in his breast pocket. "I want you to call in every day."

"Chance—"

"For my peace of mind, okay?"

She smiled. "If I talk to Taryn, does that count?"

He rolled his eyes. "Try to keep a lookout for someone and that's the thanks I get." His face grew serious. "Taryn would never forgive me if something happened to you."

"Thanks," Ellen said. "You're both good friends."

He waved her comment away.

"No, I mean it. I appreciate your friendship." She dragged the toe of her boot in a little pile of spilled hay. "When I saw you coming up that driveway with Bancroft, I thought you were here to enforce his will."

"Ellen—"

"I should have known better. You kept your promise. That means a lot."

Just as Dr. Warner was finishing his examinations, Dr. Parnell arrived. Ellen blew out a pent-up breath. The gnomelike figure duckwalking into the barn exuded warmth and cheer, and his presence never failed to reassure her.

"Am I too late?" he whispered. His peppermint-scented breath tickled her nose.

"Just in time." She led Dr. Parnell to the group assembled by Apollo. "Judge Dalton, this is Dr. Lamar Parnell. He can give you a history of the horses' injuries and care since they arrived here."

Dr. Parnell reached for the thick file lodged under his arm. He went over each horse's injuries and gave an update as to his opinion of their state of health. His genuine love for the animals came through with each word he uttered. "I've brought copies for your own files."

He handed the judge a stack of photocopies and winked at Ellen. If strangers weren't invading her barn, she might have kissed him. For the first time since she'd seen Bancroft's van, she felt a twinge of hope.

Bancroft puffed up his chest. "Well, we've seen them all, and everyone and their brother's given their opinion. Let's start loadin'." He skewered Ellen with his gaze. "You'll need to open the front gate so we can get the van up here."

"The judge hasn't passed his ruling," Chance reminded Bancroft.

"What's to rule on? Sure they're all a bit sore, but nothin' that prevents them from bein' hauled."

Ellen's body vibrated with rage. Colors faded. Shapes blurred. *Emotions won't impress the judge. Stick to the facts.* She forced herself to speak calmly. "Titan is standing on three legs. Hercules has a fractured cannon bone in his foreleg. Perseus's shoulder injury impairs his mobility. Pandora's hip was bruised and cut. She can barely walk. Calliope's windpipe was crushed and her front feet were damaged. And Apollo's back leg is still swollen. None of them can balance themselves properly in the van."

"If the driver goes slow, they should all do fine," Dr. Warner said. There was no inflection in his voice.

"Even slow speeds require a balance that none of these horses can handle without stressing them further," Dr. Parnell countered.

"The red horse seems to move freely," the judge said.

Ellen went to stand next to Apollo's head and rubbed his muzzle. Her hand bumped against Kevin's fingers and she drew a bit of comfort from their strength. "It wouldn't take much to reopen the stitches, and the swelling impairs his ability to move and balance."

"The one with the hip..." The judge thrust his chin toward the bay mare looking at them over a stall's Dutch door.

"Pandora."

"She seems to move easily, too."

"She's limping." As if to prove her a liar, Pandora chose that moment to wander to the other end of her stall in search of the hay net. Only a trained eye could see the hint of pain as she moved.

"It's not like they're ever goin' to race again," Bancroft scoffed.

"They still deserve to heal before they're transported," Dr. Parnell insisted.

"Do you know where they're headed?" Bancroft asked. His wife touched his arm with her blood-red fingernails and gave an almost imperceptible shake of her head.

"Where?" Ellen blasted the tremor in her voice.

"It doesn't matter. They're mine and I want them back. The law's on my side." He sounded like a spoilt child.

The judge ignored them as he made one more visit to each of the horses, then wandered outside to look at the pasture. Scribbling notes, he returned to the group standing awkwardly by the front door of the barn.

"The sheriff tells me there was an incident here yesterday," the judge said.

"It wasn't an incident," Ellen said. "Someone deliberately planted garbage-filled bags in my pasture."

Bancroft's jaw quivered. "Are you implyin'—"

"I'm not implying anything. I'm saying it straight out. After I sent your errand boy away, you sent him back with a message—"

"I don't need to play games. I've got the law on my side."

"That's enough," the judge said. "In my opinion, the horse named Apollo and the horse named Pandora are fit enough to travel. Mr. Bancroft may transport them today. The rest still require additional care before they are fit enough to travel. They shall remain in Ms. Paxton's care." He looked at Kevin. "I understand you're a recent hire. How long will you be staying?"

"As long as Ms. Paxton needs me."

After consulting with both vets, the judge added, "I'll return in two weeks and look at the remaining four horses again."

Bancroft's jowls quaked. "Now, you just hang on a minute. These horses are mine—"

"They're unfit to travel," Ellen said.

"Oh, for cryin' out loud, they're headed to slaughter! What does it matter what shape they're in?"

Ellen gasped and recoiled. He planned on killing these beautiful animals? "They've still got a long, healthy life ahead of them. Why would you do that?"

"They're useless as racing stock." Tessa Bancroft gave an apologetic smile.

"So you're going to kill them? Why don't you sell them to someone who's willing to turn them into saddle horses?

There are plenty of people who would buy and retrain them.''

''Ms. Paxton.'' Bancroft's face was jerky tough. His gaze was whip sharp. His tone of voice took condescension to new lows. ''They're my stock and I can damn well do as I please with them.''

''That—''

''Whatever their fate,'' the judge interrupted, ''they have the right to protection against needless suffering. Apollo and Pandora may be transported. The other four will stay.''

''Since we'll be disposing of them,'' Tessa said sweetly, ''can't Dr. Warner simply put them down here? They are, after all, our animals.''

''That would require a legal argument before the court.'' Judge Dalton closed his portfolio and removed his glasses. ''By the time the case could get scheduled, the horses would more than likely have healed. Waiting out the two weeks would be simpler for all concerned.''

''This is ridiculous,'' Bancroft bellowed.

''The judge is right, sugar.'' Tessa reached for her husband's arm, but he ignored her.

He shook a finger in the judge's face. ''You're goin' to be sorry you messed with me.''

''Is that a threat?''

''Take it any way you like.'' Bancroft zeroed in on Ellen. She took half a step back and bumped into Kevin, who steadied her. ''Open the front gate.''

Bancroft stomped outside.

She reached for the remote in the tack room. Her gaze connected with Kevin. He was petting Apollo, but he focused his attention on her. She had the ridiculous urge to nestle her head against his shoulder and receive some of the same comfort he gave the horse. Impossible, of course. Regret trickled through her.

She could read nothing on his face. He'd said little throughout the proceeding. Yet she'd felt his support and saw it now in the depth of his gaze.

Reluctantly, she stepped outside the barn. She pressed her thumb twice on the remote before she found the button. As the gate slowly opened, Bancroft whistled and gestured to his driver. The van's engine rumbled to life.

Without looking at her, Bancroft said, "Get those damn horses ready to go."

With a heavy heart, she turned and headed back inside the barn. She couldn't look at Apollo.

I'm sorry. But words would never be enough.

Not only had she failed to speak for him, she was sending him to his death.

ELLEN LOOKED so sad and fragile as she petted the two horses goodbye. Unshed tears shone in her eyes. She fought to keep her features neutral, but her internal pain showed as plain as a neon sign.

She handed Kevin Apollo's lead. "Would you load him, please? I'll get Pandora."

Kevin nodded. He wanted to hold her and reassure her that she'd done her best to help the animals. But if he touched her, all he'd earn was a swift boot right off the ranch. He was responsible for her vulnerability and wouldn't take advantage of it.

The sheriff was already suspicious. Kevin had noticed the piercing look that studied his every move, felt it down to his marrow. He swallowed the knot of emotion in his throat. Instead of clasping his twin into a bear hug and asking for forgiveness, as he'd often done when they were younger, he had to maintain his distance in order to stay and protect Ellen. He couldn't take the chance the sheriff would escort him out of town if he knew Kevin's real identity.

Apollo's hooves clopped on the barn's concrete aisle, then padded softly on the earth outside.

Ah, Pajackok, have I not taught you anything?

You have, Grandmother, but I can't take a chance. Not yet. Ellen still needs me and I can't be sure of Kent.

Pah! It's you you're trying to protect, not your brother, not Ellen.

With a hand, he buzzed at the voice in his head as if it were a pesky fly. He had to concentrate on the task at hand—load the horse and deflect the sheriff's interest.

The closer he and Apollo got to the blue transport van, the more Apollo's muscles bunched. His eyes widened. His ears twitched back and forth. He made a halfhearted try at rearing, then backed up. Kevin let him go as far back as he wanted. Halfway to the barn, Apollo stopped.

The horse was afraid of the van. After his accident last week, who could blame him? Kevin let him stand for a few minutes, then started back toward the van. He didn't force the horse to go forward, but coaxed him. He applied light pressure on the lead rope. Then each time Apollo offered any forward movement, Kevin released the pressure.

After ten minutes, Apollo stood quietly with his head inside the van. His front feet were just outside the door on the ramp. Kevin let him stand and study the spooky insides, then backed him away from the van to relieve some of the pressure.

"What the hell are you doin'?" Bancroft bellowed. "You almost had him in."

"Leave him alone," Ellen said. She stood out of the

way, holding Pandora. "Apollo's scared to death of going in there after what happened last week."

"Horses don't have any feelin's."

Her jaw moved, but she didn't answer. If she hadn't been holding Pandora, Kevin would have bet she'd have slugged Bancroft. He silently seconded the urge.

After five more minutes, Kevin had Apollo back to the top of the ramp. He noticed Bancroft's patience was wearing thin once more. The man kept looking at his watch and pacing a tight circle. He was going to have a conniption any minute now. But Kevin wasn't going to pressure Apollo to conform to anyone's schedule.

Kevin climbed into the compartment and asked Apollo to step inside.

Bancroft exploded. "Stop babyin' the damn horse and just get him in there."

"He's almost there," Kevin said, keeping his voice slow and easy. "Give me another ten or fifteen minutes."

"Oh, for cryin' out loud! It's goin' to take all day at this rate."

"Doesn't bother me."

Bancroft swiped the hat off his head and slapped Apollo's backside.

"Knock it off!" Kevin tried to steady the spooked horse. "Get away from him."

Bancroft raised his hand to slap the horse again.

"Let him out!"

The hat smacked Apollo's flank for the second time. He turned on Kevin with fire in his eyes. Ears laid back, he bit him soundly on the right shoulder. Kevin rebounded out of the way of the attacking horse. Apollo backpedaled down the ramp. He reached the end of the lead rope with such force that the rope burned Kevin's hand as it whipped out of his grip. At the end of the ramp, Apollo's injured leg went under him. He started falling, scrambled to his feet, then lit out as if the hounds of hell were after him.

Before Ellen could reach for the remote clipped to her belt, Apollo was out the gate.

The bite was so strong, Kevin's shoulder muscle throbbed. The pain spread all the way to his elbow, but he barely noticed it. Aggravated didn't even come close to describing the hot lava spewing inside him. He marched over to Bancroft and grabbed the front of his starched shirt with his good left hand.

"Not only did you ruin the trust I'd built with the horse, but you won't get him near a trailer any time soon." Raw emotions strangled his voice to a mere whisper. The need to punch Bancroft's face swelled like an infected boil. But once he started hitting, he knew he wouldn't be able to stop, and that wouldn't do Apollo or Ellen any good.

"You want that horse loaded." He shoved Bancroft back. "Do it yourself."

He turned to the judge. "I'll be glad to try again once Maverick here's out of the way."

The judge nodded. "Let's get the other one loaded."

Bancroft ordered his driver to run after Apollo and yelled obscenities at Kevin and Ellen. "This is what you call competent care?"

"Mr. Bancroft," the judge said, "I suggest you calm down. You've caused quite enough turmoil for one day."

"I don't have to stand for this."

"No," the judge agreed, "you don't. I suggest you leave now and let these people load your remaining horse. At the rate you're going, you won't be taking any of them home."

Bancroft's eyes narrowed. "You'll be hearin' from me."

He jerked Tessa's hand. Tottering on her high heels, she followed him.

Kevin strode to the barn, hoping his temper wouldn't catch up with him and make him do something he'd regret.

KEVIN HAD LEFT with Blue at his heels. Ellen knew he was looking for Apollo. The bite he'd taken to his shoulder had looked vicious. He had to be in pain, but he was doing what she would have done—putting the horse first. She wasn't expecting him to show again until after the van left. Then she'd insist he take care of his injury.

She followed Kevin's example and took her time loading Pandora. She allowed the mare to get over her fear of the van. An hour later, Pandora was comfortably settled and ready to go. Reluctantly, Ellen walked away.

Watching the truck disappear down the road made her stomach churn. She'd failed Pandora. With her gentle spirit, retraining the mare would have taken little time and would have provided someone with a fine companion. *What a waste!*

"I'm going to send someone out to cast those footprints and tire tracks," Chance said. His expression told her he didn't think it would do much good.

"Thanks."

Chance and the judge left. She closed the gate behind them. The ordeal was over—for now. She turned away. Weariness crept into her bones. When she reached the barn, Kevin and Dr. Parnell were standing at the far end, examining Apollo.

Bancroft's impatience had given the horse a reprieve. If only she could have saved Pandora, too. She shook her head. Worrying over what couldn't be changed was a waste of energy. She had eight more horses who were counting on her. She had to concentrate on them.

"Is he okay?" She studied every inch of the chestnut horse's hide.

"He'll be fine." Dr. Parnell put the finishing touches on Apollo's bandage. "You may want to ice the leg again tonight."

She nodded. "Will he be okay outside? He prefers to spend the night in the pasture." She shrugged. "And after another trailer terror…"

"He'd be better off inside, but if you keep him in one of your smaller pens, he should do all right."

"Okay," she said, "I'll do that."

"Have you noticed how easily the horses get out of breath?" Kevin asked.

Ellen frowned. Apollo's nostrils flared as if he'd just finished a race. His sides heaved. "How long have you been back?"

"A good twenty minutes," Kevin said. "He didn't go that far. With his leg, he couldn't. Blue found him by the back-pasture fence. I took him home the back way. He should have cooled down by now."

"He was under a lot of stress."

"It's not just him. Pandora, too. That short walk from the barn to the truck had her huffing and puffing."

"All the Bancroft horses fatigue easily. It's because of the stress of their injuries."

"They're young—three and four years old." A blade of hay twirled in Dr. Parnell's mouth as he spoke. "And they're coming off the track, so they're at the peak of conditioning."

"But they've been through a lot. And seeing how Bancroft has so little regard for them, maybe he overworked them."

Dr. Parnell's face pruned. "It's been a week and most

of the original trauma stress should have faded. Especially with your tender care."

"Can you run some tests?" Kevin asked, then turned to Ellen. "It's up to you, of course."

"What kind of tests?" Had she overlooked something important?

He shrugged. "Tox screen."

She gasped. "You think Bancroft drugged them?"

Kevin glanced at Dr. Parnell.

The vet spit out the blade of hay. "Possibility."

"It's been a week. Would the drugs still show up in their blood?"

"Depends."

A million questions whirled into her mind, but the answers didn't matter—only the horses' welfare.

"Okay, then. Run every test you can think of." If she could prove abuse of that kind, it would give her ammunition to fight for them when the judge came back in two weeks. "Can you do the tests now?"

A wide smile lit Dr. Parnell's round face. "I just happen to have everything I need in my truck."

Favoring his right arm, Kevin held each horse in turn while Dr. Parnell drew blood samples. Ellen handed out the noontime ration of hay. Blue guarded the barn door like some Cerberus at the gates of Hades.

Once finished, Dr. Parnell gathered his things and prepared to leave. "I'll let you know the results as soon as I get them."

"Thank you."

Ellen pressed the remote to close the gate behind Dr. Parnell, then rounded on Kevin. "How long were you going to suffer in silence?"

He gave her a sheepish grin. "As long as it took to hang on to my job."

"It's yours for at least the next two weeks." As much as she hated to admit it, he'd proved helpful. And right now, she needed every form of ammunition she could get. She gave him a light shove in the ribs, propelling him toward the tack room. "Sit. Take off your shirt and let me look at the damage."

TESSA BANCROFT STARED at the black horse in the stall of the high-tech barn she insisted be kept as immaculate as an operating room. Teeth bared, he lunged at her, nipping the metal bars fronting the upper half of the door. Then he turned his back on her, twitched his tail and tore into the hay rack in the corner.

He was mean as the devil, but he was healthy. No change had shown up in his blood chemistry. Two years was a record. Besides, temperament didn't interest her as much as results. And the black could fly.

The others had deteriorated since the accident. How long before fatigue escalated to the next stage? Soon curiosity would overwhelm even a guileless woman like Ellen Paxton. She would ask questions. She would involve her veterinarian. Then what? Would they understand what they were seeing? If this farce went on for much longer, the project might be compromised.

Getting Bradley to back away from his avenging-hero role had taken much sweet-talking. The last thing she needed was a battery of lawyers putting the horses under a microscope. The evidence had to be destroyed, but Tessa couldn't bring any attention to herself.

If at first you don't succeed, try, try again. Tessa smiled as she thought of Sister Mary Frances's cheery voice. This wasn't a shoe-tying lesson at the group home, but the advice was nonetheless wise. How else could a girl like her have gotten so far?

What she needed, Tessa decided as she strode to the offices at the back end of the barn, was an advantage. Advantage came from learning your opponent's weakness.

"How good are you with that computer?" Tessa asked the mousy technician sitting at the desk.

The girl looked up and blinked at her owlishly.

Tessa bit her tongue, then slowly articulated. "Can you get me information on people if I give you names?"

"Off the Internet?" The girl lifted a shoulder. "Sure."

Tessa scribbled three names on a piece of scratch paper, started to hand it to the girl, then added a fourth. "Get me everything you can on these people."

"The horses' data. You wanted charts and—"

"Do the search, then finish with your work." There was precious little Tessa disliked more than whining. Good help was impossible to find these days.

"I've got class tonight."

A lady never swears, Sister Mary Frances had been fond of saying. So Tessa swallowed the curse on the tip of her tongue, rubbed the locket at her throat and smiled. "Then if you want to get there in time, I suggest you stop whining and get to work."

The black would run in less than three weeks. He would win. Tessa wouldn't let anything or anyone get in the way of her goal.

I'll show you. I'll show you all.

Chapter Five

In the tack room, the fan on the ceiling swirled nothing but hot air. The back of Ellen's neck itched. Sweat soaked her feet through her socks and she wanted nothing more than to take off her boots. Her T-shirt was glued to her back. Her jeans felt like an ungainly second skin.

Because the window's stuck. Because the sun beats on the barn's metal sides. Because the room is so small. Especially now that Kevin practically filled it. She swiped a stray piece of hair from her cheek and blew out a stale breath.

Cap in hand, Kevin turned to face her. "I'm fine."

She pointed to the closed trunk that held spare pieces of equipment. "I'll be the judge of that."

He started to protest, but she stopped him with a raised hand. "You won't do me much good if you can't work."

With a nervousness that seemed out of place in such a strong man, he sat on the edge of the trunk. Turning his back to her, he removed his shirt.

Even from the doorway, she could tell the action was painful. He guarded his shoulder and brought the T-shirt down his injured arm rather than raising it over his head. The nasty purpling and swollen redness made her suck in a breath. So did the old scars crisscrossing his back like some madman's game of tic-tac-toe. "He got you good."

"That he did."

The broad shoulders veed to narrow hips. The play of muscles on his back was taut and lean, deliciously masculine. As she approached him, her breathing shallowed and her pulse sped. The dust motes seemed to fall in slow motion in the shaft of light piercing through the window.

Gently she prodded the area of the bite. The texture of his skin was smooth and surprisingly soft under her fingers. The zinging shock traveling up her arm was oddly disturbing. He flinched. She snapped her hand away and swallowed. "The bite didn't break the skin. You won't need a tetanus shot."

"That's a plus."

She strode to the fridge on the workbench where she kept her veterinary supplies. From the small freezer section, she extracted an ice pack. She fumbled with the pack before she could get a good grip and was glad the door hid her clumsiness. When she spied two smaller packs, she nearly grabbed one to cool her forehead, then thought better of it. In a few minutes, she'd head to the house and take a shower before starting on the afternoon chores. That's what she needed, a break. After this morning, who could blame her?

She snagged a towel from the battered cabinet above the bench. The off-white terry cloth fell from her grip and landed on her other arm. As if that was her plan, she placed the pack over the towel and wrapped it. As she draped the pack over his shoulder, her fingers brushed the heated skin. Her body's immediate and shockingly rapid tightening stole her breath.

She moved away, feeling a bit light-headed. "Leave that on for twenty minutes."

He shifted the ice pack and winced.

She hung on to the door frame with one hand. "You really should go to a doctor and make sure there's no permanent damage."

"I don't have any medical insurance."

Of course he wouldn't. He was a drifter, going from job to job. "My horse caused the damage. I'll pay for the visit."

"That's not necessary. All it needs is ice."

"I have to go to Beaumont tomorrow anyway."

He frowned as if a trip into the city would prove more unpleasant than the pain of a bite from an angry horse. "I'll think about it."

There was something stoic about the way he sat on that trunk—as if he was bracing himself for something unpleasant yet pretending he didn't care. *The scars,* she thought as her gaze traced the network on his back. *He thinks I'll ask about the scars.*

She looked away and busied herself straightening halters and lead lines on the hooks along the wall. The scars didn't matter. She was curious about them, of course, but they didn't matter.

"I won't ask about them," she said, rearranging brushes in a caddie.

"About what?"

She looked at him over her shoulder. "The scars. If you want to talk about them, I'll listen, but I won't ask."

His intense gaze studied her, but he didn't expand on the scars' origin. She picked at dried grass on the bit of a bridle, trying to ease the strange pressure building inside her.

Blue, who'd observed his master's confinement from the aisle, tentatively nosed his head into the tack room. Ellen peered down at him. "You can come in if you want."

The dog gave her an uncertain glance, then, tail wagging in a slow arc, he made his way to Kevin's side. Kevin seemed to relax as he petted the dog's head.

"I'm sorry Apollo bit you."

"I was the closest." He shrugged with his left shoulder. The lean muscles flexed and extended, racehorse sleek, shiny with sweat.

Her throat parched. She needed iced tea. She took a step into the barn's aisle. A dry breeze ruffled her skin, making it prickle. "I wish he'd bitten Bancroft."

"He was just defending himself."

"But you were trying to help him."

The keenness of his gaze made her insides swirl in a warm wave of feminine awareness that took her off guard. She hadn't felt this kind of heat in years. She hadn't expected to ever feel it again. Not after Kyle. Not after Garth. Certainly not for a stranger.

He's not even the settling kind of guy, she thought, raking a strand of wet hair away from her face. *You don't need that kind of complication.*

"He had no way of knowing that hit on his rear didn't come from me," Kevin said. "I was in his line of sight and he had to defend himself."

The pack slipped from his shoulder. With a hand, he dragged it back onto his swollen muscle. His fingers splayed to hold the pack in place. The sun caught the tanned skin, throwing bone and ligaments into relief.

She swallowed hard. "Still...I feel responsible."

He shifted so he could look at her more directly. "I should be the one apologizing for losing my temper."

Ellen gulped. A trick of the light, surely. For a second, she thought she saw Kyle in the piercing sadness of his eyes.

I have to go, Ellen. Why can't you understand?

She blinked and the mirage disappeared.

You're a fool. Kyle is dead. Fantasizing about Kevin Ransom won't alter the fact.

He wasn't Kyle. He was simply a hired hand. He was here for two weeks—to work—then he'd leave. If she lost sight of that, she might as well give up on the ranch, because she was obviously too feebleminded to care for these animals. They deserved her full attention.

"If you hadn't, I would have." The venom in her voice took her aback. Not since Garth's trial had she felt this base need to see someone punished. "Bancroft deserved what he got and more."

"That doesn't make it right."

She stared at him for a moment and studied the play of dusty light on his sharp features. "You're really upset about this."

His forehead creased. Elbows resting on his knees, hands dangling between them, his gaze scrutinized the ground. "It goes against everything my grandmother taught me."

"Everyone feels anger."

"But not everyone acts on it. It's a negative reaction."

"To a negative situation."

He shook his head, seeming to pluck at words from somewhere deep inside. "If I'd been in control, I could have diffused the situation in a more positive way."

The attachment he bore for his grandmother fascinated her. She must have meant the world to him to continue to guide him from the grave. Ellen's hand tightened against the door frame. What if…? She shook her head. The past was a dangerous place to dwell. "Did your grandmother expect you to stay in control every minute of your life?"

He looked up. The dark depth of his eyes robbed her breath. "She would say that control gives you freedom."

"I'm not sure I understand."

"When you're ruled by emotions, they control you. You're a prisoner at their mercy." His features twisted in a mask of pain. The words sounded almost like an apology. For what? As far as she was concerned, he'd done nothing wrong. "But when you control your emotions, you're free to choose. They have no power. They—" He shrugged and looked away.

She couldn't help feeling she'd missed something important. She took a step forward, meaning to comfort him, then stopped suddenly and reached instead to straighten a saddle pad.

"Control," she said. "Is that why you move from job to job?" She'd worked long and hard for her own independence; she could understand his need.

"No." His gaze sought the window and narrowed. She half expected him to continue, but he kept silent, lost in his own world.

Kyle came to mind again. He'd talk about horses and riding and rodeo for hours, but when it came to emotions, the words always seemed to get stuck somewhere between his heart and his throat.

He's not Kyle.

She dusted a cobweb from the corner. "It's a need some people have—to keep moving."

"Sometimes you have to go to come back."

Something about his voice made her gaze seek his once more. Something urgent. Something…needful. Her heart beat heavily in her chest and a sense of regret skimmed over her like a ghost. "Is there someplace you're working your way back to?"

He was silent for so long she thought he wouldn't answer. Then he shook his head. "No."

He stood up and placed the ice pack on the workbench.

"It really ought to stay on longer."

"I'm fine." He brushed by her. "I'll check on Apollo. See if his pulse is down. Something's not right with those Thoroughbreds."

Something wasn't right all around, she decided as she headed for the house. Somehow, she'd failed him, too.

THE NEXT DAY STARTED with an argument. His shoulder had stiffened to the point that any movement was excruciating, but Kevin had no time to baby his injury. To keep his job, he had to pull his weight around the ranch. He'd tried to hide his discomfort, but Ellen saw through his one-handed handling of the feed buckets. Each time he went back to the feed room for another ration, she dug into him.

Some things never changed.

He smiled. There was comfort in that. Comfort in knowing her experience hadn't broken her resilience, her spirit.

And comfort, too, in the soft pink light of morning speckling the barn aisle, in the slow rhythm of work before the heat set in, in the contented munching of oats and swishing of horse tails.

"Oh, that's right," she said, measuring grain into a red bucket, "I forgot. Real men don't feel pain."

He took the bucket from her, wanting nothing more than to crush her against the wall and kiss her senseless. It had once been his most potent weapon against her quick wit. He smiled at the memory of Ellen fighting his kiss while he stroked her breast until her nipple tightened and her comeback exploded into a soft curse of need and she wrapped her arms around him, kissing him back until neither of them remembered why they had argued in the first place.

His shoulder brushed against the door frame and an arrow of pain shot clear down to the tip of his fingers, reminding him of the role he had to play. "I'm feeling it all right."

"Did you ice it this morning?" She frowned up at him and the genuine care in her gray-green eyes speared a shot of guilt through him. That was pure Ellen through and through. He used to tease her, calling her Statue of Liberty because of all the strays she took in. *Give me your tired, your poor...* Your broken. Your needy. From partner all those years ago, he realized, he'd slipped to being simply one of her scarred boarders.

And that was the way it should be. She deserved a happy future.

So why did it bother him so much?

"I'll do it after the morning chores."

He entered Perseus's stall and clucked at him. The bay gelding stiffly moved over. Kevin clipped the bucket in place in the corner. The cat grooming itself on the partition didn't pause in his task. Everything was as it should be.

"By that time, you'll have ripped the muscle apart."

"I can handle it."

"Of course." Even from the aisle he heard her derisive snort. "What was I thinking?"

He took the next bucket from her, trapping her hand in his on the handle. The touch sparked a hum that vibrated through his hand and moved up his arm. "And you're not pushing yourself to prove who knows what to who knows who?"

Her chin cranked up. Her eyes challenged. Her lips pursed. And the urge to nip that lower lip and take her challenge down a notch ricocheted through him like a bullet gone wild.

"It's my ranch," she said. "I don't want to lose it."

"It's my job. I need it."

"I gave you the day off. With pay."

"I've still got one good arm. I don't believe in charity."

She huffed at him and climbed awkwardly to the hay-loft. The sight of her trim rear sashaying up the ladder made him forget the pain in his shoulder. Her footsteps in the loft shook bits of hay and dust through the ceiling's cracks onto his shoulders, calling him back to reality.

She was out of bounds.

He picked up the last bucket of grain.

All of this—the ranch, the horses, Ellen—were part of the dream that haunted him at night. They could have been his. If only he'd held his temper in check. He'd promised Nina to make things right, not make them worse. He would help Ellen keep her dream, but he would not hurt her again.

Pudge didn't let Kevin get the bucket to the hook before he devoured his mere mouthful of grain.

"Luci! No!" Ellen yelled from the loft. "Damn, she flew the coop again."

Kevin latched Pudge's stall. "I'll get her."

"It's too late. She's already rolled."

"Mud bath?"

"From neck to tail." She laughed and the sound thrummed through him, song-happy. "You'd think I was running a spa. If I could get a bridle on her, she'd make an awesome jumper the way she sails over that fence every day. Hey, maybe you can work more of your magic on her."

"It's a matter of trust."

"In her case, it's also a matter of pain. She's still very tender at the poll."

He measured out flakes of hay and stuffed them into nets. "I'll take a look at her this afternoon."

"This afternoon, you're going to ice your shoulder and rest it."

"I don't need my shoulder to look at a horse." He chuckled.

This was the Ellen he remembered, the Ellen he loved. Easygoing, bossy…in-your-face beautiful inside and out. Falling back on old rhythms was proving too easy. *Watch your step.*

"Shoot!" Ellen muttered.

"Need help?"

Blue appeared at the barn door. Worry creased the skin above his eyes. He glanced toward the front gate, then back at Kevin. A navy truck coasted to a halt. The driver leaned on the horn.

"Bancroft," Ellen said through gritted teeth as she climbed down from the loft.

She slipped on the last rung of the ladder. He steadied her with his good arm and was rewarded with an intoxicating whiff of moonflowers. Holding her was entirely too appealing. He had no business letting his hand linger on the curve of her hip, no business hungering for the feel of her skin, no business aching to kiss her. He let her go and stuffed his hands in his jeans pockets.

She nudged by him and stopped at the barn door. "It's not a van, so he's not here for Apollo. What do you suppose he wants?"

"We'll find out soon enough." He strode toward the front gate. Blue and Ellen flanked him like centurions in battle.

Bales of hay and feed sacks filled the back of the navy pickup. The cab contained only one man.

"What can I do for you?" Ellen asked the driver when they reached the gate.

"I got a load of feed for Mr. Bancroft's horses." Through the open window, he handed her a clipboard. "If you'll sign here, I can drive up and unload it for you."

Ellen and Kevin studied the form intently. Other than the greasy thumbprint on the edge, Kevin saw nothing out of the ordinary about the bill of receipt. But Bancroft didn't seem like the type of man motivated by altruism. Why had he sent the feed? Why now, so late in the game?

"They're fed," Ellen said. Her eyes narrowed. "Take it back."

"I got orders not to leave till I've unloaded the feed."

"Not my problem."

The driver shifted a wad of chewing tobacco from one cheek to the other. "It will be when I unload here."

"Why the sudden generosity?"

Chewing on his wad of tobacco, the driver shrugged. "Mr. Bancroft likes to take care of his own."

She scowled as she took the pen and signed her name. "In other words, he doesn't want me to forget they're his animals."

The driver spewed a line of tobacco juice. The brown gob landed just shy of her boots. Kevin's fingers twitched at his side. "I do what I'm told."

"That's reassuring." Her voice dripped with sarcasm. She nodded at Kevin. "I'll get the gate. You supervise his every move."

"Yes, ma'am."

An hour later, the truck bounced back out on the farm road. He and Ellen and Blue stood over the sacks of grain stacked in a corner of the feed room.

"What do you think?" she asked, hands on hips.

"An apology?"

"I doubt it." She cocked her head. "Electronic bugs?"

"Unlikely." As angry as he was, Bancroft had no reason to eavesdrop on them. The horses were well cared for and he knew it. A man like Bancroft peddled in opinion, in influence—bought and sold like commodities. Kevin straightened Blue's bandanna. The dog licked his hand. "A way to impress the judge?"

She flipped the end of her braid over her shoulder. "I hope not."

Or maybe he'd read him wrong. Maybe winning at any cost was Bancroft's goal. Maybe he wanted to discredit Ellen by hurting the horses and blame their decline on her. "Drugs?"

She frowned. "He wouldn't dare, would he?"

"Let's have a look." He took a penknife from his pocket and slit a bag open. He plunged his hand in the sack and let grain slide through his fingers. No signs of powders, but that didn't mean anything. Bringing a handful of feed to his nose, he sniffed. "Looks and smells okay."

"Still, you can't tell." The creases on her forehead deepened. She kept rubbing one wrist with her opposite hand. "Why is Bancroft suddenly so interested in the feed the horses he's sending to slaughter are eating? It doesn't make sense."

"Maybe you're chasing ghosts in the wrong place," he said, seeking to alleviate the tension stringing her so tight. Watching her shoulders stiffen by the second without reaching for her and massaging her worry away was an unexpected form of torture. But mixing duty and desire would get him nothing but trouble. He reached for the bone feather in his pocket. His thumb worried the carved ridges. *Stick to the plan.* Maybe he was letting his feelings for Ellen get in the way of his judgment. "Maybe feed is just feed."

"Maybe, but why take a chance?"

"Have the feed tested, then."

She nodded. "Bag up a sample from every sack. Break out a few flakes of hay, too." She pivoted on her heels. "I'll call Dr. Parnell."

He'd been wrong, Kevin thought as he scooped feed into plastic bags and tagged them. Nothing here was as it should be.

Whether the feed was drugged or not, it was a message. The horses were Bancroft's. He had no intention of losing them. And Ellen was getting in his way.

JUST AS ELLEN PLACED a baking dish of oven-fried chicken on the table, the phone rang.

"Go ahead," she told Kevin, pointing at the food, then answered the phone.

"You missed your appointment," Taryn said.

Ellen turned her back to her guest.

"How do you know?" She dumped the peas and red potatoes in separate bowls and took them to the table, carefully avoiding Kevin's gaze. He didn't know about the physical therapy, and he didn't need to know about her vulnerabilities. They were none of his business. He was just a hired hand.

"I was at the doctor's office with Shauna for her six-month checkup and ran into Kim in the hallway. She said you didn't show for physical therapy and weren't answering your phone."

"Something came up."

"Yeah?" The curiosity in Taryn's voice made Ellen blush.

She reached for a glass and filled it with iced tea, proud she'd hit her mark with no splashing. "Boy, you must be hard up for excitement if how I spent my day provides entertainment."

"So it wasn't a roll in the hay with the hired hand that tied you up?"

"Taryn!" The image that popped into her head was much too vivid. The scent of sweet hay, the rustle of it beneath a quilt, the light and shadows playing on bare muscles, the taste of salty skin—they were all so real that a strange liquid sensation slid through her.

"Could have been just as effective as therapy," Taryn offered.

Ellen tossed her braid back. Therapy made her sore from head to toe. Making love—what little experience she'd had with it—had left her feeling...languid. And the thought of sliding her body against Kevin's was far from relaxing. "Somehow, I doubt it."

"Okay, I'll move on. For now. There's nothing wrong with the horses, is there?"

Ellen breathed silent relief. She didn't want to talk about Kevin. That subject was too confusing. She bustled from the counter to the table with butter and bread and the pitcher of iced tea. Kevin pretended concentration on his meal. Blue snored by the door. "Bancroft had a load of feed delivered."

"What for?"

"To remind me he's in charge."

"I'll bet that sat real good with you."

"Is that Ellen?" Chance's voice boomed from the background. "Let me talk to her."

"Sorry I forgot to call," Ellen said with exaggerated contrition when Chance came on. "Bancroft sent a present."

"What?" he asked warily.

"Oats and hay."

"He's probably just trying to prove to the judge he's a good guy."

"You don't think that's odd?" She looked out the window and frowned at the blue-black darkness creeping over the ranch like a bruise. Luci, C.C. and Apollo were peacefully grazing. Everything appeared quiet and normal. But

Bancroft's delivery—with all the questions it rose—had crimped the edge of her feeling of security.

"I wouldn't worry about it. His hands are tied and he knows it. He's probably just trying to undo some of the damage he caused with his behavior yesterday."

"I hope so. The horses should be improving, but their energy level is going down. Did your deputy find anything when he looked at the tracks outside the pasture?"

"He took a cast, but we don't have cause to go to the Double B and try and match them. No one got hurt. There's no way to prove the bags didn't blow from one of your neighbors' yards." Chance paused for a beat. "I checked him out."

She frowned. "Bancroft?"

"Your Kevin Ransom."

"He's not mine." She could feel Kevin's gaze right between her shoulder blades. She rolled them once, but the skewering feeling persisted. "Find anything?"

"No, and that bothers me."

"What do you mean it bothers you? If there's nothing, there's nothing." She picked up a sponge from the ceramic frog beside the sink, wet it and wiped the counter.

"He wasn't born. He never went to school. His paper trail goes back only fourteen years."

She scrubbed at a drop of jam glued to the counter from breakfast, unnaturally aware that the man she was discussing was sitting only a few feet away. "So?"

"The only place he exists is in the world he created," Chance said.

Kevin came from a nomad family. Not everyone was born in a hospital. A lot of kids were homeschooled. There probably was a logical explanation for the gap in time in Kevin's references.

"What about the rest?" She'd talked to the horse owners he'd helped. She'd heard the honest praise in their voices. She'd seen his gift with her own eyes. But she couldn't tell Chance any of this—not with Kevin there to hear. She didn't want him to know he was the topic of discussion, that he was being judged.

"What rest?"

She turned on the water and rinsed the sponge, hoping the noise would cover the sound of her voice. "What I gave you."

"The references?"

"Yes."

"He's there, listening," Chance guessed.

"Of course."

"The references check out."

"There you go."

"All that means is that this ID is established."

Her shoulders relaxed. "That's good, isn't it?"

"He could still be dangerous."

Dangerous? She slanted Kevin a sideways glance. The hard lines of his face did give him an air of danger. But the whole effect was negated by the soft smile and gentle scratch behind the ear he gave Blue, who was resting his head on his master's knee. Animals had keener instincts than humans when it came to a good heart. "You're wrong."

"I want you to send him away. We'll find somebody else to give you a hand."

"No." Granted, she didn't know much about Kevin Ransom, and his presence had a way of putting her on edge. But he'd given her no cause to doubt him and plenty of reasons to be thankful he was around.

"Ellen, listen—"

"It's a matter of trust."

"It's a matter of safety."

Chance still saw her as the pathetic creature she'd been a year ago. But she was healing. Day by day, she was getting stronger. She had a second chance at her dream. She wanted to pass the good fortune on to someone else. "Chance…it's my turn."

"Turn for what?"

"You know." She glanced at Kevin. The light exaggerated the harsh scars on his face—just as fatigue intensified her own body's weakness.

"You don't think you've fallen for him?"

"No, of course not!" She turned back to the counter and straightened the set of sunflower canisters. No one fell in love in a few days. "Don't be ridiculous. You had Angus and Lucille. I had you and Taryn. Now it's my turn."

"It's not the same. He's not a horse in need of rescuing."

"And what are you judging by?"

"God, Ellen, it's not the scars. It's the fact you're out there alone with someone who changed his identity. Do you think people go around pretending they're someone else because they're upstanding citizens? People who change their identities usually have something to hide."

And some people who went around as pillars of society sometimes kept their wife drugged and caged in a nursing home just so she couldn't tell the world he was a cheat. She banged the potato pot into the sink. "What does Taryn think?"

Chance grumbled in frustration. "She's as stubborn as you are. And if you get hurt, I'll be the one who'll get the blame for not warning you."

"Consider me warned then."

There was a long silence. "You be careful."

"I will." She twirled the phone cord around a finger. "Say good-night to Taryn for me."

"You need anything, you call, you hear?"

"I hear."

She sat at the table and served herself a chicken breast gone cold. The spoon of peas jiggled in her hand, but made it to her plate without bombarding the table with strays. She decided she didn't need any potatoes.

"Your friend, the sheriff," Kevin said, placing his fork and knife on the empty plate. "He's very protective."

She shrugged and scattered peas around her plate with the tip of her fork. "Isn't that what friends are for?"

"I mean you no harm."

The look in his eyes was sharp and true. The depth of his gaze was unclouded. The fierceness of his features said he meant every word.

Her gaze returned to her plate. She picked at the chicken, cut off a bite. It slid down her throat like arena dust. He wouldn't consciously hurt her.

But he could.

The realization landed with a dull thud—right beside the slow churn of awareness in the pit of her stomach.

Already, he'd infiltrated her life in little ways. Already, she was depending on him. Already, he looked at home in her house.

That gave him an advantage she'd sworn no man would have over her.

Another weakness. Another vulnerability.

If she'd learned anything from Garth it was that, to fool a mark, you had to gain their confidence.

Where the horses were concerned, Kevin already had hers.

She was warned.

Chapter Six

The next three days passed in an easy rhythm that Ellen found both comforting and disturbing. Kevin seemed to read her as easily as he read the horses. He was there when she needed him. He made himself scarce when his presence started to make her tense. His head always seemed turned the other way when her hands cramped or her balance wobbled or her tired eyes forced her to blink like an old-fashioned doll being shaken.

Meals became lively discussions about the horses and the ranch. She ate with appetite for the first time in a year. He showed her a more efficient way to get water to the tank in the pasture. She showed him the massage technique she'd learned from the physical therapist for Apollo's leg. Against all expectations, she found herself laughing easily, hating for the day to end, watching his silhouette as he walked the ranch every night before he turned in.

And every night, she cursed as she slipped into bed because she could feel herself sliding down a slope she had no business contemplating. Getting hung up on him would cause her nothing but grief.

Another week and he'd leave. That was the deal. He'd made it plain he wanted no ties. If she kept seeing Kyle in him just because she couldn't seem to forget the only man she'd ever loved, his leaving would break her heart—just like Kyle's had.

Kevin had to leave. That was best. She had to be sure of her strength, of her mind, of her own possibilities before she trusted herself to anyone.

And she had to let Kyle's memory fade.

Every time she thought about her weaknesses, the feeling of impending doom came over her. Like a funereal shroud it weighed on her, heavy with the scent of death, absorbing her heat, stealing her breath. She woke up hyperventilating, her muscles paralyzed, her teeth clacking like a skeleton's, afraid that in spite of the locked doors and windows, in spite of Kevin and Blue outside like sentries, in spite of the miles and jail bars between them, Garth would find her and croon to her in the darkness while he slipped another needle in the crook of her elbow. She would stare at the glowing numbers on the clock, wishing the night away, acutely aware of time ticking—wasted...forever gone.

But as darkness faded, replaced by the cheery pink of dawn, she would awake, eager to start the day, to care for the horses, to see Kevin—to swap horse-training tips, of course. She had so much to learn from him before he left.

Watching him work was a wonder. Today, he was teaching C.C., the Appaloosa, some manners. C.C. had the bad habit of bullying his way through gates, throwing his head and jerking her off balance so he could reach the green grass before she was ready to let him go. She didn't have the strength or the desire to bully him back. Now, sitting on the top rail of the fence, she saw she didn't have to. She was starting to understand the sheer power of Kevin's simple training techniques.

"He's learned that he's bigger and stronger than his handlers," Kevin said. "He knows he can keep his head down there as long as he wants because we won't have the muscle to haul it back up.''

Especially with the shoulder you're trying so hard to pretend doesn't hurt. ''That's why he was left to starve,'' Ellen said. ''His owner couldn't handle him anymore. So how are you going to make him change his mind?''

In that rusty voice of his, Kevin explained each of his actions, the logic behind them. He rewarded C.C. for every little yield toward the desired behavior. His body truly spoke to the horse in the animal's own language.

She hung on to every word, every gesture, mesmerized. Not so much by the voice, she realized. That sound was like sand, Sahara-dry and abrasive. But by the tone, the unhurried rhythm. That slow pacing told the horse, told her, he had all the time in the world, and made them both believe it. They could count on his quiet confidence, on his consistency, on his willingness to wait for trust.

The thought stirred a longing that had her gripping the rail tight.

This time, C.C.'s attempt to lunge for the grass was halfhearted. Kevin lightly asked him to bring his head back up and C.C. obeyed.

''He's got it!'' Ellen clapped her hands once in delight.

Kevin's smile was enough to warm her all the way down to her toes. ''You can sweet-talk a horse into anything, but you can't force him into anything. Not if you want it to stick.''

He dragged his knuckles across the horse's muzzle. A series of snapshots of Kyle flashed across her mind, nearly knocking her off the fence. He was coming out of an arena, out of a ring, in from a trail. He'd jump off his horse and scrape his knuckles across his horse's muzzle as if to say, ''Love ya, horse, but I'm too macho to hug you in front of these people.'' She shook her head to dislodge the memory. Kyle was dead. A lot of people liked to rub a horse's soft muzzle.

"What next?" she croaked.

"I'll put him out with the others and we'll try again later to make sure he remembers."

As he started leading the horse, C.C. zipped ahead as if he was in charge.

"Looks like you've got another lesson on your hands."

"Yeah, someone really did a number on this horse."

Before she could comment, Blue, who was lying beneath the fence at her side, scrambled to his feet. Looking toward the road, he rumbled a hoarse and squeaky attempt at a bark. A moment later, a cloud of dust sprang up, and from it, the unmistakable navy of a Double B vehicle materialized.

"What does he want now?" Ellen slid off the fence. Thumb hovering over the remote button that opened the gate, she debated making Bancroft walk. With a sigh, she decided against it. "Might as well just get this over with."

From the corner of her eye, she saw C.C. circling around Kevin and figured she'd have to handle Bancroft alone. Kevin already had his hands full.

She squared her shoulders. She could handle it. The horses were more lethargic than when they'd arrived, but Bancroft had no way of proving the fault was in her care. Hands on hips, she waited for the intruders at the head of the driveway. Blue sat beside her. The ferocity of his gaze at the trio piling out of the truck almost made her laugh.

"If you're gonna bite," she whispered, "make it the guy with the hat."

Ambling toward her, Bancroft tipped his hat. "Mornin', Ms. Paxton."

His wife wore red today. A second skin of a dress that showed just what her older husband saw in her. Her lipstick, her nails—fingers and toes—matched the dress. Dr. Warner dragged behind like a reluctant dog on a leash.

"Mr. Bancroft," Ellen acknowledged.

His smile was meant to charm. All she saw was the cardboard stiffness of it.

"I've brought Dr. Warner to check on the horses."

"They're all doing fine. Dr. Parnell sees them every day."

"That's unfair to you," he drawled. Her skin crawled. "After all, they are *my* horses. I should bear the cost of their vet checks."

"I'll send you the bill."

His jowls reddened like steaks waiting for the grill. "I'm tryin' to be civil here, Ms. Paxton."

"What Bradley means," Tessa Bancroft said, wrapping her arms around one of her husband's and tipping her head against his shoulder, "is that the horses are used to a very strict diet and a very structured routine. At home we monitor their intake, pulse, temperature, weight, et cetera, on a daily basis. We'd like to continue with our protocol."

Protocol? What a strange word to use. Ellen studied the china-perfect face for some sign of emotion and found none. Tessa's concern wasn't for the horses. "What does it matter, since you want them destroyed."

"Well, little lady," Bancroft boomed with a voice that was just a little too fast, a bit too loud, "what you said the other day made some sense. If they improve by week's end, I might consider makin' some money off them."

Money. With people like him, it always came down to that. A life was as easily traded as a share on the stock market. He was leading her on. That much she'd figured out. He knew just which carrot to dangle to gain her co-operation. He knew she would do anything to preserve the horses' lives. The question was, why did he feel the need to manipulate her? Was it the judge he was trying to impress?

See what I mean, Your Honor. I was tryin' to be the good guy and she turned me down flat.

What did he really want with these horses? What was he trying to protect? Could it be simple as money? That she didn't understand his true intention irked her.

What she had left from Garth's settlement wasn't much—enough to keep the ranch going if she invested wisely and watched her pennies.

"I'll buy them from you." She'd tighten the belt a notch. The horses were worth it.

"Now, listen." Bancroft's eyes hardened to black diamonds. "I've been more than patient here. I've tried to cooperate. The truth is, you don't have a choice."

"They're under my care by order of the court."

He shook a sausagelike finger at her. "They're my horses and I have the right to say how they're maintained. Dr. Warner will examine them on a daily basis until they're returned to our facilities."

"I trust my own vet." She crossed her arms under her chest. "They're well cared for."

"I still own their papers."

"I'll buy them from you."

He made a show of studying her ranch, sneered. "You can't afford my price."

"I'll give you what you'd get at auction. It's more than you would've gotten by putting them down."

He breached the space between them, invading her zone of comfort. On his breath, she smelled tobacco. Mixed with the heavy sandalwood of his cologne, the effect was a noxious cloud. She cringed inwardly, but held her ground.

"The truth," Bancroft said, "is that, given the circumstances, I'd rather dispose of them than sell them to you. You've given me more trouble than I usually allow.''

The sheer hatred behind the voice made her jump inside her own skin and take a step back. Blue crouched and gave a warning rattle low in his throat.

Then she sensed Kevin's presence behind her, solid and silent. He would fight a black-hatted villain for her, face a gang of gunslinging desperadoes for her, tackle Bancroft one-handed for her. All she had to do was say the word and he would step between her and danger.

The reflection of that impression showed mirror clear in Bancroft's eyes, in his retreat. The knowledge gave her strength she didn't know she had, and in that strength, she found courage.

For the horses, she yielded.

She would watch Dr. Warner's every move, memorize, analyze. She wouldn't give him the chance to slip them a needle or a poisoned treat.

In her sanctuary, the horses would stay safe.

FROM HIS PERCH atop the pasture fence, Kevin scanned the north sky and found Nina's midnight star. The mother star. *When you pray,* Nina had told him, *it's important to still the noise in your mind and listen.*

He wasn't sure he'd ever learned the right way to pray, but he liked the deep of the night when the rest of the world was sleeping and he didn't dare. He could listen to the rhythms of nature—the grass crinkling, the stomp of a hoof, the high-pitched whine of mosquitoes. Tonight, the full strawberry moon cast heavy shadows and silvered the backs of the five horses grazing serenely. He could hear the breeze puff through the branches of the oaks, tinkling the leaves like wind chimes. If he put his feet on the grass, he could feel the slow shift of the earth beneath them, the ancient language of time.

In this quiet symphony of nature, his soul found a measure of peace.

He missed Nina, missed her wisdom, her understanding…her unconditional love. In his pocket, he sought the bone feather she'd carved for him. With his thumb, he worried the ridges.

I'm failing, Grandmother.

Pah! Your greatest failing is your inability to see what's in front of your own nose.

She's going to lose the horses. If not because of Bancroft, then because of whatever illness plagued them. He'd sensed something off in them from the moment he'd seen them. Now, the symptoms were worsening. Ellen had noticed, too, and the changes worried her. *She's going to get hurt.*

Or maybe she'll find her strength.

He wished he could believe that.

Everything has a purpose, Nina's remembered voice assured him.

No, not everything. Not senseless flashes of temper that stole other people's dreams.

He shifted restlessly on the fence. Luci, Pudge and C.C. roamed, eating a bite here, a bite there, swishing their tails lazily like normal horses. Apollo and Perseus did more standing than grazing. Each step seemed to expend more energy than eating gained them.

They were young. Their injuries were healing nicely. Why were they behaving like horses two steps from the grave?

But his mind couldn't wrap itself around the problem. Something in the air suddenly carried a new inflection, as if distant notes were modulating into a song. They pierced through him, starting a hum low in his belly. The glow of it shimmered to his heart long before the dog at his feet sensed the shift in atmosphere. Blue lifted his head, saw no cause to worry at Ellen's approach, then went back to his rabbit-chasing dreams.

What did the dog know? The want was so fierce, Kevin didn't know how much longer he could contain it. Her moonflower scent drifted to him on the breeze. The soft unhurried sound of her feet on the earth made a mockery of his racing pulse. He gritted his teeth against the hard surge of arousal.

Ellen and his feelings for her were more of a problem than anything Bancroft and his misplaced pride could dish out.

She placed both forearms on the top rail of the fence and leaned her chin on her crossed hands. She counted the horses and noted their condition. The hum inside him became a fever pitch.

He'd known from the second he saw her in the sheriff's office that he was lost. He'd never forgotten her—though he'd tried. She'd been part of his dreams, part of his nightmares, since he could remember. He could never rid his system of her. She was a part of him as surely as his blood.

How could one woman hold so much power over him?

The lunar light bleached her skin and hair of color and accentuated the silver in her gray-green eyes. She was tall—almost as tall as he. She could look him in the eye. But she cast a slim shadow that seemed as frail as the lace of cloud skimming over the moon. And like those lacy clouds, it seemed all it would take to tatter that shadow and make it disappear was a breath of breeze.

Yet, as strong as he was, all it took was a whiff of her moonflower to send his senses in a spin. And when that radarlike hum started inside him, riddling his gut with a thousand tiny knots, he had no control over the canter of his pulse, the gallop of his heart. All he could do was brace himself against the painful kick of need that tensed every muscle of his body and robbed him of thought.

"How's your shoulder?" she asked, shifting the lean of her head on her hands to look up at him.

He rolled his right shoulder. The muscles were still tight but the pain was nothing more than an aging bruise. "It's fine." He scanned the pasture, but his whole being tuned in to the low thrum of her so close. "Everything okay?"

She nodded and her braid shifted forward, liquid silver in the moonlight. He remembered the softness of her hair on his skin, felt his desire throb at the memory.

"I like to come out here and watch the horses when I can't sleep," she said.

"Does that happen often, not sleeping?" He hated to think of her rest as honeycombed with nightmares. In his arms all those years ago, she'd slept contentedly. How long since he'd felt the satisfaction of holding a woman so dear to him?

She shrugged. "Sometimes it seems like such a waste. All those hours in the darkness and nothing to show for it."

He nodded, not quite sure what to say. What would she do if he ran a finger along the curve of her cheek? Would she run from him if he offered to give the darkness meaning? Would she recognize the taste of his kiss?

Fifteen years of near vegetation, the sheriff had said. Did she still blame Kyle?

"They don't look right, do they?" The fine-boned fingers of one hand waved in the horses' direction. The remembered feel of them on his skin sent a warm shiver of anticipation down his spine, pooled a hot ache in his groin.

"The horses? No, they don't."

"Dr. Parnell says there are no drugs in the feed. I had him run the tests again."

Kevin knew she'd put all her hopes in those tests, believing they would secure her the right to their perpetual care. When the horses left in spite of her fighting spirit, how would she handle the loss? His fingers dug into the wood of the fence. His heels pressed into the lower rail. She wouldn't understand the fierceness of his hug, of his need to deflect sorrow before it touched her. "What are you hoping to find?"

"Something. Anything." She sighed. The soft sound echoed in the night, mournful somehow as it floated into the wide-open plain. His heart eddied with regret. "I don't know. A reason, I guess. Something that makes sense. Their fatigue is getting worse. Titan's all bruised and I can't figure out how he got his legs so knocked around."

He nodded. The degree of lethargy wasn't normal in horses so young, so fit—even taking into account their near-fatal accident. She was getting too attached to animals that could do nothing but break her heart. Why had she chosen this line of work?

"Dr. Parnell is running the blood tests again," she said, chin on hands. "He said there was something odd about the results and thought the lab might have processed them wrong."

For her sake, he hoped the new results gave her an answer.

"If he's not drugging them," she said, "what do you suppose Bancroft is doing to them?"

"I don't know."

"Tessa Bancroft's protocol, what do you suppose it is?"

He'd watched Dr. Warner perform his daily exam and hadn't seen anything out of place. "They check the horses' pulse, respiration and temperature."

She fell silent, her gaze focused on Apollo and Perseus. Cicadas shrilled. Mosquitoes whined. Wind ruffled leaves. "Chance says you don't exist."

Her offhand comment zinged like a cattle prod. His jaw tightened. How close to the truth was his brother? How long did he have before his twin confronted him? Before Kent escorted him out of town? "I'm real enough. You checked my references."

"They only go back a few years. What did you do before?"

This was the time. This was the place. All he had to do was open his mouth and let the truth spill out. *I'm Kyle. I've come to pay back my debt to you.*

But light had danced in her eyes in the past few days. She'd eaten whole meals, not just bites. In spite of the Thoroughbreds' deteriorating condition, there was a lightness and a brightness to her that he couldn't bear to see dimmed. The truth would sting. So he turned away, peered into the night.

"I was in an accident," he started. The words stuck in his throat as a flood of memories swamped him.

The terror in his brother's eyes flashed before him. Kent couldn't swim and Kyle had shoved him in the fast-running Red Thunder River—all because he couldn't tell Ellen he loved her, couldn't listen to her fears, couldn't stand to have his own brother intercede for him again.

The responsible one. The rebel. They'd carved out those roles early and never quite managed to shed them. As little as Kent thought of him, Kevin still cared for his twin. He'd tried to save him. God, he'd tried.

"Grab it!"

The tips of Kent's fingers skimmed his. The water carried him away. He choked on a mouthful of panic as the dead paraded before him. His mother. His father. "Kent, no, Kent, don't leave me!"

The root of a submerged tree caught Kent, held him safe for a moment.

Thrusting out his hand, Kyle threw himself against the bank. "Grab it!" The sandy soil crumbled beneath him. Gravity pulled him forward. He smacked headfirst into the turbulent water, taking Kent with him.

He held on to Kent's waist as the water tugged at them. "Hang on!" But, panic-ridden, Kent had fought him. Then another dead tree appeared and Kevin swam for it with every fiber of his being, thinking that, for once, he'd win.

Then the river tossed Ellen his way. He snatched and brought her back to the shore, worried, so worried because of the bleeding cut on the side of her head, because her eyes were closed, because her moan had spoken of pain.

He wanted to stay by her side, but his brother's terror called to him. Garth, his best buddy and partner in mischief, had come crashing through the brush.

"Take care of Ellen," he'd said, then he'd plunged into the water again to find Kent. The rocks. He had no choice. He pushed Kent and the ballast of dead tree he refused to release out of the path.

Then nothing but blackness until he'd woken up in a hospital more broken than whole. Racked with pain and guilt, he'd wanted nothing more than to let himself perish, but Nina had dragged him back into living.

The memories weighed on him, had him gasping for air. He jumped from the fence.

"I spent a couple of years recovering," he said, thankful the shadows hid his torment. "Then I worked for my grandmother."

"Why did you change your identity?"

Did she know? Had the sheriff already told her? He glanced at her over his shoulder. Her gaze studied him. He held his breath. Did she see through his scars, through his deception? If she did, he could read no fear, no hatred, no recognition in her moonlit eyes, only curiosity. He swallowed hard. "Because a new face deserved a new name."

"Because of the accident?"

He nodded.

Perseus coughed, making a hacking sound that startled Apollo, who stumbled sideways before catching himself. Blue got up, sniffed the air.

"The cough, that's new." Ellen frowned.

Blue started forward toward the shed, then stopped, turned and looked at Kevin. "I'm sure he's okay."

Kevin thrust his hands into his jeans pockets. Someone was out there. So involved had he been with Ellen that he hadn't sensed the dark and cold malignancy now tainting the air. "Why don't you go back to the house? I'll check on Perseus and see you in the morning."

He didn't want to alarm her, but he wanted her out of harm's way—just in case.

"I'll wait," she said, cranking up her stubborn chin.

He tensed, torn between protection and action. "I'd feel better knowing you got some rest."

Her frown deepened. "Something wrong?"

She scanned the pasture, took in the grazing horses. *Speak in her language.* He knew the one weapon he could use to ensure her cooperation. With reluctance, he let a slip of truth escape. "Moonlight becomes you."

He heard her sharp intake of breath, saw her eyes grow wide, her pupils darken in the glow of the moon. He could almost hear the quickening beat of her heart. He turned until the moon enhanced the drape of denim below his waist, let her see his body's response to her. As he'd hoped, she trusted him with the horses, but not with herself, and withdrew.

She nodded, backed away from the fence. ''Okay, I'll see you in the morning.''

Blue's ears pricked toward the clump of mesquite at the back of the pasture. Who, what was hiding in the shadows? Blue's tail raised and bristled. His nose wrinkled and his lips curled.

Kevin watched until the door of the house closed and the light went out. Then he set out across the pasture, Blue at his heels.

He loved her. Always had. Always would.

But love had to be earned. He'd failed her. Now he had to fix his mistakes.

The hair on Blue's back stood up, reminding Kevin danger lurked in the shadows. He had a job to do and it didn't include seducing Ellen Paxton. He had to keep her safe.

Loneliness howled inside him.

His silent bay went unanswered.

WHY HADN'T ELLEN PAXTON simply fed the horses the grain she was sent? All this wasted time could have been avoided. Nothing could save these animals. They were the walking dead. But Tessa needed them alive and she needed them at the clinic to safeguard the project's integrity and dispose of them properly. Otherwise, too many questions would be asked.

She waited in the dark in the truck while the task was done. This time nothing would go wrong. Even Ellen Paxton's sexy ranch hand couldn't work miracles. Not against the wrath of nature's fury. *Or a woman scorned,* she added with satisfaction. How would Ellen Paxton react to the little secret the mousy technician had unearthed? Tessa's trump card. She would hold on to it for a bit longer.

In the meantime, they would be overwhelmed. The judge would have no choice but to return the horses immediately.

After that, one well-placed whisper into the right ear would put the final nail in the coffin. Betrayal, she knew, was the bitterest pill to swallow.

Through the trees she could see them. Her fingers itched to reach for the revolver in the glove compartment. Bradley thought her only skill was her beauty. He would die of shock if he knew how well she could handle a gun. Handling a weapon was one of the many survival skills she'd learned on the streets.

Against the moonlight, the man and the woman made solid targets. She could drop him first. Then before he even hit the ground, she could plug a second round into her. There would be a certain satisfaction in that. But it would be messy, and right now she needed a measure of discretion—for the black, for the goal.

Footsteps hurried around the truck.

"Is it done?" she asked, anticipation making her lick her lips. This time, she'd chosen the right help. Young and champing at the bit for a slice of excitement, Bradley's most recent cowpoke did not fear deportation. Little did he know that once his usefulness passed, he would find himself looking for new employment.

"It should give at any time."

"Are you sure?"

He smiled. "Want to watch?"

She glanced out at the quiet ranch, so serene in the moonlight. The proposition was tempting, but she needed to set up her alibi. "Go."

Chapter Seven

"Park by the bakery," Ellen said, and he eased into a space by the front door.

After morning chores, they headed to town to refurbish supplies. She said nothing about his inappropriate behavior last night, but Kevin noticed a new stiffness about her, a new distance. With all she'd gone through, the last thing she needed was to have her heart broken by a hired hand, so he, too, pretended nothing had happened.

While waiting for her friend Taryn to finish waiting on another customer, Ellen pretended to shop the clear cases lined with croissants, sweet rolls and hard rolls and the racks of still-warm sourdough boules, French baguettes and multigrain loaves. Girl talk. He was sure he wanted no part of that.

Ellen planned a visit to the grocery store, the feed store and the hardware store. That gave him a couple of hours on his own. He headed for the gas station on the guise of filling the tank of his truck. He pumped and paid, then headed for the pay phone by the rest room.

He trusted Stanley Black Bear, that wasn't the problem. The problem was the waning pang of need to return to Colorado. The lack of urgency felt like a betrayal of Nina and the roots she'd finally put down. Stanley said he had everything under control, but that didn't make Kevin feel any better.

When he returned to the truck, the sheriff waited for him, one elbow lazily lounging on the back panel, one battered hiking boot propped on the bumper. "Mr. Ransom. I don't believe we've been properly introduced."

His gaze was direct, thorough—purposeful. Control, Kent had always had it. Even in the heat of an argument he could stay cool.

But not Kyle, never Kyle. He'd taken all of his anger at himself for not finding the right words, at Ellen for not understanding, at Kent for interfering, and channeled it into a shove. And with it, changed all of their lives.

An eel of apprehension snaked its way through Kevin's gut. For a second, he was seventeen again, the rebel to Kent's responsible one, feeling somehow lacking. Almost-forgotten anger simmered, just waiting for a flame to fire it to boil.

Kevin stared at the hand thrust in front of him. He had no choice but to take it.

His brother's hand was firm and strong. He wasn't prepared for the wave of emotion that crashed through him. *I'm sorry, Kent. I never meant to hurt you.*

But there was Ellen to think of. The fresh—and different—footsteps he'd found in the dirt last night put her in jeopardy. Then there'd been the sounds of a truck engine close by. What reason would a truck have to sneak around with no headlights at that time of the night? For her sake, his apology would have to wait. "Kevin Ransom."

"How long were you going to hide, Kyle?"

Kent knew. Kevin's heart leaped as if jolted with a bolt of lightning. He tried to jerk his hand from his brother's grasp, but Kent didn't let go of his bone-crunching grip. "As long as I had to."

They glared at each other, eye to eye. The bite of Kent's gaze found its mark. "At least you have the decency not to lie when you're caught in the act."

Did Kent remember that Kyle never had dodged the bullet when it pointed right at him? "How did you know?"

"Anonymous tip. The prints checked out."

Kevin fell back on old habits of indifference and feigned distance to build a carapace over the dueling love and resentment roiling in his gut.

Kent's gaze narrowed. Pain or reproach? "I thought you were dead. I looked for you."

"I couldn't come back."

"No, I don't suppose you could." He dropped Kevin's hand as if it was suddenly no more appealing than week-old garbage. "You were never one to accept consequences."

Old bitterness soured his mouth. Kent, like everyone else, had seen only the troublemaker. "That's not it."

"What are you doing here, Kyle?"

Once again words failed him. "I saw the wreck on TV. I saw you. I thought— Ellen—"

Kent frowned, dragged in a breath as if he, too, were struggling with some internal tension. "She's been hurt enough. Leave her alone."

"I owe her."

"You got that right."

Kent's accusation punched him straight in the stomach, dousing the burning fury. "What happened to her?"

His brother eyed him up and down, then he leaned his back against the truck as if they were two friends shooting the breeze. His voice was low and full of censure. "Garth tried to kill her. When he couldn't, he kept her prisoner in her own body."

Fifteen years of near vegetation.

Kevin looked down Gabenburg's main drag. Where was she now? The hardware store? The grocery store? Having her out of his sight suddenly had him sweating. Could someone get to her here in town? The depth of his protective need rankled him. "How?"

"Drugs. He kept her drugged so he could use her to control her father and skirt the law. Sound familiar?" Kent's hands flexed, but remained at his side. "Your good buddy was a yellow-bellied varmint. He showed his true colors that day by the river. When he saw we were in trouble, he turned tail. When Ellen tried to get him to help, he walked away. She was so worried about your worthless carcass, she tried to blackmail him." Kent tipped his head, clenched his jaw, accusing again. "Did you know he cheated to get his scholarship to college?"

Kevin shoved his hands in his jeans pockets, searched for the feather at the bottom of the right one, found no comfort in the ripple of chiseled ridges under the pad of his thumb. He and Garth had shared all the major milestones of their lives, but in the end his love for Ellen had carved distance in their friendship. Kevin shook his head. "No."

"When Ellen threatened to expose him, he tried to kill her."

"The cut on her head."

Kent nodded. "She was in a coma. You know how Garth was, always wheeling and dealing. His first year in college, he hit it big with one of his schemes. Big enough to get himself into trouble. In exchange for some bending of the law, he promised Carter Paxton he'd marry Ellen and give her the best care his money could buy."

"Sheriff Paxton allowed that?" Ellen's father was an overprotective bull, keeping a tight rein on his daughter's every movement. He'd never approved of Ellen's interest in Kyle and had made sure to catch Kyle's every transgression. Not once had he cut him any slack.

"He wanted the best for Ellen. The marriage was to ensure Garth wouldn't renege on his word." Kevin read the rebuke in Kent's eyes. "He didn't know about the drugs your friend was slipping her to keep her mind scrambled."

"How could Garth get away with that? Didn't anyone notice anything at the nursing home?"

Kent shrugged. "They say the drug was experimental and didn't show up on any test."

Kevin swallowed hard, trying to make sense of all Ellen had endured. The strength of her spirit to survive filled him with awe.

"She's had a tough go this past year," Kent said. "She's still weak and in no condition to deal with your lies."

It's my fault.

Pajackok, what are you responsible for? He remembered Nina's eyes shining bright, her small hands anchoring his shoulders, her body vibrating with conviction after the one and only time he'd tried to discuss the accident with her. Though few words had come out, she'd sensed his turmoil and tried to use his anger to get him out of it. *You're quite arrogant to think the earth revolves by your power, that your thought set the fire on the mountain, that you can influence any part of my happiness.*

This is different.

Pah! You are responsible for your actions. Leave others to carry their own burdens.

He was responsible for pushing Kent into the river. For that he owed him an apology. He was responsible for Ellen's rescue attempt. For that he owed her a debt of honor.

But he was not responsible for the torture Garth had put Ellen through. "I can't do anything about what Garth did to her—"

Kent whirled on him and grabbed the front of Kevin's shirt. "When are you going to take responsibility for your actions?"

Kevin lifted both his arms at his sides, surrendering. Kent had always been the more stubborn of the two. Once his mind was made up, there was no knocking him off the deep rut his conviction had created. Arguing was useless. "I already have."

"You're still the same." Kent shoved him away and raked a hand through his hair. "What do you think's gonna happen when she finds out who you are?"

She would feel betrayed, she'd have every right to. "She won't." *Unless you tell her.* The silent gauntlet didn't go unnoticed.

Kent's gaze bored into him as if he were trying to lift the scars off his face to find the irresponsible twin of their youth. "For your sake, I hope she doesn't. If any harm comes to her, you'll pay."

"I wouldn't have it any other way." Knowing his own heart, Kevin stood tall. "She's in danger, Kent. Someone was prowling her ranch last night."

"I'll look into it."

"I've got it under control." Kevin's jaw tightened. Kent had never given him enough credit for anything. "Did you get anything off the castings you took?"

"I'm tied by the law."

Kevin pressed his lips tight, swallowed back the acid words burning his throat. "My first priority is Ellen."

Kent drilled a finger into Kevin's chest. "Those horses are leaving in six days. You'd better follow them out."

"She needs me."

"If she still needs help, I'll get it for her."

"Kent—"

"Chance. My name is Chance."

Kevin nodded, meeting his brother's dark gaze. "I've changed, too."

"Not from where I'm standing."

And the truth of it was in his brother's eyes. Kent—Chance—still saw him as the family screwup. "Fair enough."

Sensing this was his last chance to prove his worth, Kevin hurried to rejoin Ellen. He'd show his brother he could keep Ellen safe. He found her at the grocery store and helped her load her supplies.

"What did Chance want?" Ellen asked as she clicked her seat belt in place.

"He was just checking up on you."

"He worries too much."

As Kevin turned the key, the engine growled to life. "You're lucky to have a friend like him."

She smiled. His heart wrenched. "I know."

When they drove into the yard fifteen minutes later, the quiet hit him first, then the stir of unrest.

"Blue?" Kevin warily exited the truck. He closed the door, heard it snick gunshot loud. Using two fingers, he whistled. "Blue!"

The baleful *screak-squeak* coming from the barn ran chills down his back.

They both started running. In the barn, water spewed from a severed pipe. A geyser churned and frothed from the mangled artery spouting into the four nearest stalls.

The thunder of the pouring water swept him back sixteen years to the raging Red Thunder. His breath rasped through his throat. Images of Kent drowning swamped over him as the remembered current pummeled him.

For an instant, he held his twin safe in his arms. All they had to do was swim for the shore. The boulders spiked out of the undulating water. He had no choice. He had to let go. Just before he slammed full force into the rocks, he pushed Kent away. Then pain and darkness engulfed him.

"Oh my God!" Ellen's high-pitched whisper fished him from the whirlpool of memories.

Titan and Hercules stood helplessly, feet mired in a muck of soaked wood shavings and debris. Calliope was down on her side, half submerged. Her breathing was a wretched opera of choking gurgles. The only thing keeping her nostrils above water was Blue's body pillowing her head.

Kevin hadn't been able to stop the river then, but maybe this time he could stop the flood.

WATER FLOWED from the burst pipe in Calliope's stall like music from a mad maestro. It thundered and boomed, lashing out in every direction in an endless outpouring of fury. The gush filled the confines of the stall, overflowed the baseboards and spilled into its neighbor. Wave after wave spread in reptilian writhing onto the concrete aisle. It gurgled down the drain in the wash stall, but not fast enough. Dark tentacles expanded and multiplied, creeping into the feed room and tack room.

When had the pipe broken? How long had the horses been forced to stand in this flood? The weight of the horror anchored Ellen for a moment. Blue's croaky whine snapped her into action.

"Hang on, Blue," Kevin said, and disappeared outside.

She splashed into the stall and knelt by Calliope. Blood pounded in her ears. Her heart tripped like a runaway train. Hands shaking, she reached for the downed horse. She tried to lift the mare to her feet. But even adrenaline couldn't give her strength she didn't have. The dead weight crumpled her like paper.

Bent over, she tugged on the mare's neck. "Get up! Come on, girl, you can do it. Get up!"

All her desperate pleas got her was a shaky exhale of breath. Water kept springing around them. Tears swam, distorting her vision. *I can't save her. I'm not strong enough.*

She whispered into the horse's ear, holding the mare's head out of the water. "Come on, Calliope, get up." Her insides bled when she got no response.

When Kevin reappeared in the stall, she spewed her frustration at him. "What did you do to the pipes? I should never have let you mess with them."

Kevin grabbed her shoulders and pulled her up. Water slopped between them.

"Let go!" She drove a fist into his chest. "Can't you see Calliope needs help?"

"I'll handle her."

As her gaze swung to his eyes, she caught sight of the suffering there. She sucked in a breath.

Not Kevin. A nip of guilt. How could she have thought Kevin would hurt the horses? A tick of relief. Someone else had sabotaged the pipe. A burn in her solar plexus. "Who? Why?"

He shook her slightly to get her attention. "Where's the shutoff valve?"

Shutoff valve? Of course, the shutoff valve. They had to stop the water. Her hand flopped, pointing to the front of the barn. "Outside the feed room."

He aimed her toward the door. "Turn off the water. Call the vet. Call the sheriff."

Ellen hesitated, drawn to the bay mare struggling to keep her head out of the water. "Calliope."

"I've got her. Go!"

Nodding, she ran in a wobbly line toward the outside of the barn. He was stronger. He spoke the horses' language. He could work magic with his hands. If anyone could get Calliope on her feet, it was Kevin.

Alternating between cursing Bancroft and worrying about Calliope, she searched for the access panel. A smooth layer of earth covered the side of the barn. Ellen frantically dug until she found the usually accessible panel. She tore open the valve cover. The bright blue handle sheared off in her hand when she tried to turn it. She roared her outrage and shot to the garage. Her thighs burned. Cramps knotted her calves. Her fingers felt like rusty hinges as she tried to punch in the code.

"This is not the time," she yelled, and attacked the buttons once more.

The door groaned open. She fell to her knees and rolled beneath it. Grabbing the toolbox, she whirled and raced back outside. At the valve, she dumped the contents of the toolbox and reached for the wrench.

Her vision began to blur. She blinked furiously as she reached for the valve stem and ordered her stiff fingers to adjust the wrench. Nothing she did could make the wrench grab onto the metal. The tool slipped on the stem as if it were greased.

"I can't shut it!" she called to Kevin.

"Keep turning."

Grunting, she put her weight behind the turning action, but even the aggressive teeth could find no purchase on the battered metal. "It's not turning."

"Keep trying."

"It's not working."

Dropping the wrench, she ran back into the barn. Calliope was standing. Despite his bruised shoulder, Kevin supported her. Her throat swelled. *Thank you for being here. Thank you for saving her.*

Blue flanked the mare's other side as if his presence there could keep her upright. Calliope's legs shook as though they would buckle under her at any moment. They had to get her out of the water.

"The handle sheared off and I can't get the stem to turn," she managed to say. "Will she walk?"

"How's the stall across the aisle?" Kevin asked.

Sweat and dirt streaked his face, blending away the scars, deepening the color of his skin. For an instant she thought of Kyle, of her last view of him, muddied and wet. Man merged with boy, tugging at her heart. *Don't go there!* She shook her head and squinted at the stall.

The water current flowed the other way—for now. "Mostly dry."

"Move Perseus. I don't think I can get Calliope to walk much farther than a few feet."

The process of moving Perseus was excruciatingly slow, but she couldn't rush the injured gelding. By the time she'd settled him in the corral outside, Kevin and Calliope both looked ready to collapse. Such courage, such strength. Her heart squeezed with admiration at his determination to help the mare.

Ellen opened both stall doors. Reaching under the mare's belly, she joined a hand with Kevin. The solidity of his fingers bolstered her.

"Ready?" he asked.

She nodded. Blue shepherded from the back, nipping gently at the mare's fetlocks. Kevin crooned at the horse in nonsense words. Calliope's ears flicked. Her eyelids crept open. She gave a weary snort, then took a shaky step forward.

Ellen cheered as she huffed and gritted her teeth to carry her share of the burden.

"That's it, that's my girl, one step at a time, there you go," Kevin's voice droned on, casting its spell.

Soaked from head to toe, they supported-dragged-cajoled Calliope across the aisle to the relatively dry stall.

Silently, they each fitted halters and moved the remaining horses outside. Like an extension of herself, Kevin knew exactly what to do and did it. She never should have doubted him. He'd proved his loyalty time and again. Hiring him was the best thing she'd done for the ranch.

"The pump," Ellen said as the last of the horses was settled outside. "I should have thought of it earlier."

"Where's the circuit breaker panel?"

"At the house."

While he found the pump circuit breaker and shut it off, she placed a call to Dr. Parnell, one to Chance, another to a plumber, and reluctantly, a fourth to the judge. Better he hear about this latest mishap from her than the Bancrofts.

As she hurried back to the barn, dappled gray clouds scoured the sky. Dampness rode on the breeze. The unease of a storm settled in her bones.

Rain was the last thing she needed.

The pasture's shed wasn't big enough for eight horses. The barn was ankle-deep in water, but none of it was drinkable. Five of her eight stalls were too soaked to use. Her wooden grain bins were no match for the skulking reach of unleashed water.

Was that the plan? If she couldn't see to the horses' basic needs, would Bancroft swoop in, bare her failure to the judge and take the horses away?

She had no feed, no fresh water, no shelter to give to

the horses in her care. Calliope was worse off now than when she'd arrived. Given the circumstances, would she also lose Luci, C.C. and Pudge?

Her step faltered. A hand went to her heart. Her limbs shook. Tiredness, she told herself. But even as she strode forward, she recognized the zigzag of fear snaking through her. She couldn't lose them. She couldn't let these beautiful animals be taken away only to be put down.

All those years in the nursing home, she never gave up. As long as she'd woken up to the sight of sunshine dancing rainbows in her collection of crystal horses on the dresser, she'd had a ray of hope that she would one day escape. But now a cloud of despair blackened her heart.

You've already lost fifteen years. You can't give up.

She jutted her chin forward, defying the darkening sky. Whoever had messed with that pipe wasn't going to win. She'd go down fighting. She'd have more feed delivered. She'd rig up makeshift stalls in the outside sheds. She'd haul water from the pond if she had to. But she'd meet the horses' needs.

She had Chance and Dr. Parnell on her side. She had Blue to guard her. She had Kevin to help her. At the thought of him, a warmth radiated to her chest and a smile lit her lips. She wasn't alone. She had people she could trust.

She might still lose, but at least she'd have the satisfaction of knowing she'd done her best.

Somewhere after the storm, there had to shine a rainbow.

WEARING A DISGUISE of jeans, T-shirt and a Rangers baseball cap, Tessa Bancroft huddled at a pay phone beside the 7–Eleven. Wind clubbed the booth's glass with skeletal knocks, making it hard to hear over the noise.

This was all Ellen Paxton's fault.

Without water, the judge shouldn't have let her keep the horses. Fixing everything should have taken her at least a couple of days. She should have had to pass an inspection before she could turn the system back on.

The plan had been perfect. No one could connect Tessa with the "accident." By all rights, the judge should have handed the horses back to her. They should be at the clinic by now.

But something had gone wrong. And they were still under Ellen Paxton's meddling care.

"She's endangering the project," Tessa said. "The black is running in less than two weeks. I can't have those five horses ruin my chances at winning."

"Tessa, darlin', you chose the wrong woman to mess with. She's got more lives than a cat and you don't stand a chance of taking anything she has her heart set on."

"Don't you understand how close we are?"

"We?" He had the gall to laugh. "Now, tell me again why I should help you win something that belongs to me in the first place."

She gritted her teeth. "Because your horses are involved. Do you really want to see the Royal Legacy name associated with a scandal?" Her reflection in the booth's glass showed a wicked smile. "Think of the shame. Like father, like son."

He tutted. "But see, now they're *your* horses. You stole them from me. You stole my research. You'll have to take the blame as well as the glory."

She'd always known he played dirty. Getting involved with him had been a calculated risk from the beginning. But the lure of winning, especially in Sheree MacQueen's backyard, especially with the horses, had won over caution. Her blue-blood mother might have abandoned the bastard daughter she'd produced with her stable hand, but she could not deny her her rightful place in the winner's circle. "I'll bring you down with me."

"Sorry, darlin', but I've got enough problems of my own without takin' on yours."

"You have no choice."

"I don't take kindly to threats."

Before Tessa could say anything more, he hung up. She slammed the receiver into its cradle. There was only one thing left to do.

Eliminate the problem.

Without Ellen, there was no reason for the horses to remain at the ranch. And the poor woman had already proven she had a propensity for accidents.

As for the connection to the research, she had the perfect solution.

Chapter Eight

"Are you two done in there?" Ellen asked over the corral fence.

A gust blew strands free from her braid, setting them in motion like golden streamers. Kevin's fingers actually twitched at his side, such was his need to touch a curly spiral and wind it around his finger. He hitched his thumbs into his jeans pockets, then glanced at his brother. "Almost."

He hadn't expected to have to deal with Chance again so soon, but here he was with his antagonistic eyes and his features pinched tight. Together they'd walked every inch of the barn and the surrounding paddocks while Ellen dealt with the plumber and the vet. They'd found nothing. Yet a part of Kevin still felt he had to prove his innocence in this matter.

"Is it all right if I put a horse in here?" Ellen asked. "The plumber wants to pump the water into the field and the noise is scaring Perseus."

Kevin deferred to the sheriff.

Chance nodded. "Go ahead."

Fatigue bruised her eyes. The streak of dirt across her cheek looked like dried blood against her moon-pale skin. The wave of tenderness cresting through Kevin caught him by surprise. She shouldn't be working so hard, but he had no right to suggest she rest. And before he could relieve her burden, he had his critical brother to appease.

"How's she holding up?" Chance asked as she left to fetch Perseus.

"She's tough—tougher than you give her credit for."

"You're not still in love with her," Chance said. The statement was more a warning than a question. Kevin knew there was no right answer.

The obligation born of guilt had become something else altogether over the past few days. Kevin had thought he could help her in a time of need and wipe the slate clean knowing she'd go on to succeed. But all the old complicated feelings were coming back, tumbling into a great big ball of confusion.

He wanted her in a different way than when they'd both been seventeen. He tried telling himself he hadn't fallen for her all over again, that this wasn't love, but simply caring. Then the invisible connection between them would click and the hum of contentment that filled him whenever she was near would purr to new heights.

Chance hitched a foot on the lowest rail. "She's missed two physical therapy sessions since you've been around."

"She's had plenty going on to work out her muscles." Wind kicked up the sand in the corral and spun it in small eddies that skittered along the ground. The sound of the blast against the denim of his jeans was a hiss.

"I'd hate to see her progress slow."

"I'd hate to see her lose her spirit. She needs to do this. She needs to care for these horses."

Chance's elbows splayed at his side like an old-time gunfighter reaching for his side arm.

Shaking his head, Kevin gave a dry laugh.

"What's so funny?"

"Remember the movie *The Good, The Bad and The Ugly*?"

Chance frowned. "What about it?"

"Whenever Clint Eastwood found himself in a tight spot, they'd play that eerie whistle."

Chance's gaze narrowed.

"I just heard the tune whine in my head."

Ellen and Perseus shuffled into view from the back paddock. "You've always been the good. I was the bad."

"Kyle—"

"It's best if you call me Kevin. For Ellen's sake. I love her, Chance. I always will." He ran a hand over the warped lines of his scars. "But she doesn't need this."

"It's not your scars I'm worried about."

"I know. She deserves better all around. But I need to apologize. This is the only way I can do it without hurting her." Kevin went to the gate, opened it for Ellen and took the horse from her.

"I've got him." His chin jerked toward the front gate. "You've got company."

A black truck drove up and parked by the barn. The woman from the bakery exited and waved. Ellen ran to meet her and fussed at the baby while Taryn unfolded the tonneau cover. Carrying her daughter, Taryn headed toward them. Her long brown hair was caught in a ponytail and her blue eyes sparkled as she looked at her husband.

"I brought some drinking water and sandwiches." She gave Kevin a nod of greeting and Chance a quick kiss, then handed him his daughter. "Here, since y'all are just standing around doing nothing, you can hold Shauna while I give Ellen a hand unloading everything."

With a wave and a smile, she left. Both women seemed to talk at once as they lugged jugs of water to the house.

Their laughter drifted on the breeze. Something inside Kevin constricted.

A gurgle from the baby made him tear his gaze from the women to the girl in his brother's arms. She was a little butterball with a fluff of black hair, big blue eyes and a killer smile. Chance will have a hell of a time when she started dating. Looking at his niece dressed in her watermelon sundress and hat, Kevin could almost understand Carter Paxton's protectiveness when it came to his daughter Ellen. If this little girl were his, he'd hate the thought of having someone like the cocky teenager he'd been come knocking at his door.

Then his gaze drifted to his brother, and for the first time he saw him in a different light.

Gone were the harsh lines, the cold eyes, the predator tightness. One small woman and an even tinier girl had transformed him into a giant teddy bear. Love shone from his eyes as he watched his wife disappear into the house. When his daughter batted at his cheek for attention, he met the tiny fist with a loud raspberry into her palm that sent her into a fit of laughter. Shauna's joy brought an adoring smile to his face.

"You're happy," Kevin said through the tightness in his throat.

Chance looked up, contentment radiating from him. "I am."

"I'm glad."

Kevin looked away, found his gaze straying to the house and the light burning brightly in the kitchen against the gathering storm clouds. That safety, that contentment, that happiness was what he wanted for Ellen. "Bancroft is behind this."

"There's no way to prove it. He certainly wouldn't have

done the job himself. And the water's washed away any evidence.''

"Take a good look at what he did." Kevin ticked off each point with a finger. "He messed with the water supply. That hurts her operation. It overwhelms her with extra responsibility. It puts the horses' welfare in jeopardy. One call to the judge and he can get the horses back."

"So why hasn't he done it?"

"Because he can't admit he knows about this." Kevin stared at the slate skies. The wind carried the scent of rain. More water would only make Ellen's life more miserable. "You're from here. What do you know about Bancroft?"

Shauna reached for her father's hat, grabbing the brim with two fists. Chance took the hat off his own head and put it on his daughter's, playing peekaboo with her while he spoke. "Only what I see in the papers and on television. He's good at what he does. He's a man who likes the camera and plenty of attention. He talks big. He plays hard. He plays to win." Chance swept his gaze around to the barn. "But this looks like just an accident. The plumber said it looked like the pipe had a weak spot that gave way."

"Why is he fighting for horses he doesn't even want?"

Chance shrugged and crammed his hat back onto his head, much to Shauna's disappointment. Next the baby tackled the star on his chest with fingers and mouth. "Some people just hate to lose."

Kevin's jaw tensed. He couldn't just stand here and wait for the next disaster to happen. "There's got to be something more. He could have manipulated the media to get his way, but since the initial report, there's been nothing on the news. Why not?"

"It doesn't exactly show him at his best."

"Or maybe he's got something to hide."

Chance shot him a lethal glance. "Let it go. If you're right, if it is Bancroft, then it'll all blow over in a few days when the horses go home."

"Unless he can't wait that long."

The wind picked up and Chance shielded his daughter from the blowing dirt. "He will. He doesn't want the bad publicity."

"There's something wrong with these horses. What if he's trying to hide the fact that they're sick."

"What does that get him?"

"I don't know."

"You're asking for trouble when there's no need to."

Kevin caught sight of the house, of the warmth of the light, of the women in the kitchen. "Trouble. According to you, that's my specialty. But if it was Taryn who was fighting to speak for the horses, you'd do all you can to make sure her voice wasn't silenced."

Chance pressed his little girl tight to his chest and kissed the top of her watermelon-slice hat. "I'll see what I can dig up."

Chance started to walk away, then stopped. "You should tell Ellen who you are before she finds out. Whoever sent me the anonymous tip could use that fact to hurt her."

As his brother joined the women who were heading toward the barn, Kevin couldn't decide if Chance had given him a blessing or another warning.

"How's she doing?" Ellen asked later that night as she entered Calliope's stall and handed him a plate of sandwiches. Sitting on the stall partition, Kevin grabbed a triangle of smoked turkey on multigrain bread and took a bite. He hadn't realized how hungry he was until the first satisfying mouthful hit his stomach. The judge had come and gone, and for now they had a reprieve. He'd be back in a few days, then everything would be up for grabs again.

"She's breathing easier."

Dr. Parnell had given Calliope a shot of antibiotics and another to help open her airway. To keep Ellen busy, he'd also suggested a steam inhalation.

The mare had given up by the time they'd found her that afternoon. Only Blue's dedication had saved her. Ellen thought his manipulation of the horse's survival instincts was magic. What she didn't realize was that the selfless love reverberating from every cell of her body had given back the mare her fighting spirit. Not anything he'd done. Not the drugs Dr. Parnell had injected into her.

There was so much more to this woman than kindness and gentleness. There was a core strength in her that put him to shame.

"What do you know about the horses from the wreck?" he asked, to direct his thoughts on less treacherous grounds.

She sat in the thick nest of wood shavings by Calliope's head and stroked the mare's muzzle. Blue was beside her, keeping his faithful guard on the horse he'd rescued. "Not much except that they belong to Bancroft and were on their way back to his ranch from the track in Houston."

"Where's his ranch?"

"The other side of the Gabenburg county line toward Beaumont."

Kevin frowned and reached for another section of sandwich. "So what was he doing out this way?"

"Maybe the highway was closed because of the storm that night."

But that didn't make much sense. "What do you know about their pedigrees?"

"Not much. My background is in barrel racing and

Quarter Horses.'' She plucked hay from the net and tried to entice Calliope into nibbling. Eyes half-closed, head hanging low, the mare ignored her.

He took another bite of the sandwich and chewed it slowly. "I noticed a computer in your living room. Does it have Internet access?''

She nodded.

"I think we should do a little background research on Bancroft and his horses.''

She frowned and glanced at her watch. "Dr. Parnell got the results from the second round of tests.''

"Anything show up?''

"The blood count came in low. He says the horses' symptoms—dull, lethargic demeanor, tiring easily, pale membranes in the eyes and mouth—all point to anemia. He thought that was odd, because the feed had an elevated amount of iron.''

"Maybe they're getting worse because they're not getting their regular feed.''

"I thought of that.'' She frowned and twisted the hay in her hands.

"You can't blame yourself. You were right to test the feed first.''

"Maybe. We'll switch tomorrow and see if that helps.''

"If the feed is high in iron, that means Bancroft knew the horses were anemic. The feed is just to cover the symptom.''

Her head jerked up. "You're right. So where is the anemia coming from?''

"I think we need to look into their pedigrees and their race records.'' He polished off the last sandwich quarter. "I think we also need to take a look at Dr. Warner's book.''

"The 'protocol' book.''

"Yeah," he sneered. "The 'protocol' book. When he gets here in the morning, you divert him with Calliope and I'll see what I can see."

"What if you get caught?"

He smiled. "Maybe that forkful of manure just happened to fall into his bag, and naturally, I was making sure none of his belongings got stained."

She laughed and the sound of it heightened the crazy hum inside him. "I don't know. That sounds risky."

He ran a hand over his face. "Hey, with a face like this, what's not to trust?"

She lifted her hands and exaggerated the tremor of her tired muscles. "I think he'd be more apt to believe my shaky hands than yours."

"It's your call."

The mare coughed. He slid from the rail. Ellen stood up. He tried to move out of her way, but misread her intention and ended up nose to nose with her.

Her arms were small and delicate beneath his hands, all bones under that soft pink skin. Her moonflower scent, subtle and feminine, was enough to fog a man's brain with thoughts better left unrealized. His breath hitched. There, right there, were her lips, ripe and soft, parted in invitation. All he had to do was lean forward and taste her.

A sudden hunger for her ripped through him. Her eyes had gone blurry. Her body seemed to soften before him. She wouldn't push him away.

But he wasn't who she thought he was and he'd promised Chance not to hurt her.

"Ellen." Shaking his head, his hands gripped her arms tighter. He started to push her away.

Then she leaned in, eroding his resolve. One taste. Just one taste. He could steal that bit of memory to keep him company on cold Colorado nights, couldn't he?

He was an idiot. But then, when it came to Ellen, he'd never been able to think quite straight.

ELLEN HAD FANTASIZED about the taste of him all evening. Leaning forward now that he was so close seemed natural. She brushed her lips against his, feather-light. Just to see how soft they were, she told herself. But if she thought the impulse would ease her curiosity, she was wrong.

Two sensations hit her simultaneously: she felt like a fool for being so forward and taking what wasn't offered, and she felt a delicious ache stir her with astonishing need.

More, she had to have more.

The taste of him was dark and dangerous, like Kyle's had been. It ignited a fire she'd thought too dead to revive. The flames blazed so fast and furiously, she had to hang on to his shoulders or fall. Without meaning to, she deepened the kiss. His body jolted hard against hers. The shock of the spark it created vibrated inside her in helpless echoes.

What have I done?

She jerked away. He stepped back. In a clumsy dance, they shuffled until Calliope and Blue stood between them.

Ellen fussed with the inhalation station they'd set up for the horse. Breathing deeply, she took in a bracing whiff of eucalyptus. Still the remembered feel of him burned against her, still the bone-deep pulse of him thrummed inside her, still her heart struggled to slow its runaway pace. What must he think of her?

"The water's cold," she said. "I'd better get a refill."

Mind lost somewhere between the heat of his kiss and the brute force of her reaction to it, she grabbed for the bucket. Her hand missed, knocking it over and sloshing water all over Kevin's shirt and jeans.

He bent down to pick up the empty bucket. One hand

clutched around the handle, he lifted it and gave a rusty chuckle. "Since I'm already wet, why don't I take care of it?"

Face burning hot, she couldn't quite meet his gaze. Her useless fingers twisted in front of her. Her tongue tangled in a knot. "Sure."

She'd made a right fool of herself. Kissing a ranch hand. What had she been thinking?

As he walked out the stall, she wrapped one arm around her quivering stomach, then touched her lips with two fingers. She could still feel the throb of his kiss. Shivering, she hitched in a shaky breath.

God help her, she wanted more.

She couldn't explain why her natural reluctance to being touched seemed to fly out the window when Kevin was around. All she knew was that she wanted to be near him even now when her brashness had him seeking escape.

She followed him to the tack room where his bed was set up. A layer of muddy slime still coated the floor. The blankets on the cot hung soaked from the sides. He couldn't sleep here tonight. "You can move your stuff to the guest room in the house."

"I'll stay with Calliope tonight. Why don't you go in and get some rest? Tomorrow's going to be a long day."

He had his back turned to her and was taking off his wet T-shirt. The Xs and zigzags of anger carved on his back, the fading bruise on his shoulder, brought reality back to life. He'd been hurt badly. She could understand the self-preservation instinct to avoid more pain. And what could she honestly offer him when she was still in love with a dead man? Without thinking, she reached out and touched the marks on his back. "I'm sorry."

He flinched as if she'd burned him and whirled to face her.

She rubbed one wrist with the opposite hand and shifted her weight from one foot to the other. "I—I didn't mean to startle you. I—I just—"

"It's really not a good idea for you to stay here right now."

At the tightness in his voice, she looked up. He held the wet T-shirt tight in both hands. The muscles of his chest were taut as if on guard. In his eyes, she'd expected to see hurt or anger. Instead, attraction glimmered, hot and strong, and oh, so primal. The fierceness of it took her breath away. The heat of it shot an arrow straight to her core. Her body answered without her permission, softening, lubricating…yearning.

"I, uh." She licked her lips, trying to find thoughts in the strong stir of desire engulfing her mind, her body, her senses. "I wanted to apologize."

"You already have."

"I thought…"

"What?" He cocked his head. With a finger he reached out and stroked her cheek. "I'm not what you need."

Fight sprang up from old hurts. Was another man trying to tell her what was best for her? "What do you know about me or what I need?"

"You seem like the type of woman who'd want a fairy tale—a prince who'd come home every night, two point five kids and a dog. Not a one-night stand with a drifter."

"You're wrong. About the fantasy, I mean."

"Am I?"

She'd always thought of black as cold, but Kevin's eyes were the hottest things she'd ever seen as he stepped closer. With a finger, he stroked the crooked fall of a curl, skimmed her cheek. A delicious tremor shivered down her spine, making her head light, her blood warm, her body scream for release.

"Tell me the truth," he crooned as if she were one of the horses. "Weren't those the dreams that filled your head as a little girl?"

"I had big dreams once." Her voice croaked from the dryness of her throat. Once, she was going to be a vet. She was going to marry Kyle. Together they were going to raise horses and children and live happily ever after. "Dreams change."

"And now?" His breath whispered against her lobe, sending a shower of delight fluttering through her. "What do you want?"

She wanted to lie, to tell him a pretty tale to prove him wrong, but could think of nothing but the truth. "I'm not sure what I want."

He looked around. "Seems like you're on your way to something solid."

"Maybe." She scanned the barn. The walls were good and strong. Her house was the home she and Kyle had once imagined. The land was rich enough to support her horses. They weren't the purebreds of her childhood dreams, but they needed her. And she needed them. Wasn't that what was important? "When I heard about Luci, I got mad. I, I…"

She had the urge to tell him everything about Kyle and Garth and the lost years, but even a man who wore his scars on the outside for all the world to see might not understand the helplessness of fifteen years without a voice.

"She needed a home, so you gave her one."

The gentleness of his voice constricted her throat. "Yes."

"You have a good heart, Ellen Paxton. Don't waste it on a man who has none."

Even as he spoke, she saw the hard hammer beat in his

chest. She placed a hand, fingers splayed against it. He sucked in a breath. The heat of him seeped through her palm. "You're wrong. You have a generous heart. Your dog knows it. The horses know it. Maybe one day, you'll figure it out and stop running away."

He pulled her hand from his chest. She felt the rip of the connection and cringed. "Sometimes the idea of things is better than the reality."

"And sometimes reality can surprise you." Not knowing what to do with her bereft hand, she tugged at the rubber band holding the end of her flyaway braid. "My behavior earlier was inappropriate. I'm not looking for…anything."

"I didn't think you were." He reached into his duffel bag for a clean shirt. "But I'm human and I need a bit of space now."

"Oh, okay, then. As long as we understand each other."

He gave a curt nod. "I'll heat the water."

"Thank you."

As she strode away, the heels of her boots clicking on the concrete aisle, she muttered a curse. She'd handled this all wrong. Raking a hand through her hair, she tore apart the loosened braid and walked back to Calliope. She sat in the thick nest of wood shavings in the stall and cuddled up to Blue. But even hiding here couldn't dispel her awareness of Kevin.

His every movement in the tack room brought pictures of him into her mind. Not just of his body so lean and sexy, and his eyes so dark and hungry, but of his strength, of his gentleness, of his seemingly tireless energy. Everything about him was wrong for her. But her body, for so long stiff and hard like forgotten clay, had found a new malleability under his gaze, and wanted to explore this new feeling of aliveness.

"The last thing I need is to make a fool of myself over him." When the horses left, so would he. Unless she managed to keep them... She growled and shook her head. No, she wasn't ready for that. Not with so many unresolved feelings still trapped inside her.

She reached for Blue's head and scratched behind his ear. He plopped his head on her thigh and looked up at her with soulful eyes.

"It's too complicated," she told the dog.

Her anger, her guilt, her enduring love for Kyle still hid in a corner of her mind. Part of her feared opening herself to the sorrow she'd find there. Part of her knew she had to let go.

Twenty minutes later, Kevin entered the stall and set the steaming bucket of water he carried onto the upturned garbage can. The scent of eucalyptus wafted on the visible waves of steam. Speaking in low, sandy tones, he wrapped a clean towel around Calliope's nose and encouraged her to breathe deeply.

Watching him murmur to the horse, she suddenly knew what it was about him that disturbed her so much. Her hand stilled on the dog's head. Her chest tightened. Her heart melted.

This was the man Kyle could have grown into given time and love.

Chapter Nine

The sound of an engine woke Kevin from a fitful sleep filled with disturbing dreams of cutting rocks and raging rivers and wild lovemaking. Remembering the reason for his stiff back and the crick in his neck took him a minute. He'd fallen asleep sitting in Calliope's stall while he was supposed to keep an eye on the horse.

Through slitted eyes, he focused on the mare. She was nibbling hay from the net. Her sides weren't heaving. Her breathing was normal. She was going to be all right. Relief slumped through him. Losing the mare would have hurt Ellen too much.

Then he became aware of the weight on his shoulder, of the hair tickling the side of his neck, of the heat molding his body so perfectly it might have been a blanket. Ellen. He couldn't remember sitting so close to her. He'd argued long and hard with her to go back to the house and get a decent night's sleep. One of them should. And with the memory of her tender kiss stirring his blood into chaos, he doubted he'd get one.

There'd always been something addictive about the feel of Ellen. He should have known one kiss wouldn't be enough. He wanted more, but he didn't want to frighten her with the fierceness of his need. So he'd savored what she was willing to offer. Now he'd have to keep his distance, because her guard would surely catch up with her impulse. Her regret would make things awkward and he wasn't ready to leave yet. Not until Bancroft was out of her life and she was out of danger.

The engine noise came closer. Blue didn't stir from Ellen's side. Kevin scowled. Had they missed morning feed? He looked out the window. No, the sky was too dark. Gently, reluctantly, he eased Ellen from his side and settled her into the soft bedding. She mumbled something in her sleep. It sounded like ''Kyle'' and had him holding his breath for a second. But she didn't wake. As he went by the feed room, he glanced at the clock by the feed bins. Five-thirty. Who would visit at such a time?

At the barn door, he paused and watched the navy Double B truck splash through puddles and halt before him. Rain pelted against the barn's tin roof in drowsy splats. Catching sight of him, Luci and C.C. left the shelter of the shed and trotted to the gate, expecting breakfast.

''What are you doing here?'' he asked as Bancroft and his wife exited the truck.

''We've come to check on the horses.'' The wife's smile reminded him of a robot playing at feeling. ''The front gate was open.''

The front gate was *always* locked. ''What happened to Dr. Warner?''

''His wife is ill. He's with her. I'll be collecting the data today.''

Collecting the data? There was a coldness to the woman that didn't sit well with Kevin.

Bancroft crammed a hat onto his head and hiked the collar of his rain duster over his thick neck. ''We don't owe you an explanation. Get on with it, Tessa. I don't have all day for this.''

"Of course, sugar. I'll be done in half an hour if you'd rather wait in the truck."

Bancroft stuffed himself back into the truck's cab and reached for a steaming mug of something. Tessa stalked into the barn as if she owned it. At least today she'd dressed the part of the equestrienne—somewhat. Paddock boots covered her feet. Tight riding jeans showed every well-toned curve from hip to calf. A brown silk blouse, wet from the rain, clung transparently to her, leaving nothing to his imagination.

"Why are most of your stalls empty?" She extracted what looked like a blue accounting book from the black bag she carried.

Wood shavings sticking to her hair, Ellen silently questioned him over Calliope's stall door. He raised one shoulder and let it drop.

"Because someone tampered with the watering system yesterday and the stalls are drying out."

She shoved the book back in the bag. "I'll call for my van then, and take the horses home."

He shook his head. "Afraid not. The judge has already been by to see the damage and approved of the care they're getting. You'll have to wait."

Without looking at him, Tessa dug the book back out and turned the pages. Her jaw tightened. Her teeth seemed to grind in slow circles while she tamped down her anger. "Please fetch the horses for me."

He grabbed a halter and lead rope from the tack room and handed them to her. She held them by two fingers as if she didn't understand their use. "You want 'em, you get 'em. I've got chores to do."

Her features pinched. "Do I need to get my husband?"

"If he wants to help, he's welcome."

She thrust the halter at him. "Have Ms. Paxton fetch them."

"She's busy tending to one of your horses who's come down with pneumonia."

"Pneumonia?" Tessa's high-and-mighty eyebrows curved into a reproachful arch. "How could she let that happen?"

Like you don't know. "You can thank whoever flooded the barn for that."

"I'll talk to the judge."

"Knock yourself out. He already knows she's too sick to move."

Kevin turned away and headed to the feed room where he noisily set about mixing the morning rations. Interesting that the horse's condition held no concern for her other than a way to fault Ellen or get them back in her clutches. From the corner of his eye, he saw Tessa steam, nostrils flaring like a Thoroughbred filly after a race. But he'd left her no choice. If she wanted the horses to "collect her data," she'd have to get them herself. How important was the data to her? What information did it give her?

Tessa bent down and replaced the book in the black bag. When she exited the barn, he grabbed a bucket of feed and headed down the aisle. Ellen hurried out of Calliope's stall, trapping Blue inside. The dog scratched at the door.

"We don't have long," Kevin said, examining the bag. Tessa had left the zipper just so, cracked open three-quarters of an inch, a wood shaving balanced on the pull, an "S" crease in the leather on the side. "Look out front and make sure Bancroft doesn't surprise us."

Ellen went to her post and laughed. "This you should see."

Crouching beside the bag, he removed the shaving and carefully slid the zipper open. "What?"

"Bancroft singing along with the radio."

Chuckling, Kevin extracted the book. "Any good?"

"A lovely froglike bass."

The paddock gate squealed a warning. Thank God he hadn't gotten around to oiling it yet. Kevin grabbed the knife from his pocket and cut a page as close to the binding as he could. He shoved the paper in his back pocket, hiking the hem of his T-shirt out to cover the bulge. Then he returned the book to the bag, the zipper to the three-quarter-inch mark, made sure to crease the "S" and balanced the shaving as he'd found it.

By the time Titan's hooves clopped onto the aisle, Kevin was in Calliope's stall and Ellen was stuffing hay nets in the feed room.

A soaked Tessa took pulse, respiration and temperature readings and made entries into her mysterious protocol book. She scratched notes on a pad and handed them to Ellen.

"I've altered their feed rations," Tessa said. "Make sure you see to the changes. It's important they're fed the grain we sent."

Ellen glanced at the new schedule. "Why?"

Tessa huffed with barely suppressed impatience. "Because it's balanced specifically for their needs. *You* are harming them by feeding them ordinary oats. Is that what you really want?"

"Of course not." A pang of worry creased Ellen's forehead. Kevin wanted to shake Tessa for deliberately stabbing at Ellen's weakness.

"Then stop being obstinate and feed them their proper rations. I'll send another load to replace what you lost in your unfortunate flood."

Tessa breezed away like a queen done with her lowly subjects.

Kevin went to stand by Ellen at the barn door.

"Well, that was weird," Ellen said, hands on her hips.

"Yeah, weird." Had the Bancrofts arrived early in hopes of catching them still asleep? If so, why? He'd have to take a look at the gate. He withdrew the pilfered page from his pocket and ironed it with the side of his hand against his thigh. "What do you think?"

Beneath the date, eight months ago, each horse—or he assumed the code stood for a horse—had a series of numbers entered in columns. Twelve horses in all. Two horses had red lines and no data in the spaces beside their names. Dead?

"What does it mean?" Ellen asked, frowning.

His fingers tightened on the page to keep himself from reaching for her and pressing her head against his shoulder. "Beats me."

They looked at each other, then down the aisle at the row of horses waiting expectantly for their breakfast.

"You finish the feeding," he said. "I'll start on the stalls. The sooner we're done with the chores, the sooner we can start looking for the answers."

Before he filled the wheelbarrow with fresh shavings to cover the bared stalls, he trotted to the gate and examined the mechanism. Not a scratch. He pressed the remote button. The gate hesitated, then swung closed smoothly.

In all the chaos yesterday, had they left the gate unlocked? The answer was a resounding no. He and Blue had walked the perimeter before the rain and the gate had been closed and locked.

THE RAIN and the constant interruptions for chores and consultations with the vet and the plumber hampered their research. They'd found a Thoroughbred-pedigree query page and left their request for all six of the Bancroft horses' lineage, but hadn't gotten very far on the rest of their investigation.

The data on Tessa's logbook page still remained a mystery. So far, they'd deciphered the entries for temperature, pulse and respiration. The numbers in the other three columns didn't seem to relate to anything they'd seen Dr. Warner or Tessa do. Ellen had copied the information on a fresh page for Dr. Parnell to examine. He'd promised to look at it after his rounds.

By nightfall, the rumble of the sky was a reflection of the growl reverberating inside her. Ellen was dying for a shower, for an hour of uninterrupted Internet time, and mostly, for answers.

A knock sounded on the kitchen door. Without moving from her spot next to Kevin on the hunter-green corduroy couch, she called, "Come in."

The plumber peeked through the door, rain dripping from his slicker onto the kitchen floor. "Everything's back in order."

"I can take a shower?"

He smiled. "Might want to let the water heat back up first."

"You're a miracle worker." She cheerfully wrote out a check and thanked the plumber profusely.

"You go first," she told Kevin as she sank back into the comfortable seat. He started to speak, but she interrupted him, leaning toward the screen of her laptop propped on the mission-style coffee table. "I want to run a load of laundry, so I'll need your clothes."

Shooing his hands from the keyboard, she placed her own fingers on the keys. "Where are you?"

He leaned in too close. She shut her eyes and inhaled the scent of horse and man and tried not to think about how good he'd tasted last night. "Checking the racing schedules. Something doesn't work. You said they were racing in Houston, but the Thoroughbred-racing season at the Sam Houston Race Park ended in April.''

"April?'' She stared at the screen and scrolled up and down on the displayed page. "That doesn't make sense. If they weren't there, where were they?''

"Didn't Bancroft say they were on their way to slaughter?''

"Yes, of course. Maybe they were going from the ranch to…there.'' She waved him away. "I'll check that angle while you shower.''

Half an hour later, he came back smelling of soap and toothpaste and that unique scent of his—something like sunshine on first-cut hay. If she hadn't felt so grimy, she might have given in to the temptation to curl herself on his lap and drink in the clean scent of him. The urge to run a hand over his chest was nearly overpowering. The yearning to taste him again almost impossible to resist.

"I've been checking on where else they might have raced.'' She cleared her throat and squinted at the screen. "Thoroughbred racing doesn't start for another week at Louisiana Downs. I've got the page for Lonestar Park in Grand Prairie loading.''

Tripping on the edge of the braided rug, she left before she could make a fool of herself, and scrubbed away what felt like an inch of dirt and sweat from her skin and hair. But as hard as she tried, she couldn't wash away her desire for his touch.

Fresh clothes and a glass of iced tea gained her back some composure. She joined him on the couch, flinching at the unexpected jolt of thigh brushing against thigh.

"They were racing at Lonestar,'' Kevin said, moving closer to the edge of the cushion, creating space between them. "None of them won.''

"Well, that's enough of a reason to kill them all," she huffed. "If they were coming from Grand Prairie, then they had to be heading south, so that works. They were probably going home."

"I doubt it." He turned the screen so she could see the page displayed. "That's the Double B."

Head after head of cattle. Not a horse in sight. "So, where were they going?"

He seemed to hesitate, playing with the keys. Deep ridges formed on his forehead. "Kevin?"

"Legacy's Apollo, Legacy's Pandora, Legacy's Calliope, Legacy's Titan, Legacy's Hercules, Legacy's Perseus." He rubbed the thigh of his jeans, his fingers lingering on the small lump where the pocket would end. "The pedigrees came back while you were in the shower. They all have the same sire. Legacy's Prometheus. He's standing at the Royal Legacy Ranch."

"Maybe they were going there."

"Maybe." He typed in an URL. Slowly, the page loaded. Thoroughbreds galloped across the top border. A ranch house with a fieldstone front and a stained glass-adorned door appeared. A picture of foals frolicking in a pasture bordered by a blinding-white fence popped up on the left. A black horse crossing the finish line by a length took up the middle spot. On the right, a head shot of Legacy's Prometheus—a black devil with an attitude.

Below, line by line, her nightmare came back to life. Blond hair, brown eyes, a smile that could dazzle and kill in one breath. *Hello, darlin'.* His drawled endearment echoed in her head and grated along her nerves. He seemed to pop right out of the screen and stand beside her as he'd done so many times over those helpless years. *Remember, darlin', when you thought you could manipulate me as easily as you did your sweetheart? You learned your lesson, didn't you? I always win.*

"Royal Legacy is owned by Garth Ramsey."

Her heart stopped beating. Her blood seemed to drain right out of her. Her skin went cold and clammy. When she found her breath again, it jarred her heart into overdrive. She jolted up, swayed, found her footing and scrambled sideways.

"Ellen?"

"I—I…" She ran a hand through her still wet hair, not quite sure what to do with herself. Not Garth. Not again. How could he? He's in jail. The horses belong to the Bancrofts not to him. "I need to check on the horses."

"Let me do it."

He stood behind her as if ready to catch her should she fall. *Don't touch me. Please, don't touch me.* She strode to the kitchen, reached for her baseball cap on the hook under the bar mirror, caught sight of her ghost of a face and looked away. Stuffing her feet into boots, she concentrated on breathing. *Breathe in. Breathe out.*

"I'm fine." *Breathe in. Breathe out.* "I want to make sure everyone's settled in for the night."

"I'll go with you."

"No," she said through gritted teeth. *Breathe in. Breathe out.* "Keep looking."

"Ellen—"

She slammed the door in his face and hoped to God he wouldn't follow. She could barely keep herself from flying apart, let alone handle an explanation.

Would Garth never stop haunting her? Rain pelted down, but she didn't feel its sting. Somewhere along the way, her cap blew away and her already wet hair became soaked. Slipping and sliding, she managed to find her way to the barn.

Busy, she had to keep busy or thoughts of Garth would drive her crazy. She had to force him out of her mind. Jamming her brain in neutral, she moved from stall to stall. Her legs jerked stiffly as she walked. Her hands shook as she fumbled with the latch on each stall. She couldn't feel her fingertips. The weight in her chest grew, but she refused to think, to cry, to feel. She checked each horse, but couldn't have said if they were dead or alive. She stuffed hay nets, swept the aisle, cleaned the tack room.

Move, move, keep moving.

But exhaustion caught up with her. Her tired muscles rebelled, cramping, twitching. She crawled onto Kevin's stripped camp cot. She drew her knees to her chest, felt herself fall into a dark pit. Despair wrapped around her, choked her, sucked her will, leaving her limp.

Garth.

Even in jail, the man responsible for her coma, for her imprisonment in a nursing home, had the power to ruin her progress into health. She thought she'd put him and his cruelty behind. She'd sworn nothing he'd ever done would touch her again. Then this. Was the accident no accident at all? Had he "given" her the horses to build her up, then tear her apart?

I always win.

If he'd searched for a hundred years, he couldn't have found a more perfect way to torture her.

A raw, strangled wail ripped straight from her soul. She held it in with both hands. "How could you? How could you? How could you?"

Her stomach heaved with each suppressed sob. Her throat felt raw from her stifled cries. She gulped in air. The brutal images of Garth, of his anger, of his murderous intent returned in full, living color. They swirled in her mind, dragging her deeper into endless black. If he was willing to kill her to keep his secret, if he was willing to drug her to influence her father, wouldn't he be willing to use the horses to have the final say? He blamed her for being in jail. As they'd led him away, chains jangling at his wrists and legs, he'd sought her gaze and mouthed, *I always win.*

"No." She sat bolt upright, hanging on to the edge of the cot as if it were the only thing that could keep her sane. "I can't give up. I can't let him win."

A burst of lightning filled the tack room. Thunder exploded, shaking the ground. A frightened whinny pierced through her pain.

"Apollo." The gelding had refused to come in, even as his herd mates were snugged inside, away from the elements in freshly dried stalls.

With leaden legs, Ellen forced herself to stand, then to walk, then to run outside. Apollo paced the pasture gate.

"What's wrong?" Rain drenched her to the skin.

As another boom of thunder rattled the ground, Apollo stood shaking. Was he reliving the night of the accident? Ellen opened the gate, slipped on a halter over his head. "Come on, Apollo, let's go in."

But the chestnut gelding just stood, trembling with fear. Helplessness filled her. "Please, Apollo, follow me."

She begged. She cajoled. She pushed and prodded and begged some more. Soaked and scared, all Apollo would do was stand, eyes wide and panicked, limbs shaking as the ground shuddered beneath them after each crash of thunder.

"Apollo." The word rasped raw out of Ellen's throat. She flung her arms around the gelding's neck and squeezed hard. "Please, Apollo."

All the tears she'd tried to hold in came flooding out, mixing with the rain and the lightning and the thunder. She pressed her hands on both sides of Apollo's cheeks.

"Now you listen to me. I can't help you unless you come with me. You got that? You want out of this nightmare, then you've got to follow me inside where it's nice and dry."

She grabbed the side of the halter, then stepped out, confidently expecting Apollo to follow her. The leather slipped from her fingers. With a sob, she let go and kept walking. *Apollo, please.* One step. Two. In the next, she felt Apollo's nose press against the small of her back and a stream of fresh tears flowed. "That's it. We can't let him win, Apollo. We just can't."

A few minutes later, Apollo settled down, munching on hay. Ellen grabbed a grooming caddie. With a scraper, she sloughed off the excess water from the gelding's coat. Then she twisted hay into a wisp and massaged the horse.

Sobs racked her body. Pain and despair keened out of her. She kept rubbing, refusing to stop even when gentle hands tried to pry the tool free from her fingers.

"I won't let him win."

KEVIN CRADLED the weeping Ellen in his arms and carried her into the house. He sat her in the overstuffed chair in the living room, draped the afghan on its back around her shivering body.

"I'm fine," she said. Her tears had finally run dry, but the flatness of her voice and her shaking limbs told him otherwise.

He wasn't sure how he'd expected her to react to Garth's name. Anger, maybe. Resentment. But not this complete devastation. He needed to hold her, to wrap his arms tightly around her, but sensed doing so would only suffocate her. Still, he couldn't let her go completely, so he tugged off her muddy boots.

He hunted through the kitchen, looking for something

strong, but had to settle for chamomile tea. He brought her a steaming mug. She wrapped her hands around it, hunched over until it rested on her knees and her nose was over the rim. Rain dripped from her hair and plopped onto the braided rug at her feet.

From the bathroom he retrieved a kiwi-colored towel and a wide-toothed comb. Gently he towel-dried her hair. Then strand by long strand, he combed it out. Bit by bit, her shaking subsided.

"I grew up with Garth Ramsey," she said, still holding on to the cup as if it was an anchor. "He was my—I don't know what you'd call Kyle. He wasn't quite a fiancé, but certainly more than a friend." Kevin's hands stilled at the mention of Kyle. He forced himself to go on. "I tolerated him *because* he was Kyle's friend. He had these weird ideas about how I should wear my hair and clothes. He gave me the creeps sometimes. But Kyle liked him. So I said nothing."

Kevin's breath caught in his throat. His chest tightened. He didn't want to hear about Kyle. It would only increase his guilt. But she needed to talk, so he pushed himself to relax his touch and keep combing.

"I loved Kyle."

He closed his eyes, swallowed hard. The bruise over his heart ached with every breath he took. *I loved you, too.*

"But he had this notion he had to prove something to somebody. I was never quite sure who. Maybe my father. Maybe his grandfather. Maybe even his brother. He always felt like he didn't measure up."

Carter Paxton hadn't thought him good enough for his daughter and missed no opportunity to tell him so. He wasn't too likely to have approved of their planned engagement. John Henry Makepeace cursed him every time he bailed him out. *You're going to turn out just like me.*

Is that what you want with your life? Why can't you be more like your brother? And Kent had made it plain enough that he was tired of acting like a buffer between him and the world so hard up to bite him on the heels.

Kyle thought he'd hidden that hole in himself from everyone. The brash cowboy, flashy and fast. Everyone had believed the tough image he'd projected. How could she have seen through it so clearly?

She swallowed a gulp of tea. "He was everything I wanted, but he didn't believe me. 'Someday I'll make you proud,' he'd say. And I'd say, 'I'm already proud.' But he had to go. For himself. I understood, really, I did. But I was scared. I'd already lost so many people I cared for. I couldn't lose him, too."

Kevin strangled the comb in his hand. He needed to hold her so much, to tell her was sorry. Instead, he continued stroking her hair. "Maybe he had to go so he could come back."

She shrugged one shoulder. "He never got the chance. We got into a stupid fight. Said things we both regretted. Then I made things worse by pretending I didn't care. I tried to make him jealous. Instead, I got him drowned."

"You can't blame yourself."

She shook her head and let out a throttled sound. "If I hadn't gone to the river that day… If I hadn't tried to make him jealous, then none of this would have happened."

And if I'd been able to bare my soul, he thought, *if I'd been able to tell you I wasn't quite ready to settle down yet, that I needed a little time and a little distance, that I would come back because my heart was full of you, and that it was that fierce passion that scared the hell out of me, then there would be no reason for you to try to make me jealous.*

And her deep emotions had scared him as much as his own. Scared him still.

He knelt beside her, hooked a finger under her chin and lifted it until she looked at him. How could she even think she was to blame? "Whenever I railed about my fate, my grandmother used to tell me there was a reason for everything."

"Did you believe her?" Her gray-green eyes looked at him with such hope for release.

He dropped his hand and shook his head. On that score, Nina's words had brought him no comfort. "No."

"Maybe she's right. I've certainly paid for my mistake." She drained the mug.

He took it from her, set it on the coffee table and sat on the corner, knee to knee, but not touching her. "You didn't do anything wrong."

"I tried to blackmail Garth into helping Kyle when he got into trouble with the river. Garth turned on me. He bashed my head against a rock, then rolled me into the water to drown. I'm still not quite sure what happened after that. The doctors say I might never remember. I was in a coma for a long time." She lifted a hand. It spasmed. "That's why I twitch like an old fish when I'm tired. Some of the connections still haven't woken up."

"I hadn't noticed."

She gave a dry laugh. "You're a bad liar."

He hoped he was good enough of one to play his ranch-hand role for another few days. The last thing she needed was selfish Kyle showing up at the wrong time in her life.

"When I started coming out of the coma," she went on, a small frown rucking her forehead, "Garth started visiting."

She gulped in air and started shaking again. Kevin clasped her hands between his and rubbed warmth back into her icy fingers. "You don't have to explain anything to me."

Gazing at her feet, she ignored him.

"Twice a week. Regular as clockwork, he'd visit. Once in a while, he'd slip a needle into the vein of my arm. I couldn't stop him. I was too weak. When I close my eyes, I can still see him there beside me."

Her breath shuddered. Her eyes were fixed and fuzzy, her gaze frozen somewhere in inner landscape. He blew on her fingertips to warm them. "You were strong. You didn't give up. You survived."

"I could hear and see and understand everything that was going on around me, but my muscles seemed to belong to someone else. And I could feel. God, I could feel. Hurt and anger. Hate. So much hate."

She gulped in air. "But I couldn't scream. I could barely move without help. I couldn't find the words to speak, the tears to cry. It was like there were two of me. The heavy me in the body and the light me in my head, and the two couldn't connect."

He squeezed her hands harder, wishing he could extract and absorb all of her pain.

Her breath hitched. "Garth would come in and drawl in my ear. He'd tell me how beautiful I was, how lucky I was, how he would always take care of me because he loved me so much."

Kevin gritted his teeth, said nothing. He wanted to kill Garth with his bare hands, watch his eyes bulge, his face turn blue, his tongue swell. Then he wanted to choke him all over again.

"When I finally got away, he told me that I'd never be free, that I'd always belong to him." Tears streamed silently down her face. They clawed at his heart, ripping it to shreds.

With the edge of the towel, he wiped her cheeks dry. Her gaze speared his with fiery desperation. "I can't let those horses go. I can't let him win."

"He can't hurt you."

She shook her head. "You don't know him. He'll do anything to win and I'm responsible for him being in jail."

Kevin swallowed hard. Her torture at Garth's hands had filled her life for sixteen years. That it had instilled him with capabilities he didn't have was normal. Letting go would take time. Now was not the time to point out her faulty logic. All he could do was reassure her. "We won't let him."

Chapter Ten

"Do me a favor?" Ellen asked. She trapped his hand against her cheek, the towel a calming barrier between the voltaic charge of her touch.

"Sure. Anything."

"Make love to me."

Lightning flashed. Thunder rattled the windows. The shock of her request jolted him backward on the coffee table, knocking a pile of catalogs to the floor. Kevin swallowed hard and shook his head. "No."

"Why not?" She blinked madly as she tried to fold the towel on her knee. "Do you have a problem, you know, in that department?"

A big problem. I'm in love with you. "No—"

"A sexually transmitted disease?"

"No, that's—"

"If it's protection that's worrying you, there's no problem. For a couple of reasons, the doctor put me on birth control pills last year."

Frustration whined along his nerves. "That's not—"

"Don't you want me?" She lifted her gaze to meet his. A frown of confusion creased her forehead. Her fingers nervously knitted together above the folded towel. Her bare feet, with their moon-pale skin, curled protectively against one another. "Last night. I thought…you might."

"Wanting is not the problem." Far from it.

"Then what?"

"The timing's wrong." A decade off, at least.

"How?" She cocked her head to one side, setting the riot of drying curls on her head in motion. They played with the light, sparkling gold, tormenting him with their promise of silk. "You want me. I want you."

"You've had an upsetting day." He shoved both his hands in his jeans pockets, reached for the bone feather, thumbed the carved ridges and prayed for strength. "You should go to bed—"

"I'm trying to maneuver you there." One side of her mouth quirked up. "You'll have to help me out, though. I'm not very experienced in the art of seduction."

"Trust me, you don't need any help," he muttered. He took in a long breath, then leaned forward and tried for a brotherly pat on her knees. "Ellen…"

"Yes?"

His fingers curled around the caps of her knees as he tried to figure out what to do next. He wanted her more than he'd thought possible. And here she was asking for what he most desired. Holding her, kissing her, loving her had become an obsession that tormented him day and night since he'd walked onto her ranch. But this wasn't the way. She was upset over Garth and would surely regret her brashness in the morning.

Sweat prickled his neck, slid down his spine. His blood pounded through his veins. His want for her was a wildfire he needed to contain—for both their sakes.

Aroused and angry for even contemplating her invitation, he shot up from the coffee table. In the kitchen, he poured himself a glass of water at the sink and drank it in one shot. Might as well have spit into an inferno for all the cooling relief it provided.

"Kevin." Her hand skimmed over his back. Every muscle in his body tensed, trying to hold back the kick of need to his belly. She drew closer, skated her lips along the side of his neck, slid her hands around his waist. Her busy fingers played with the button of his fly. He tried to muffle his groan, but it chugged through him locomotive loud.

Swearing, he spun around and grabbed her by the hips. The pupils of her eyes blazed wide open, nearly buckling his knees. He hiked her onto the counter. Driving her knees apart with a check of his hips, he pressed his erection hard against her. "Is this what you want, Ellen? Hard and fast on the kitchen counter? Hot sex with the ranch hand. That's so cliché."

He'd hoped for embarrassment, a flick of pain to prevent the deeper cut. But the fever in her eyes matched the one boiling through his blood. Her voice became whiskey smooth and twice as potent. "If that's the way you want me, then yes."

"Why?" he rasped, digging his fingers through her hair, spearing her with his gaze.

She swallowed hard. "You don't scare me. I've seen you with the horses, with Blue. I know how good and gentle and caring you are."

"You don't know anything about me."

"I know the important things." She wrapped her arms around his neck. "I trust you."

"Don't." *I'm lying to you.*

Lightning bleached the sky out the window. One, one thousand. Two, one thousand. Three, one thousand. Thunder growled. He licked the dryness from his lips. "There's someone out there for you. Not me."

She brushed a finger along his wet lips. He tried to find

his breath. "I loved Kyle, but he's dead. I've been free for a year, but part of me is still stuck in the cage of my past. I need to forget him."

"By using a stranger for sex?" The irony of the situation wasn't lost on him. She wanted to use the man he pretended he was to forget the boy he'd been.

"Not a stranger. A friend." Her fingers wreaked havoc on his nape. Her gaze suddenly blurred and filled with sadness. Her voice hitched. "Kyle, he's stuck inside me and I need to know I can go on without him."

"It's a mistake," he whispered as he held her close. He wasn't sure if he was telling her or reminding himself. The scent of her seeped into his him like a poison, clouding his mind until he could make out no thought. Everything became pure sensation—heat, love, passion.

"But it's my mistake to make," she said.

If she was going to do this, if she was going to use a man to forget the boy still living in her heart, then it might as well be with someone who loved her. "Then let's do it right."

He carried her to the bedroom, peeled back the quilt with a rainbow of stars in primary colors covering her bed and set her down on the edge. Looking around, he spotted the fat blue candle on her bedside table. He lit a match from the box beside the ruby-red glass holder. The flame flickered to life. Lightning shimmered through the curtains, but the thunder's roll was nothing more than a distant murmur.

As he turned around, a warm, heavy feeling filled his heart. He was in love with her. Had always been. He'd get over it. He'd get over her. Had to. There was no other way around it. But for tonight, he could give her the gift of his love and wrap it into the goodbye to the boy she'd once loved who no longer existed.

WHEN KEVIN TURNED, her breath caught in her throat. With the candlelight burning behind him, he was faceless. He pulled his T-shirt over his head. The soft light burnished his skin. Her heart skipped unsteadily. Her pulse jumped as if she were a skittish filly.

What were you thinking? What are you doing?

His hand hesitated at the zipper of his jeans. "There's still time to change your mind."

Unable to speak, she shook her head.

"Ellen?"

"What?" she whispered, and swallowed hard. As she peered into his darkened face, Kyle's ghost arose from his blank features, teasing her, taunting her. *I told you I'd always love you. I'm not going to let you forget me.*

"What do you want, Ellen?"

"I want…" She gulped in air. "I want to feel like a woman, not a broken body." Not a broken spirit.

Kevin offered her a hand. She took it, rose to her feet. He peeled off her damp T-shirt, dropped it to the floor. He rained a trail of kisses down the side of her neck. With a finger, he slid the strap of her bra off her shoulder. His lips followed, drawing a ripple of shivers. His thumb brushed against her nipple, reaping a small gasp of pleasure from her.

"You like that?"

"Yes," she said breathlessly. Her arms snaked around his neck. Her fingers raked into his hair. "Don't stop."

His mouth so soft, so hot, so unexpectedly hungry, spread a delicious warmth through her. The scent of lavender, howood and clary sage from the burning candle further relaxed her. A languid melting overtook her bones, shaping her to the hard lines of his body.

Lost in the sensation of his hands on her skin, she wasn't quite sure how the rest of their clothes got to the floor, how they maneuvered to the bed, but suddenly the solid weight of him was over her, enveloping her. She should be afraid, but she wasn't. For the first time in sixteen years, she felt safe.

She kissed the fingertips brushing along her cheek. "I knew your hands would be like this."

"Like what?" he said huskily.

"Like magic."

"Not magic," he said, proving himself wrong with a long, slow caress down her back that sparked an electric pleasure from head to toe and had her coiling herself around him.

With this selfish act of love with a stranger, she thought she'd be saying goodbye to her past, to Kyle, but found she was instead saying hello to herself.

Each touch, each murmur, each kiss awakened a new part of her. Her body became alive, truly alive. Every fiber, every cell, every atom. Echoes of the past, the feel, the taste, the scent of sex, mingled with the present, filling her with melancholy. But the boy's hesitation had become the man's experience, and her girl's innocence was becoming a woman's appreciation. Kyle was dead. Kevin was alive. She was alive, so alive.

Sensations coursed through her, one jumping right over the other, leaving her quivering and desperately wanting more. Her moans of pleasure mixed with the sound of feral delight low in his throat and thundered like runaway horses into her, over her, until reason seemed to race right out of her.

Holding his gaze, she opened herself to him, arched up to meet him, took him inside her. As he cradled her face with his heavenly hands, the look in his eyes was so fiery, so dark, so deep, she fell into it whole and wasn't sure she'd ever want to escape.

The slow rhythm of body learning body quickly turned into a canter, then a mad gallop of pleasure. Under the spell of his gaze, his hands, his mouth, everything inside her gathered, strained, waited.

He whispered her name. It reverberated inside her ear, inside her heart, inside her soul.

Then against the thunder of his pulse, the sheer ecstasy etched on his face, the shuddering of his body, she fell apart, giving into the rolling rush of madness charging through her wild horse fast.

WHEN ELLEN AWOKE, he was spooned around her, a hand curved possessively around her belly, a leg draped lazily over hers, and she'd never felt such deep contentment. The pink of dawn was just beginning to color the horizon.

In his arms, she'd discovered a physical hunger she'd never expected, her body's ability to accept a man with a purely feminine response—and love for a man she barely knew.

There was no getting around it. She'd gone and fallen for a man who'd made it plain he was a cowboy who didn't want to be fenced in.

That headlong pitch into something so vital certainly hadn't been part of her plan when she'd set out to seduce Kevin.

She'd banished Kyle to a tender place in her heart only he could ever fill, but found she had plenty left to give. Her feelings for Kevin were different than the ones she held for Kyle, but no less potent. Kyle was the past; Kevin the future.

A dash of panic raced through her. No, not the future, the present. She pushed the wisp of anxiety aside and concentrated instead on the joy singing through her newly awakened body.

She turned in Kevin's arms. His features were soft in sleep. Remembering the feel of his kiss, she leaned across the pillow and tasted him again. The light brush of her lips on his reignited a rush of sensations. She skimmed a fingertip down the length of his side, heard the sleepy sound of pleasure deep in his throat.

She was stepping into dangerous territory, but she didn't care. She loved what he did to her, how he made her feel alive and strong. She would enjoy the moment while she could. There'd be time enough later to sort through the consequences of loving a man who couldn't stay anchored too long in one place. She slid her body against his, felt a wholly feminine satisfaction when his body responded to hers.

Slowly his eyes opened. A smile touched his lips at the sight of her. She loved how it went all the way to his eyes and made them sparkle with fire, the way it made her belly flutter. He wrapped a corkscrew of her hair around his finger and rasped a good-morning into her ear.

"How's your shoulder?" she asked, not quite knowing what to expect from him.

He rolled it once and chuckled. "It's fine."

She loved that sound, the way it seemed to brighten all the dark corners inside her.

Last night, Kevin's loving had shown her the possibilities of life. For the past year, she'd cocooned herself, afraid to look at the hurt she'd suffered, afraid to get lost in it. Now she knew she was strong enough to face it.

She rolled onto Kevin, lost herself in his deep, dark eyes. "There's time enough for a short ride before we have to get up to feed the horses...if you're up to it."

He was.

HE LOOKED GOOD on a horse, Ellen brooded as she sat on the fence watching Kevin work Luci in the soft dirt of the ring. Just looking at him made her tight and edgy and needy all over. One night with him and she was already dreaming of something...more.

You're a fool. She frowned, trying to concentrate on Luci, seeing only Kevin. Attraction was one thing, need quite another. He was leaving soon. She wasn't in love. She'd simply rediscovered she was alive at the hands of a capable lover. Nothing wrong with that. Healthy, even. Her hands gripped the fence rail tighter. Mad butterfly wings fluttered in her stomach.

Her plans for the future included many things, but they didn't include falling in love. *Concentrate on what he's doing so you can do it yourself once he's gone.*

Luci wore no saddle, no bridle, just a rope around her neck—and Kevin on her back. She'd tossed her head up and down for the good part of an hour. She still couldn't pass for a relaxed horse, but she was walking forward and her eyes weren't quite as glazed.

He brought Luci over to the fence and Ellen fed her sections of apple. "She did good."

"She did wonderful." Kevin vaulted off and knuckled Luci's muzzle, catching the side of her hand. The double-barreled blow of tingling skin at their accidental touch and the spark of the memory of Kyle doing the same gesture made her snatch her hand to her side.

Blue thumped his tail and Kevin bent down to scratch the jealous dog's ear. The jolt of the past faded and all that was left was the present. Kevin, not Kyle.

"Do you think you can handle the ranch for the rest of the day?" Ellen asked as she maneuvered Luci through the gate. Her decision, she thought, was what was making her see ghosts all around. Last night, she'd made peace with Kyle. Now she had to continue the healing.

The horses were fed. The stalls were mucked. Tessa Bancroft had done her daily collection of data. If Ellen was going to get back home before dark, she had to leave soon. A leaden weight settled in her stomach. She had to do this. If she couldn't, then her life wouldn't be her own. Fear would tinge the corners of her newfound strength. And that was the last thing she wanted.

"Why?" Kevin tossed the question offhandedly as he closed the gate behind her. But when he followed her into the barn, his body carried a subtle tension. Like a spring winding, his edginess coiled her own.

Though she couldn't use them with Luci, she stopped the mare at a set of crossties. Kevin held her while Ellen grabbed a caddie of grooming tools.

"Are you going somewhere?" he asked when she returned. The corners of his smile were tight.

With a chuckle, she tried to make light of fingernails of anxiety suddenly scraping down her back. "You're not going to go all protective on me, are you?"

"It's a male thing."

She could practically smell the testosterone wafting from him. She liked it. Feared it. But she wasn't ready to wear the shirt of dependence again. And it would be too easy to lean on someone like Kevin. She had to do this alone. She picked out a rubber currycomb and rubbed gentle circles on Luci's back. "I don't know why I bother. She's just going to roll in the pond as soon as I let her out."

"Natural sunblock. She's got sensitive skin." He massaged the mare's neck until she lowered it for him, then started inching ever so slowly toward the poll she protected so dearly. Magic. If she didn't watch it, she'd get caught up under the spell of his charm, too.

"I know." She switched sides but could still feel Kevin's gaze boring into her. "I need to go out of town."

"I'll go with you."

"I might not be back in time for the evening feed." She traded the currycomb for a dandy brush, resumed grooming Luci, and couldn't understand why she tiptoed around the issue. "Look, I don't owe you an explanation. I was merely letting you know that I was putting you in charge of the horses for the rest of the day. That's what I'm paying you for, isn't it? To take care of the horses."

He reached for a strand of her hair, twirled it around a finger. "I thought we'd moved a step up from that last night."

She nearly melted, but forced herself to keep brushing Luci. "Last night doesn't change anything. You're still leaving in a few days."

She glanced at him, dared him to deny the fact. He didn't.

"I have a bad feeling."

"So you're psychic now?" She bent and traded the dandy brush for a body brush, feeling as if a net were tightening around her.

"No, but something doesn't feel right."

Luci flinched under the brisk stroke of the brush. Ellen lightened her touch. Was he simply feeling her unease? "I'll be leaving as soon as we're done here."

"I'll go with you."

She swallowed, counted, and still had a hard time keeping a leash on her temper. "I need you to take care of the horses."

Resting his hands across the horse's back, he closed his eyes. When he looked up, frustration was etched on his face. "You're right, you don't owe me anything. I want to know where you're going because I need to know you're safe.''

The need didn't sit well with him and that made it easier to accept. ''Thing is, I've had all of my decisions made for me for too long. I need to do this for myself.''

''Last night you called me a friend.''

She had, but that didn't change anything. ''It's something I need to do.'' But he was right. If Taryn had asked her, she would have told her. She switched the brush for a hoof pick. ''Ashbrook.''

''What's in Ashbrook?'' She felt the tension in his hand reverberate through Luci's skin as she picked up a foreleg.

''Garth Ramsey.''

He muttered a curse. ''The same Garth Ramsey who held you prisoner?''

She shrugged carelessly and returned the foot to the ground. ''He's in jail. He can't hurt me.''

''Why?'' he rasped, and she wondered at the intensity of the question.

''I've got some questions for him.'' There was a snarl in her voice.

''I hear you, Ellen.'' He reached across Luci's back and cupped her cheek with a hand. The tenderness of his touch had her throat constricting. ''But you don't have to do this.''

Silently she implored for his understanding. ''I want him to see I'm not afraid. I want to look him straight in the eyes. I want the truth.''

''The truth of what? What is worth torturing yourself that way?''

She lifted Luci's rear foot and picked it clean. ''I want to know how he's drugging the horses.''

''Ellen, you're not making sense. How can you think he has anything to do with what's happening to the horses?''

"He drugged me and got away with it. The drug was experimental. It didn't show up on any tests. Why wouldn't he do the same thing to horses? Winning means everything to him."

"He's in jail."

She moved to the far side and cleaned out both feet. "He owns them."

"They were bred at his farm. I'll give you that. But that doesn't mean he owns them. The Bancrofts hold their papers."

"So where were the horses going then? There's not a horse at the Double B. But Royal Legacy is in the same area."

"Maybe they keep the horses with their trainer. A lot of people do that, Ellen."

"You think I'm paranoid."

"I think you're taking a leap of logic that's too big."

Fists clenched, she whirled on him. Last night he'd given her strength. Today he was trying to take it away. "You don't understand."

"I do." He huffed out a breath and thrust a hand into his jeans pocket. "I understand Garth hurt you. I understand you want control over your life. But I don't think facing him now will get you anything. Dr. Warner and the Bancrofts are responsible for these horses' condition, not Garth Ramsey. You're looking at the wrong place for your answers."

She dropped the hoof pick back into the caddie. "Then there's no harm in going to see him and asking him a few questions."

"Ellen…"

She spritzed Luci with fly spray. "Garth is a fine actor. Everyone sees him as a smiling good old boy, but he's not. He's calculating and controlling and manipulative and very possessive. If he got into the breeding business, it's because he wants to get into that winner's circle. The getting there is more important than the how of doing it. Even if it means seeing someone else gets them there for him. If he's chosen to race, he's chosen to win and nothing will stop him. Not even being behind bars.''

''It's a mistake.''

''He acquires things. He doesn't let them go.'' Perseus nudged her back pocket when she got too close to his stall. She turned and rubbed his muzzle, then turned back to Luci. ''I've got to know what he's done to these horses so I can help them.''

He trapped the hand fiddling with Luci's mane beneath his, forcing her to look at him. ''How long can you drive before your eyes start blurring?''

''That's below the belt.'' She jerked her hand from beneath his, then hid the awkwardness by returning the fly spray to the caddie.

''You get under my skin,'' he said.

Her head jerked up. His intense gaze made her swallow hard. ''Does that bother you?''

Hell, yeah, the look in his eyes said. Not practical for a man to have an itch he couldn't scratch. And it wasn't practical either for a woman like her to fall for a drifter.

''Let me go with you, Ellen. I'll drive and make sure we get back before feeding time. You can ask the sheriff to patrol the place while we're gone.''

''They're getting worse.'' Ulcers were appearing in their mouths. Even with restarting the high-iron feed, the fatigue lingered.

She didn't want to give in, but the look in his eyes had her teetering on acceptance. This ranch was all she had. It was a symbol of her health, her future. These horses all counted on her. If she wasn't here for them and something happened, she'd never forgive herself. "What if I'm right? What if Garth holds the key to their health?"

"What if you're wrong and all that happens is you get hurt again?"

Then she'd find out how strong she really was.

Chapter Eleven

The last thing Kevin wanted was to come face-to-face with the man who'd done such harm to the woman he loved, but if he couldn't stop her from going, the least he could do was stand by her. As a guard led them to the visitors' room, the surreal clinks and clangs of keys and doors, the dissonant tattoo of heels on sand-colored tiles, the harsh light casting stark shadows on the puke-green walls did nothing to ease the tension stringing him tighter than a cinch on a bronco.

That's enough, he wanted to say. *You've proved your point.* He couldn't see how this confrontation could help Ellen or the horses. He wanted to haul her right out of this prison compound and back to the ranch where she belonged. But here she was, straight-backed and determined, and he'd promised to let her handle Garth on her own.

He reached for Nina's feather, rubbed the talisman as if it held answers. But the memories of this town, of his relentless teenage anger, of his failures, proved stronger than Nina's medicine.

"Ten minutes," their guard escort announced.

Ellen was granted the interview only because of the sheriff department's respect for her late father. Kevin had found out during the drive to Ashbrook that Carter Paxton had died of a heart attack while he'd fought to fast-track Garth's trial.

"Thank you," Ellen said. Her voice sounded so small it wrenched his heart. She wouldn't thank him for reaching for her and trying to shield her with his arms.

She sat in the molded-plastic chair facing the wire-reinforced glass. On the other side, a door opened and an orange-garbed prisoner entered. A smile curved Garth's mouth as he spotted Ellen. Kevin had always hated the way Garth looked at her as if she were one of the pecan pralines he favored but could rarely afford to buy at Tio Rio's. Sixteen years later, the urge to punch that smirk right off his face was still just as strong. A guard led Garth to a chair, sat him down, then stood at the door, arms crossed over his chest, pretending to hear nothing.

Kevin's stomach churned. Seeing Garth behind the glass, he recognized that the friend of his youth had turned into a hard stranger. There was something cold about Garth's gaze, something spiteful about the way he now looked at Ellen.

Standing his ground took everything Kevin had. Every muscle strained. His jaw tightened. His hands coiled into white-knuckled fists. He desperately wanted to stand between Ellen and Garth, to shout at his old friend—to strangle him. *You won't ever hurt her again.* But he knew. The ache in his heart told him. Given a chance, Garth would find her weakness and skewer her with it.

White-faced and scared to death, his brave Ellen had the courage to confront the man who embodied her worst fears. Her internal strength awed him.

What does that make you? A chicken-hearted, lily-livered, yellow-bellied coward.

He saw it then, the error of his way. Nina was right. The only one his secret protected was himself. Ellen deserved the truth. She deserved an apology. She deserved to render whatever punishment she saw fit. By lying to her, he'd cheated her of the closure she was trying so hard to find.

As soon as they were back on the ranch, where she felt safe, he would tell her the truth about his identity—and accept whatever fallout came of it. Then he'd face Chance and ask for his forgiveness. Just as Ellen was doing, he'd face his fears. Only with the truth could all of their lives stand a chance to flow a true course.

SECRETLY, Ellen was glad Kevin was standing by her. His solid presence and protective stance just beyond her shoulder calmed her. She recognized the intense look in his eyes, the stark set of his features, and almost smiled. The cowboy hero who'd ridden into town on his white steed would certainly jump between her and the outlaw named Garth. That and the reinforced glass between her and Garth gave her the courage to confront him.

Feet flat on the floor, hands twined on the black strip of counter jutting from the wall beneath the glass, she watched him approach. The orange jumpsuit was a far cry from the silk shirts and custom-made suits he favored, but it did nothing to douse the arrogance stamped in his features. His blond hair was still styled perfectly, his nails skillfully manicured, his teeth brilliantly white. And the smooth ease of his gestures might still fool someone else into thinking he was a harmless teddy bear.

Not her.

She saw the new darkness etched in his brown eyes. She felt his hard anger through the protective glass. She knew the depths he would delve to conquer. He was a man-eating Kodiak. And he'd surely try to sink his claws into her.

Everything inside her turned to jelly. She wasn't strong enough for this. Not yet. Maybe not ever.

"Hello, darlin'." Garth's voice warbled eerily over the round speaker that allowed communication between them, reminding her of his visits at the nursing home. Goose bumps raced up and down her arms, but she refused to rub them away. "How's my lovely wife today?"

"I was never your wife." His slave, his prisoner, but never his wife.

"An annulment doesn't change the facts. You were my wife for thirteen years." He leaned back in the chair and lazily draped an arm over the back. He slanted her left hand a glance. "What did you do with my ring?"

A small smile twitched her lips. She glanced down at the bare ring finger. Her first act of freedom was to hawk the marquise-cut diamond Garth had slipped on her finger while she was comatose. "I bought a manure spreader for the tractor. I thought it fitting."

A muffled chuckle sounded behind her. Garth's gaze narrowed, then he laughed out loud as if he'd never heard anything funnier. "Hey, you're growin' some spunk. It's about time. So who's your shadow?"

She felt Kevin stiffen behind her, ready to pounce. It gave her comfort. "A friend."

"A friend," he mimicked, then smirked like a cat well fed on canary. "Have you screwed him yet?"

Heat flamed up her neck and fired her cheeks. She knew he was trying to shock her, to throw her off balance. "This isn't a social call, Garth."

"Just inquirin' after your health." He feigned a serious look and leaned forward. "Well, then, what can I do to help you, darlin'?"

His tone said help was the furthest thing from his mind. "You can answer a few questions."

He waved her comment away as if she were an insolent child. "Ah, we've been all through this before. What happened wasn't personal—"

"It was to me, but that's not what I want to know."

"Well, then, darlin', you've got me trembling with curiosity." His smile widened and he exaggerated a shiver. He still thought of her as a puppet whose strings he could jerk at will. She'd show him.

"What did you do to the horses?"

He frowned. "Horses?"

"Royal Legacy."

"Ah, those horses." He leaned back again, studying her beneath eyebrows that now shaded his eyes. "I sold all my stock a while back."

"Before you sold them, what did you do to them?"

He eyed her narrowly until the skewer of his gaze made her want to jump from her chair. But she held her ground, not blinking once.

"Do you remember my father?" he said finally.

Percy Ramsey, along with his brother, Weldon, were heirs to the Archer Ramsey lumber and oil fortune. Weldon hung on to his half and multiplied his holdings through real estate. Percy squandered his through fly-by-night schemes, booze and gambling. He was found dead in a ditch on Garth's thirteenth birthday. Drunk, he'd drowned in an inch of muddy water. "I remember."

Garth gave a dry laugh. "He loved the ponies, but his system for picking winners, well, it wasn't much of a success."

"What does that have to do with Royal Legacy?"

His smile deepened. His eyes burned. "My system *guarantees* winners."

And winning had always been everything to Garth. Because of the ridicule his father's losses had garnered the family? Her fingers tightened against each other. Kevin's shadow fell across her shoulder as if it were a shield. Bolstered, she pressed on. "How are you drugging them?"

"Druggin'. I don't do drugs." He acted as if such an act was beneath him.

"I saw you." She couldn't help it, she looked at the crook of her elbow and the invisible puncture wounds that had kept her mind locked and her body frozen. He thought he was so slick. If he didn't watch out, he'd slip right out of his chair, greased by the ooze of his lies. "I know what you did—"

He waved away her comment. "That was only a booster."

"A booster?" Her mouth gaped open in disbelief.

He leaned forward and whispered, "A little jump to deepen the spell when it looked like you were comin' out of it. I couldn't let my Sleeping Beauty awaken, now, could I?"

Kevin spit out a low curse. A wave of nausea had her clutching her stomach. She cycled through half a dozen breaths, reminding herself he was trying to push her buttons and draw a reaction. She could not give in to his taunts. She swallowed hard and gave a half shrug to dislodge the spidery film of his evil trying to spin itself around her. "So, what does your winning system entail?"

He hitched a leg over his knee and stared at her through the glass. "Do you know who Prometheus is?"

"I'm surprised you do," she blurted before she could stop herself.

"Now, see, darlin', that hurts. If you want answers, you're gonna have to play nice."

The horses had to come before her own personal need to land a few digs in Garth's thick hide. She nodded, looked down at her hands and noticed how jagged her nails had become since she'd settled at the ranch. "I know who Prometheus is."

"Prometheus brought fire to man." He smiled. "Those ancient Greeks knew how to live life to its fullest. They were ambitious, hard-living and visionary. They knew the answer to death was to carve out magnificent deeds."

They were also touchy about their honor and vengeful when they felt wronged. Just like Garth. She put her hands beneath her thighs and sat up straighter. "Prometheus also suffered terribly for having brought the gift. What did your Prometheus bring you?"

"Speed." The word hissed out of him like air rushing out of a punctured balloon.

Now they were getting somewhere. Keep him bragging. Keep him showing off his "magnificent deed." "How?"

"Research. The best money could buy." A smug look crossed his face.

"Could?"

Half his mouth curled up. His eyebrows scrunched in pseudo sadness. "I've had to divert my funds because of you."

A perverse need to cut down his arrogance gripped her. "It breaks my heart."

"After all I've done for you, it should."

She ignored the sharp edge in his voice, gentled her own. "What were you researching?"

He pressed his forearms against his side of the counter and leaned forward so that his fiery gaze filled her field of vision. His voice took on a tone of the possessed. "Possibilities."

"Possibilities?" She knew she couldn't rush him, but she had to keep him moving forward.

"Did you know that you can splice the gene of a fish onto a tomato to make it more frost tolerant?"

"Garth..." This was not the time for sidetracks.

"There is a point to this. Indulge me, darlin'. Answer my question."

She huffed out a sigh. "No, learning about genetic engineering hasn't been on my list of priorities."

"That's too bad."

Her fingers curled tighter around her seat and she forced herself to speak in a calm, even voice. "What does this have to do with the horses and their illness?"

"Who's ill?" Garth frowned with mimelike overkill.

"Your horses—Titan, Apollo, Calliope, Hercules, Perseus. The ones you sold to your neighbors, the Bancrofts."

"Ah."

She waited, but he didn't amplify. "What did you do to them?"

"It's a long story."

She made a show of looking around the small room and the chicken wire-reinforced glass between them. "Looks like you've got plenty of time on your hands."

He slunk back in his chair, draping his arm carelessly over the back. "You know, darlin', I do like this spunky side of you. It's too bad you were so out of it all those years. We could have had some fun."

Not in a million years. But she wasn't going to get anywhere trading barbs. She wanted answers, and for that, she'd have to appeal to his vanity. "It takes someone brilliant to gain speed without drugs. How did you do it?"

Garth smiled and gave a low chuckle. "It takes more than brains. It takes vision. And patience."

"Considering how much you achieved in your life, you must have both." The words scratched her throat, chicken-bone sharp.

"More." The smile lingered. A light gleamed in his eyes. "I can shape a vision into reality."

Low self-esteem had never been Garth's problem. "Is that so?"

The gleam in his eyes quickened. He'd caught on to her game, but for now was willing to play. "Senior year in college, I met two very interesting people. They wanted to change the course of history. One concerned herself with the question 'How can I feed the hungry?' The other with 'How can I make livestock sturdier?' I gave them the space and the means to make their dreams come true."

"I don't understand." Behind her, she felt Kevin's hands curl around the back of her chair. His tension coiled around her, but she shrugged it away. She needed answers.

"Drugs can be traced," Garth said. "That does me no good. Plus, they make for a short career, and good racehorses don't come cheap. I wanted predictable performance enhancement. There are two ways to get there."

He was going to make her pull every bit of information out of him. She clenched her teeth. "How?"

"Breeding for speed. And feeding for speed."

"You forgot training."

"Training is incidental. Raw talent gets the glory every time."

Slowly, his "system" dawned on her. The fish gene spliced into the tomato. "You used genetic engineering."

"You were always a smart girl." He tilted his head and looked away as if he were seeing his dream in living color. "I found the best stock available, paired it with the best research team available. And what I got was a winning combination."

"Tell me more."

He lifted an eyebrow in what looked like amused improbability. "Why should I?"

"Because they've got nothing to do with what's between us.'' She swallowed her pride and resorted to a bit of honest begging. ''They're dying, Garth.''

He shrugged. ''What can be done has already been done.''

Frustration buzzed down her spine. She flicked her watch a glance, flipped her braid back. Her time would soon be up and she wasn't even close to the answers she needed. Her shoulder blades brushed against Kevin's fingers. The touch sparked renewed strength. She licked her lips and tried a new tack. ''Who's on your research team?''

''Lillian Harmon and Silas Warner.''

Dr. Warner. The Bancrofts' vet. Tessa's protocol book. ''Are you involved with Tessa Bancroft in any way?''

''Did I screw her, you mean?'' He didn't give her a chance to reply. ''Yeah, I screwed her. So has everyone else. She'll spread her legs for any man she thinks can give her something she wants. She thinks she can buy respect, but she's usin' the wrong currency.''

''She's married.''

Garth shook his head. ''You are still so naive. Sex is nothing more than a commodity. And a good marriage is nothing more than a business transaction. Love just confuses things.'' He grinned jovially. ''Look where it got me.''

''You being here has nothing to do with love—''

The smile melted from his face. His gaze narrowed. ''I loved you. I still do.''

His admission repulsed her, but she tried not to let her disgust show. ''Then answer my question. What's wrong with the horses?''

He waved at her dismissively. ''There's nothing wrong with the horses. At least not as far as I know.''

She leaned forward. ''The Bancrofts aren't continuing your project?''

"Darlin', the only project I'm involved in now is tryin' to free myself from this unfair incarceration."

"Unfair?" She swallowed the bile surging in her throat. "You earned every year you're going to spend here. You're not going to beat this."

"I've still got a few aces up my sleeve."

The law's straight flush still beat ill-gotten aces. But that was neither here nor there. "What about Harmon and Warner?"

Garth shrugged. "Without money they won't get far."

"They're not working for you?"

"I let them go last year."

Had the Bancrofts hired them and taken over Garth's "system?" Now she simply had to decode it. "So your research and breeding got you speed. But something went wrong."

"A few glitches," he admitted, then leaned forward. "One that proved useful." His eyes danced with perverse pleasure. Involuntarily, she shivered. His lips seemed pressed against the speaker. She leaned back against the poison they would spew and pressed into Kevin's fingers on the back of the chair, seeking reassurance. His thumbs skimmed her collarbone. She relaxed a notch. "Do you still like oatmeal cookies, darlin'."

His laugh reverberated through the room. The tentacles of his evil crept through the glass, wrapped themselves around her and seemed to crush her. A helpless cry escaped her.

"That's enough." Kevin's voice came low and strong from behind her. His hands clasped protectively around her shoulders. She leaned into him, drawing strength from the solidity of his taut body. "She asked you a simple question. Answer it."

Garth eyed Kevin up and down, amusement still evident

on his face. "Have you heard about the salmon project up in Canada?"

"Just get on with it," Kevin snapped. The tips of his fingers tightened around her shoulders.

"They've engineered it so that a year-old salmon now weighs the same as a four-year-old salmon. That way they go from egg to table faster." Garth shifted in his seat, clasped his hands in front of him. "If a two-year-old has the heart of a four-year-old, if his lungs have more breadth, if his muscles have more mass, then he's going to win more races.

"And that's exactly what we did. Look back at the records and you'll see Legacy horses have won all the major Thoroughbred races in the area for the past eight years." He ground a finger on the counter. "That, darlin', is called success."

That, idiot, is called arrogance. "What went wrong?" Ellen asked, her voice catching past the constriction in her throat. All this manipulating of genes so he could feel like a winner. But the deep lines carving the side of his face also told her that winning all those races hadn't been enough. Maybe nothing ever would.

"Thoroughbred breeding has to be done with live cover. Genetic engineering would have required artificial insemination. So we had to find a way around that. We tried the feed. For whatever reason, the genetically engineered oats tend to cause anemia. So we added extra iron to the feed and that seemed to work for a while."

"But there was something else."

One of his shoulders jerked up. "The big heart and muscle mass that made them winners as two-year-olds started to become a liability by the time they turned four or five."

"So you killed them." Her heart sank. So much sacrifice for nothing.

"An autopsy's the only way to learn what went wrong and improve the next batch."

Simple as that. Life was disposable. Use and discard. If the horse doesn't fit, well then, there was always next year's foals to splice and design. Then the cruelty of his manipulation doused her like a bucket of cold water.

"You used the same oats for the cookies you brought me." Every week. And like a fool, she'd eaten them. There'd been something irresistible about the buttery sweetness of the treat against the nuttiness of the toasted oats. A bit of heaven in hell. Nausea rolled in her stomach.

"An early version that caused the horses' mind to fog." He crossed his arms. "I had some put in reserve just for you, darlin'."

She hesitated, knitted her fingers together and frowned. "Am I going to age prematurely, too?"

His voice held a surprising gentleness. "I don't know. It's all research."

Ellen's mind reeled. The whole room started to spin. She wasn't sick all those years; she'd been rendered catatonic by Garth through the oatmeal cookies he brought her in order to keep her mind scrambled so he could avoid punishment for his crime. Her. The horses. Dr. Warner and his partner. They were all pawns in Garth's pursuit of validation. Disposable.

Swearing viciously, Kevin stepped forward, coming between her and Garth. "Haven't you done enough damage?"

Garth slanted Kevin a dismissive glance. "I was wonderin' how long it would take you to spring to the rescue. You held out longer than I thought. Only reason for a man to be so patient with a woman is that he's whipped."

Kevin's jaw twitched. "You haven't changed. You're still picking on those who can't fight back."

"It's called survival of the fittest." A feral spark glinted in Garth's eyes.

Kevin pounded a fist against the glass. Garth flinched. "You feel safe picking on her because you're behind bars. You wouldn't be so brave if it was just you and me face-to-face. You always incited fights, then left me to catch the punches."

Ellen gaped at the man standing in front of her. Leaving him to catch the punches? What was he talking about?

Garth stood and narrowed his gaze. "Well, well, well. So Tessa was right. Another Makepeace has come back from the dead."

Silence, heavy and thick, filled the room. Everything seemed to flow in slow motion. The shock of realization on Kevin's face. The spreading grin on Garth's. The bottom falling out from under her. She bolted out of the chair. The metal frame clanging against the tile joined the cacophonous ringing in her ears.

Kevin stood still, staring at her. "Ellen."

Everything suddenly became clear. All the emotions he could arouse in her. All those times she'd thought of Kyle in Kevin's presence. All those times she thought she'd seen a glimpse of him under the scars. That familiar gesture. They hadn't been wishful thinking, but clear vision.

His shoulders had broadened. His muscles had defined. His body had hardened. He'd been a lean and lanky boy sixteen years ago and he was a solid man today. The black hair was cut differently, shorter, less shaggy. But those dark eyes looking at her now held the same look they had all those years ago when she'd begged him to reconsider leaving and he'd implored her to understand.

"Kyle?" Her voice sounded far away. She barely heard herself over the thunder of her heart.

"You didn't know?" Garth's satisfied smugness jabbed her like needles. "This is rich."

Kyle was alive. Kyle was here. And Kyle had lied to her. All those days, all those nights, they were a lie.

"Ellen..." His face contorted into the picture of anguish. He reached out for her.

She spun on her heels, wobbled to the door and yanked it open. Her boot heels pounded against the hallway tile, gunfire fast. Garth's laughter chased her. Kyle's curses battered her. Hands pressed against her ears, she shut them both out and sprinted past the guard and into the breath-robbing heat.

For a moment she hesitated on the front steps. The asphalt road leading into Ashbrook shimmered under the sun, unbalancing her. Hands on knees, she forced herself to breathe in and breathe out.

Kyle was alive. He'd helped her. He'd loved her. But he'd said nothing. Knowing her feelings for him, he'd still chosen to pretend he was dead. He'd made love to her. How could he have done that with the lie between them? Her hands fastened around her stomach as if letting go would allow her guts to spill out over the stairs, her heart to roll out onto the road. He'd made her fall in love with him all over again, then betrayed that love—just as he had all those years ago. Unshed tears bled her throat raw. "Kyle!"

With a growl, she strode forward. She had survived before. She would survive this time, too.

She wasn't going to let this betrayal shake her. She couldn't. She had to drive home. She had to find Dr. Warner. He was the key. From him, she'd get an explanation, some help. Getting those horses healthy again was her priority. Then she'd force him to testify on the horses' behalf to the judge.

And later, much later, she'd let herself sort out what had happened with Kevin.

The horses would never suffer again.

She had no other choice. To let anything other than the pressing need to help the horses crowd her mind would invite a breakdown. And she was never setting foot inside another institution. The horses, her ranch, were her link to sanity.

Hands shaking, mind blank, she stepped into the truck, turned on the engine, then drove off. But try as she might to outrun him, Kevin mutated into Kyle, and the man and the boy rode as passenger ghosts beside her.

Chapter Twelve

Stranded in Ashbrook, Kevin shoved his hands in his jeans pockets and started walking with no destination in mind. He hunched his shoulders against the sun beating down on his bare head. His boots were made for riding not walking. Each step jarred boot heel into bone and concussed all the way to his calves. Sweat soon stained his dark T-shirt front and back. Nina's feather went round and round in his hand, but provided little comfort. Every muscle braced against the assault on his mind, but he couldn't stop the flow of thoughts.

Like a truck mired in mud, his mind grooved deeper and deeper into what had gone wrong at the jail. Anger had once again gotten the best of him. He'd love to hold Garth accountable for this mistake, but he knew he had no one to blame but himself. He'd never forget the look on Ellen's face, her helpless cry, the instinctual rounding of her body as if he'd punched her. He'd hurt her, cut her where she was most vulnerable.

What right did he have to follow her home?

Nina was wrong. He wasn't healing his past. He was reopening wounds. Coming back to Texas had been a mistake. Chance and Ellen had carved new lives for themselves. All he'd managed to do was upset their balance.

On the edge of town, he found himself turning down Gum Springs Road. After a long stretch of pine lots, he came to a white picket fence. He hesitated, then went through the cemetery gate.

In the thick heat, no birds sang, no insects chirped. Only the dull thump of his boots on the sun-softened asphalt path made any noise. The creek on his left was nothing more than a layer of green slime on cracking mud. The stench of rotting vegetation seeped into him and abscessed in the gangrene of his errors. The sun scratched out black fingers of shadows, crooked like the limbs of the oaks they mimicked. Too tall, yellowing grass encroached on tombstones, obliterating dates beneath names.

He came to a statue of an angel, patched green with moss, and turned off the path. Beneath an oak, he found the markers he'd come to visit—and three more he hadn't expected.

Lloyd and Sarah Makepeace. When things got unbearable as a child, he'd found his way to this back corner of the cemetery and opened his heart to his dead parents, especially his mother. When she was alive, she'd always known what to say to soothe his sorrow. Dead, she'd given him no answers, but still provided a safe place to cry. He crouched beside the granite and ran a finger along the letters chiseled into the stone. Tears burned his eyes, but refused to fall. He wasn't a boy anymore.

Then his gaze fell onto another marker inscribed with John Henry Makepeace.

Buck up, boy, his grandfather's hard voice came to him. *Real men don't cry—only sissies. Are you a sissy, boy?*

Kevin's jaw tightened. An army of unexpected emotions blitzed him, rocking him back on his heels. His mind conjured up his grandfather, stern and unyielding. His ghost scowled at him as he had in life. A slice of rebellion rose from the ashes of childhood submission.

"I hated you for always taking Kent's side." The words ripped out of him like scabs peeled from a ragged cut. "I hated you for liking him better than me. I tried, you know. I tried to make you proud. But you didn't care. You expected trouble and that's all you saw."

Kevin punched the ground beside him. "I hated you for living when Mom and Dad died."

His childhood anger festered and oozed until the infection finally ran clear. Drained and spent, Kevin swiped back hair wet with sweat, then he reached out for the two smaller plaques bearing his and Kent's names. Dead, but alive—both of them. Kent was Chance now, and it suited him better. And Kyle had found a measure of peace as Kevin.

"That little boy deserved your love."

A breeze ruffled his cheek and Nina's voice whispered to him, *It was safer not to love, Pajackok. A lesson you learned much too well.*

"I can love. I loved you. I've always loved Ellen."

Then take off your armor and leave it here. Go back and finish what you started.

He shook his head, frowned. "I hurt her."

Ah, Pajackok! What is the basic lesson?

Kevin shot up from his crouch, turned away from the graves and stepped back onto the asphalt path, hoping to outrun Nina's voice on the breeze of his memory.

How do you turn a horse into a partner?

He ignored the voice of Nina playing conscience, hunched his shoulders and strode on.

The basic lesson is trust, son of my heart. Only when you trust enough to open your heart will you find your peace.

He sneered, kicked at a rock on the path. "What about Ellen? Hasn't she been hurt enough?"

What has she got now but half a lie? The truth is basic. What works for one works for all. Trust.

"She'll never trust me again."

Open your heart and trust.

His pace slowed. Ellen would never trust him. But truth *was* simple. Whether she wanted to or not, Ellen still needed help handling Bancroft until the horses' fate was settled. She didn't have to like him. She didn't have to forgive him. She simply had to accept his help for the horses' sake.

And for the horses, she would do anything—including get herself in trouble.

Nina was right. He had to finish what he'd started.

As he reached the white gate, Kevin started running toward the highway. He had to get back to her. Fast.

THERE WAS NO TIME for thinking, no time for planning. Ellen worked on adrenaline and instinct. As soon as she walked back into the ranch house after checking on the horses, she tore the kitchen apart for Dr. Warner's card and placed a call to him. The horses were getting worse. They was no time to waste.

How much of what Garth had told her was true? Truth for Garth had boundaries that shifted to suit his purposes. Dr. Warner had the answers. Would he share them?

"I need to talk to you," she said without preamble.

A long silence greeted her. She heard the thumping of her heart, her pulse beating in her ears, her breaths ragged with raw emotion.

Finally, Dr. Warner's resigned voice said, "I can't leave right now."

"I'll come to you."

He gave her an address. As she stepped to the truck, Blue danced around her, tail wagging, begging for attention. He was a blatant reminder of Kevin's betrayal and she couldn't bear to look at his scarred hide.

"Not your fault," she told the dog. Fighting a fresh crop of tears, she gave him a distracted pat on the head and sent him back toward the barn. "Later."

She'd deal with Kevin later, too. She swiped at the moisture in her eyes and started the engine. Only when she reached the main road did she realize she'd taken Kevin's truck instead of switching to her own car. The cab smelled of horses and sweet hay—of him. Reminders of him were scattered here and there. One of the black T-shirts he favored, stained and discarded. An Indian blanket crumpled behind the seats. In the holder, an empty coffee cup with the imprint of his lips.

Something squeezed her heart. *How could you lie to me? How could you love me and pretend you were dead? How could you pretend we were nothing more than strangers?* She tightened her grip on the steering wheel and forced her attention on the road.

Later. She'd deal with Kevin later. For now, she had to think of the horses. Half of them had developed a fever. Their heads hung low as if holding them up required more energy than they possessed. As if eating was more trouble than it was worth, they'd barely touched their breakfast.

Checking the scrap of paper, she slowed in front of the long one-story building that looked like a Spanish mission house. White walls and a red tile roof sat in the shadows of tall trees and a carpet of well-tended gardens. By the front door, a small fountain gurgled, caught rays of sun and spilled rainbows onto the brick walkway. A discreet sign read, Arco Iris Hospice.

She double-checked the address. It was the correct one.

The truck's engine rumbled under her feet. Her palms grew sweaty. Shivers raised goose bumps along her spine. A hospice. She'd thought she was heading to a veterinary clinic. Why was Dr. Warner at a hospice?

Her heart thundered in her chest. Had Garth called him? Was this a trap? He'd worked for Garth. He was responsible for the drug that had caged her in her own body. If she walked through those doors, would she find herself a prisoner again?

He was also the one responsible for the horses' condition. He knew what he'd done. He knew how to help them.

For an instant, she wished for Kevin's support. Then she remembered his betrayal. She could handle this alone. She was strong enough.

She exhaled long and slow. "Stay focused. For the horses." She knew who Dr. Warner was, what he'd done, what kind of man he'd worked for. She'd keep up her guard. If she could stay together after Kevin's betrayal, she could handle anything.

Grasping her purse, she exited the truck and ignored the thudding weight dropping to her stomach. She clutched at the bag as if it were a weapon and strode through the arched wooden doors at the entrance. The reception area with its lush vegetation and fountain gave the impression of a vacation resort. The scent of coconut oil and gardenias wafted on the paddled waves of slow-moving ceiling fans.

She licked her lips, swallowed hard and forced herself to walk calmly to the round island that served as a welcome desk. A woman with the liveliness of a cruise-ship recreation director pointed her down one of the three halls spoking from the hub of the front desk.

Memories pecked at her as she slowly made her way down the hall. Her helplessness, her silent cries and her endless fear beat down on her like bat wings in the night.

Garth's face, his drawling croon, his sharp needle in the crook of her elbow joined the fray. She tightened her grip on her purse, quickened her steps and shaded her eyes with a hand as if that would keep away the echoes of her ghosts. She focused instead on the remembered rainbows of hope that had whirled in the crystal horses on her dresser, on her present mission. *For the horses, for the horses,* she kept telling herself, *for the horses.*

Taking a deep breath, she hesitated in front of room 322. Stiffly, she knocked on the door. Immediately, it opened and Dr. Warner greeted her with a nod and a hello. Behind him, a woman slept on a bed. Her sallow skin draped over sharp bones. Skeletal arms rested on a pale blue blanket. A peach kerchief covered an otherwise bald head.

"My wife," he said, seeing the focus of her attention.

Something clicked in her mind. "Lillian Harmon?"

He nodded and gestured to an easy chair in the corner. "What can I do for you?"

Still unsure of where Dr. Warner's allegiance lay, she remained standing. "I want to know about the horses. What's wrong with them?"

He sat on the edge of the hospital bed. Reaching an arm around his dying wife's shoulders, he cradled her gently. The deep lines grooving his forehead, bracketing his eyes, dragging down the corners of his mouth made him look older than he was.

"Greed," he said, and his voice sounded dead. "But it wasn't always like that. Lilly and I, we had a real dream once. We were going to make a difference."

"I'm not here to judge," Ellen said. "I just want to help the horses. I saw Garth today. He told me about the genetic engineering of the oats."

Dr. Warner nodded, then he rested the side of his head against Lilly's. "Feed them the oats I sent, that's a start.

They need the extra iron and B_{12} vitamin to stabilize the hemoglobin production."

"I need to know what's wrong with them."

His eyes went blurry. "We were just starting out and needed money to pay back our student loans. Garth, well, he's got charisma. When he talked, he made you believe. We all seemed to want the same thing, share the same vision. He was giving us everything we wanted, so we agreed."

His voice faded, but Ellen didn't prod him.

"At first the research was exciting," he continued. A faraway smile spread over his face, giving him back youth. Light sparked in his eyes at the memories he pictured. His voice brimmed with passion. "We truly believed we were doing something worthwhile. What we discovered with the horses could eventually be applied to agriculture and farm stock and solve the hunger problem worldwide. Think of it! No more pictures of starving children in Africa on the evening news. No more bleating of half-starved cows. Can you see what drove us?"

She nodded, but doubted he noticed.

His forehead suddenly pinched and a hitch of raw pain tore from his throat. "Then things started going wrong."

"Wrong, how?"

He didn't seem to hear her.

"When the situation started to get uncomfortable," he said, "we wanted to stop the experiments, but Garth reminded us that we were no longer in a position to walk away."

"You were his prisoner." Just as she'd been. Legs trembling, she sank into the easy chair, then perched on its edge.

"He threatened me with blackmail." Dr. Warner pressed a tender kiss on his wife's temple. "I wouldn't have cared, except that, the week before, Lilly was diagnosed with cancer and I had to keep my job in order to pay for her treatments.''

"Then Garth went to jail.'' Elbows planted on knees, Ellen leaned forward. ''Is that when you started working for the Bancrofts?''

"It was Lilly's only chance for survival.'' Lilly's face contorted with pain in her sleep. Gently, he soothed and rocked her until her face slackened again. ''But I have nothing left to lose now. She's dying.''

The look he gave her bore sadness of such depth, Ellen wanted to cry.

He glanced at the clock on the dresser. ''It's almost time for her next treatment. Give me a couple of hours and meet me at my office.'' He reached for the wallet in his pocket and handed her a card. ''I'll give you what I have. Who knows, maybe you can find a way to keep those horses alive.''

"Thank you,'' she said, but he'd already forgotten she was there. Lilly was the only inhabitant of his world.

WHEN KEVIN ARRIVED at the ranch, the sun was kissing the horizon, making the sky blush orange, and Ellen was tidying up after a late feed. He'd gotten lucky and managed to hitch a ride from outside Ashbrook to the end of Ellen's road. Finding her at home doing ordinary chores was a relief. He'd half feared seeing her crumpled on the side of the road because of her blurry vision or her uncooperative muscles. His admiration for her resilience went up a notch.

Blue spotted him first and galloped to meet him. Kevin greeted the dog with an all over good pet and sought to order his thoughts.

Ellen stiffened at his entrance into the barn, and the

movements of her broom on the concrete aisle became choppy. He loved her. Always would. But a strange confusion, a cross between panic and helplessness, filled him now and he didn't quite know how to deal with it—how to deal with her.

Colorado and Nina's ranch seemed a faraway blur. Ellen and her scraggly rescue ranch were more real than anything he'd lived through in longer than he could remember. He was at home here—as if he belonged. The past two weeks with her had felt…right.

But they couldn't pretend nothing had happened; that he was simply a ranch hand to her ranch owner. Though Kyle no longer existed, he stood between them.

She stowed the broom in the tack room, then walked by him as if he wasn't there.

"You have every right to be mad at me," Kevin said, following her into the twilight.

She stopped in her tracks and spun on her heels. "Mad at you? I'm not mad at you. I'm furious. I *trusted* you."

His burst of anger at the jail had slashed the fragile bonds they'd woven over the past two weeks. After all she'd gone through, she'd risked opening herself to him and he'd rewarded her with betrayal.

"I couldn't tell you, Ellen. I—"

"Of course not, *Kyle*." The coldness hardening her eyes cut him. "Why should anything have changed? You didn't trust me then, either."

A fresh flame fanned his anger to life and dulled the edge of his guilt. He tamped down his temper and gave her the truth. "I didn't want to hurt you."

She scoffed. "Well, that plan sure worked wonders." Both her fists pressed against her chest. "It feels like you cut my heart right out of my body and stomped on it."

"You're the one who insisted I make love to you." He

raked a hand through his hair and took a calming breath. "All I wanted to do was protect you."

"By lying to me? By pretending you were someone else? How was that supposed to protect me?"

She stood stiff, both fists hard at her sides. He reached for her, wrapped his arms around her rigid body and held her tightly. *Please, Ellen, please.* He placed one cheek against hers, felt his heart hum and whispered, "You knew. Part of you had to know. If you didn't, you never would have trusted me."

Hands braced against his chest, she said nothing, but he felt her shiver.

"You needed help to keep the horses. It was my way of saying I was sorry."

"Sorry!" She backed out of his embrace. The sound keening out of her tore at his gut. "I don't need your pity. After all the lies, I need the truth."

"You're building something good here, Ellen. I didn't want to ruin it with memories of a past best forgotten."

"I've never forgotten," she whispered, shaking her head. "You were with me all those years. You and the horses."

He scanned the ranch with its cozy house, quaint barn and fenced fields. "I'd give my life to make your dream come true."

She shook her head. "Kevin…Kyle…"

"Kevin. I'm Kevin. Kyle died in that river."

She stared at him, blinked, opened her mouth, then closed it again. She flipped her braid to her back, then rubbed the watch on her wrist. "What happened? All those years ago, what really happened?"

The worst of the damage was already done. She deserved the truth. He gestured to the fence, perched on the top rail. Hesitatingly, she joined him, keeping the post between them. Blue settled at their feet, his worried gaze ping-ponging from one to the other.

"The river was running fast," Kevin said, looking over her shoulder at the setting sun. A thin wound of red knifed the horizon as the rest of the sky deepened to navy. Just as it had sixteen years ago. "Kent was fighting me. I couldn't control our path. He was holding on to that damn branch and wouldn't let go."

"In the end, that branch saved him."

Kevin nodded. "I know."

"Then what?"

"We were heading straight for a bunch of boulders. I pushed him away but couldn't avoid the rocks." His only thought had been to save his brother. He was the good one, the one worth saving.

She reached toward his face, then pulled her hand back. "The scars, that's where they come from?"

"I smashed just about every bone in my body. My jaw was wired shut for a year. I wanted to die. Thought I deserved to die, but Nina, she wouldn't let me."

"Nina?"

"Nina Rainwater. My adoptive grandmother. She's the one who found me." He shook his head. "She used my anger to make me fight for my recovery. Then with the horses, she taught me how to control it." He shrugged and gave a weak smile. "Well, mostly. She called me a work-in-progress."

Ellen's forehead knitted. She wrung her fingers in her lap and seemed to fight for words. "Why didn't you come back?"

"How could I? I thought I'd killed Kent." He trapped her chin in one hand. "Look at my face, Ellen. I thought I was doing you a favor."

Her frown deepened. Her gray-green eyes swirled with

pain. "Your looks wouldn't have mattered to me. It wasn't the shiny cowboy I was in love with. It was the gentle boy beneath the show I fell for."

Letting his hand drop back to the rail, he closed his eyes against the rawness of emotions playing on her face. "You wouldn't have wanted to have been saddled with a murderer. You had plans. You were going to be a vet. I couldn't take those things away from you."

"None of those things mattered. Just your love. That's the only thing I really wanted. You made me feel...special."

Touched by her simple admission, he swallowed hard.

"What we had, didn't it mean anything to you?" she asked, her voice cracking.

It meant everything. "I was young. I was scared. I loved you so much, it terrified me." He looked away, saw the first star of the evening wink at him. "I thought if you knew how much I loved you, you'd be taken from me, too. I had to put some space and some time between us to see if my feelings were strong enough to..."

"To what?"

He stared at her deep and hard. "To stand being caged. That's why I had to take that summer job."

"I understood, you know. I just needed reassurance. I was afraid, too."

"I never meant for any of this to happen."

She hopped off the fence rail. "I could have handled the truth then. I could have handled the truth now."

"I know." He slipped off the fence and shoved his hands in his pockets. "When I heard about the horses, I just wanted to keep you safe."

"What about what I needed?"

"To find your feet. I did hear you, Ellen. But by

then…'' He shrugged and kicked at a stone. Blue scampered after it. ''The lie was already there.''

''I can hold my own.'' She glanced at her watch, fumbled with the band. ''I've got to go.''

An edge of nerves shot down his spine. ''Where are we going?''

She planted her fists on her hips and faced him like a gunslinger at a duel. ''*We're* not going anywhere. I've got an appointment with Dr. Warner.''

''You can't go there alone.''

''Why not?'' Her mouth twisted in a sardonic grin. ''Because I'm too weak? Just like you thought I was too weak to know the truth about you?''

Her barb hit right on target, making him wince. ''Okay, you've made your point. But this isn't negotiable, Ellen. I have to know you're safe.''

''You're right,'' she said crisply, gaze narrowing. ''It isn't negotiable. This is my ranch and I make the decisions here.'' Her scowl flashed a warning not to pursue his stand.

He wanted to give her the rest of the truth still lodged inside him. To tell her he loved her still. That he admired her strength of spirit, her resilience. That he could think of nothing better than to spend the rest of his days next to her, working the ranch, the rest of his nights in her arms, loving her. But she wasn't ready for any of it.

She still had to prove her own strength to herself—even if it meant walking into danger. He knew he'd lost her trust. Rebuilding it would take time he didn't have. He simply couldn't let her walk into danger alone.

''Wait till morning,'' he said, desperately reaching for a compromise she could live with. ''The judge is due out then. We'll talk to him.''

''They're getting worse, Kevin. Tomorrow might be too late.''

"One night. What difference can it make?"

Ellen never got a chance to answer his question. From the barn came a loud thump, as if a load of feed sacks had fallen from the back of a truck, then the wild thrashings of hooves against a stall wall.

They both ran into the barn. Blue charged ahead and whimpered at Titan's stall. Titan had fallen in his stall and couldn't get up. His big heart seemed to want to beat right out of his body. Each pump bulged his chest. His eyes rolled frantically. The membranes were pale, the whites yellow.

"It almost looks like he fainted and it caught him off guard," Ellen said. "He's been acting weird since dinner."

Kevin stepped into the stall and calmed the gelding. Taking great care, he finally got the horse back on his feet. Titan's balance seemed affected by his ordeal.

Like Ellen. The horror of the thought made his stomach lurch. The oats Garth had fed Ellen were the same he'd given the horses. Was she in danger of dying from Garth's experiment?

Titan swayed for a few steps, then he braced his legs beneath him and started shaking. His breaths came in ragged spurts as if he'd just run a race at top speed.

"Oh, God, he's bleeding," Ellen said.

Gently, Kevin made his way to the gelding's mouth. Titan tried to fight him, but didn't have the energy. Kevin pulled back the lip. From Titan's gums appeared narrow strings of blood.

Ellen ran from the barn and reappeared a few minutes later. "Dr. Parnell's on his way. I've got to go."

"You can't. Not now."

"Stay with Titan until Dr. Parnell gets here."

"Ellen—"

"I'm trusting you, Kevin. I'm trusting you with Titan, with the rest of the horses, with the ranch. Can't we start with that?"

Start. She'd given him an opening, a possibility. But what good would it do him if she got hurt? "Not when it means sending you alone into danger."

"There is no danger. Dr. Warner is a broken man whose wife is dying. He doesn't want to hurt me. He didn't even want to hurt the horses. He's going to give me his research so we can help the horses." She shook her head slightly. Her eyes silently pleaded for understanding. "Dr. Warner has the answer. The horses can't wait. Please, Kevin, promise me you'll stay and keep the horses safe."

There it was. The impossible deal. It was what he'd wanted, wasn't it? A chance to gain back her trust. If she was right about Dr. Warner, she was in no danger and her effort would bolster her confidence. "If you're not back in an hour, I'm coming after you."

"Give me two. It takes half an hour to get to his clinic." Before he could say anything more, Ellen sprinted out of the barn. "I'll be back soon."

Still holding on to the frightened horse, he couldn't go after her. She'd entrusted him with her horses. She'd hinted at the possibility of starting over fresh. But could Dr. Warner be trusted? The vet had too much at stake to let one woman stand in his way.

Kevin swore. He tried to convince himself he was doing the right thing, but he couldn't shake the dread clawing at him like attic mice. Would he ever stop making mistakes?

As soon as Dr. Parnell arrived, Kevin relinquished Titan's care to him. He gave him a brief rundown on what had happened, then raced to the house and placed a call to Chance.

"Chance, I need your help. Ellen might be in trouble."

Kevin gave him the bare bones of facts. Naturally, Chance read between the lines, adding the missing meat and a generous portion of fat.

"How could you let her go alone?"

"I had no choice—"

"That's the story of your life. It's always someone else's fault—"

"No, I take full credit for it." Kevin understood Chance's anger, but there was no time to argue right now. "You can ream me up and down later. Right now Ellen needs your help."

"I'm on my way."

Kevin had done all he could to protect her. Rubbing Nina's feather, he reluctantly returned to the barn to keep his promise.

Chapter Thirteen

Ellen drove as fast as she dared on the dark country roads. A headache had wormed itself around her temples and pounded a timpanic beat. She longed for a shower and the relaxing blast of hot water between her aching shoulders. But it would be a long time before she could soak the tension from her tired body.

She glanced at her watch, but didn't see the time. The image of Kevin standing at the barn door floated into her mind. She shook it away.

She'd half expected Kevin to head out of Ashbrook in the opposite direction, back to Colorado or Montana—anywhere but Gabenburg. That's what Kyle had done when the going got tough. That way, she might never have had to deal with him again. At the moment that seemed the easiest solution to the whole unreal situation. He'd have faded from her memory as she got more involved with rebuilding her life, with the horses and with the ranch.

"Yeah, right!" She snorted. "Just like before."

As much as she wanted to deny it, part of her had sensed the truth from the moment Kevin had walked up her driveway and sent her senses spinning out of control. No one but Kyle had managed to touch her so easily, so deeply.

And now? Now, the feelings were still there, enmeshed

with the anger, and she wasn't sure at all how to handle either. Her life had suddenly become a sweater unraveling from both ends. She wanted him here. She wanted him gone. She didn't really know what she wanted. What did that say about her mental health?

Thinking hurt too much. She didn't want to do it anymore, didn't want to feel anything. She just wanted to find a way to heal the horses.

With a shake of her head, she put Kyle and Kevin out of her mind and forced herself to concentrate on Dr. Warner and the help he could afford her horses.

The Warner house was a modest ranch-style made of beige clapboard and brown brick. No light burned through its windows. A single spotlight on the corner of the high-tech barn illuminated the dirt path leading to the house. The rest of the property lay in shadows. The whole place had a feeling of abandonment. Was Dr. Warner here? Was Kevin right? Was this a trap of some sort?

"Knock it off!" Kevin had her spooked with his talk of danger.

Maybe a complication had delayed Dr. Warner at the hospice. Maybe he'd fallen asleep because *she* was late. He'd looked so wrung out this afternoon, she'd actually felt sorry for him.

Dr. Warner had said he'd meet her in his office and his defeated expression had looked real enough. His office was probably in the barn where a light glowed from a window toward the back of the structure. Making as much noise as she dared, Ellen made her way to the barn.

"Dr. Warner?" Safety lights on the ceiling lined the middle of the aisle at regular intervals. The smell of disinfectant burned her nose. Empty stall after empty stall greeted her. The sudden thump of a hoof on metal gave her a start. Then a dark head lashed at her from a steel-reinforced stall.

Ears flattened, teeth bared, the horse lunged at her again, stopped only by the bars on the door. He bore a startling resemblance to Legacy's Prometheus, except that he had the gangly appearance of a two-year-old. Why was he alone in this huge barn? The tag on the door bore no name, simply a number.

"Dr. Warner?" She continued down the aisle, passed a series of closed doors she assumed where the clinic part of the building, until she reached a door from which a crack of harsh white light protruded.

Hand in midair, she hesitated. Something didn't feel right. The air around her was thick, unbreathable. Even the black demon in the stall now stood still, leaving nothing but silence to wrap around her like an itchy mantle.

She knocked on the door. The metal beneath her fist gave. She pushed the door all the way open. The hinges squealed. "Dr. Warner?"

At first all Ellen saw was blinding light bouncing against white tiles. From the glare emerged a row of glass-fronted, stainless-steel cupboards filled with instruments, a stainless-steel counter, then a large stainless-steel table on some sort of lift. Above the stinging scent of antiseptic arose the sharp bite of copper. Out of the corner of her eye materialized a large dark shape. She turned toward it and gasped at the stark scene that unfolded before her.

Propped against a wall sat Dr. Warner holding his beloved Lillian in his arms. From a gash on her neck, a wash of blood tracked down her front, soaked into the white material of her gown. It snaked down her side to the slanted floor and disappeared into the drain in the middle of the room where another thin red trail joined it.

Ellen followed the jagged line back up. It widened and

flowed around an object. A scalpel. The wrist above it bloomed dark red.

Time, her heart, her breath—everything seemed to stop. "No!" She rushed toward the couple posed like rag dolls. With a trembling hand, she felt for a pulse and found none. Tears rolled down her cheeks as she tried to make sense of the scene before her. A wave of nausea came over her. Dizziness made her stumble backward. And the full horror of the macabre portrait punched her in the gut.

I have nothing left to lose now. Had Dr. Warner killed his dying wife, then taken his own life? "No."

Hand over her mouth to keep herself from retching, Ellen staggered out of the room into the aisle. She was rushing down the concrete, when the word *office* caught her attention. She skidded to a halt, closed her eyes, held her breath and, pulse pounding, pushed the door open.

She could do nothing to help the Warners, but the horses still depended on her to find an answer. She flicked on the lights, half expecting another gruesome scene. The severe order gave her back her breath.

She wiped her clammy hands on her jeans, then went about the task of searching the file cabinets flanking the wall. They were empty. Drawer after drawer held nothing more than dust and the occasional stray paper clip. The thick binders stacked above the cabinets offered no more help. Rings still opened, whatever they'd once held was gone.

Ellen rubbed the wrist holding her watch and stared at the empty drawers that would do her no good. Then on the desk, from beneath the blotter, she spotted the edge of a slim file. Sliding it out of its hiding spot, she saw that the file bore the same number she'd read on the black horse's stall earlier.

Code numbers like the ones in Tessa's protocol book under the heading "subject."

She glanced at the clock on the wall, thought about calling Kevin to reassure him, then decided against it. With as little belief in her abilities as he had, he'd insist she come home. Besides, she had no phone in her barn. Instead, she dialed 911 and reported the deaths, then swiped the black horse's file and raced to the truck.

With Dr. Warner dead, her only hope to help the horses was to confront the Bancrofts.

FOR THE HUNDREDTH TIME, Kevin glanced at the clock in the tack room as he paced by it, hands deep in his pockets, fingers frantically rubbing Nina's feather. Ten minutes. He'd give her ten more minutes, then he'd drag her home kicking and screaming if he had to. He'd let her go too many times already. She'd be upset. He'd lose all chance of the new beginning she'd hinted at. But at least he'd know she was safe.

Dr. Parnell had come and gone. He'd pumped Titan full of drugs to stabilize him, but Kevin had listened to the explanations with half an ear. He kept listening for the sound of his truck, for Ellen's voice—for this torturous wait to end.

When Blue's ears pricked toward the house, Kevin stopped in his tracks and caught the light jangle of a ringing phone. He sprinted for the kitchen, cursing himself for not waiting by the phone for Ellen's call.

"We've got trouble," Chance said. "Looks like a murder-suicide—"

Kevin's gut knotted. "Ellen—"

"No, Dr. Warner and his wife."

The breath Kevin didn't know he'd held rushed out. "Ellen's all right then. Let me talk to her."

"She's not here."

"What do you mean she'd not there?"

There was a pause. "Her fingerprints, hand prints and footprints are all over the scene. She was here, but the truck's gone."

Shaking his head, Kevin gripped the receiver tighter. "She wouldn't have—"

"I know, but this isn't my jurisdiction. The farm sits on the other side of the Gabenburg county line."

Kevin swore. Chance would have done all he could to protect Ellen, but now it was out of his hands. "Where is she?"

"If she's smart, on her way back home."

Kevin closed his eyes. A dull sensation weighed him down. "The Bancrofts. If she found Warner dead, she'd still want answers."

"I can't leave here." To protect Ellen's interest, his brother had to stay at the scene and deal with his peers.

"I'm on my way."

He'd lost her long ago. A broken promise wasn't going to change anything. And a promise kept was meaningless if something happened to her.

"THIS BETTER be important," Brad Bancroft said as he pounded through the French doors of the living room where a uniformed maid had ordered Ellen to wait.

High ceilings made a dramatic impression, as did the white marble fireplace, the two skylights and huge bay window. Detailed molding and wainscoting in shades of cream accentuated the pristine whiteness of the walls. White-upholstered antique chairs looked as if they'd never supported a body. The cherry coffee table held oversize books whose covers nobody had probably ever cracked.

The only footprints on the thick carpet were her own—and now Bancroft's.

"It's about the horses," she said, suddenly unsure about the wisdom of her impulse. The sleeves of his shirt were rolled up. The top button was undone. His mood looked murderous as he poured himself a drink from the bar. "I want to know what's going on with them."

His frown wasn't one of confusion, but one of anger. "You disturbed me for this?"

"The horses aren't doing well and I need to find out what you've done to them."

He stared at her as if she were a creature from another planet. As his expression darkened and his jowls shook, her mouth went dry. Stalking across the room, drink in hand, Bancroft dismissed her. "I have no idea what you're talking about. I've got an important meetin' in the mornin'. I don't have time for this."

"Wait! What about the racing? The protocol book—"

"The horses are Tessa's little project. I just show up in the winner's circle to indulge her."

Tessa, dressed in formfitting black leather pants and a black-fringed halter top to match, appeared and touched her husband's arm in the doorway. His adoring gaze at his wife told Ellen that indulging Tessa was as much his weakness as the horses were hers. Were those indulgences Tessa's reward for staying with a bull-ugly husband twice her age?

"Why don't you go back to your preparations, sugar, I'll deal with Ms. Paxton."

He nodded once and slanted a rushed kiss across Tessa's cheek. After a brief, heat-filled admiration of his wife's chest, he left.

"Now, why don't you tell me what this is about." Tessa

glided over the carpet noiselessly and headed toward the bar.

"The horses. I want to know what's going on with them. Why are they getting so sick?"

She shrugged and poured a generous inch of amber liquid into a crystal glass. "Maybe your ministering leaves something to be desired."

"I saw Garth today. He told me about the genetically engineered oats."

"Is that so?"

"I think the answer to the horses' illness has something to do with your 'protocol.'"

"Temperature, pulse, respiration." Using silver tongs, she dropped two cubes of ice into the glass. "What's so evil about that? All good trainers keep track of their horses' well-being."

Tessa was as much a horse trainer as Ellen was a fashion plate. No, it was something other than the satisfaction of training a good horse that drove Tessa. Once she discovered what, Ellen would find her own answers. "Blood count, liver function. No mere trainer is quite that zealous. What's the last number you're keeping track of? Even my vet couldn't figure it out."

A sly smile touched Tessa's lips. "Really, Ms. Paxton, do you always have such wild delusions? I understand you're still recovering from a tremendous trauma." She arched her eyebrows. "Perhaps a visit to a therapist is in order…"

Tessa's avoidance only served to prove to Ellen that she was on the right track. She pressed on. "Why are they developing a fever? Why are their gums bleeding? Why are they so lethargic?"

Tessa took a sip, then pressed the glass against her chest and closed her eyes as she savored the liquor going down.

"My guess is the subpar feed you insist on giving them. As I recall, I had my own high-quality blend sent to you."

Fine, you want to play that way. "What does RLP–045913Z mean to you?"

Tessa's jaw tightened. Her dark eyes narrowed. She slowly put the glass back on the bar, then cocked her head and gave Ellen a smile that sent chills scurrying down her spine. "It means you've bitten off more than you can chew."

When she came around the bar, her hand held a black, alien-looking semiautomatic handgun aimed at Ellen's chest.

Chapter Fourteen

"Now," Tessa said, her voice overly sweet, "you and I are going to take a little ride."

"I don't think so." Going anywhere with someone holding a gun was a sure recipe for disaster. Ellen hadn't survived fifteen years of drugged imprisonment to die so soon. She tried to edge out of the room, but one leg hooked on the arm of a chair. She lost her balance and found herself sprawled awkwardly on one of the pristine white cushions.

Before she could regain her balance, Tessa shoved the muzzle of the gun under Ellen's chin. "Yes, I think so."

Ellen swallowed hard and bluffed. "My ranch hand and the sheriff know where I am."

"If they did, you wouldn't be here alone. Those two are much too protective of you." Keeping the gun's muzzle pressed against Ellen's neck, Tessa whipped Ellen's arm behind her back, jerked her to her feet and shoved her forward. "Besides, I don't want to kill you."

"Sure could have fooled me," Ellen muttered, trying to ease the strain in her shoulder from Tessa's hold.

"I don't want that kind of attention right now." Tessa pushed her into the empty hall.

"Then why point a gun at me at all?"

When Tessa grabbed a leather backpack off the small table beside the door, Ellen tried to twist out of Tessa's grasp. Tessa wrenched Ellen's arm higher on her back, nearly throwing her shoulder out of joint. "Because I want *your* attention."

You've got it, Ellen thought, biting back a yelp at the sharp stab of pain. "Where are you taking me?"

"You want to know what's going on with the horses, don't you? We'll have a heart-to-heart chat on the way back to your ranch."

Home. Advantage. Kevin was waiting there. "Have you got the safety on that thing?"

"I didn't get where I am by being cautious. One wrong move, sugar, and that pretty little neck of yours is going to sport a couple of extra breathing holes."

They met no one on their way out through the marble foyer. Ellen thought of faking a spill and racing up the turned stairway with the red oak tread and carved balusters. But she would do the horses no good with a bullet in her back.

Tessa must have sensed her intentions. "Don't even think about it. You'd be dead before you reached the first step. We've got plenty of acreage to make you disappear." Then she chuckled. "Scream if you want. No one will answer. The maid is illegal and Brad has had enough of you for one evening."

Tessa's turf. Tessa's people. Ellen needed to save her energy for her own playing field.

Once in the truck, Ellen's knees trembled as she engaged the clutch. As she drove, she conjured up and rejected a dozen escape scenarios. She didn't want to give Tessa any reason to press the trigger. As much as Ellen hated to admit it, she wasn't strong enough to manhandle the gun out of Tessa's grip. With the night so thick, she couldn't attract another driver's attention—not that they'd come across anyone yet. The headlights swept across nothing but rolling fields and the occasional cow or horse grazing close to a fence. And stopping Tessa by provoking an accident wasn't the answer either. To help the horses, Ellen still needed answers.

Patience. She'd heard that caution almost every day since waking up at the nursing home. Now she'd have to dig down and heed the warning. Tessa's eyes were much too determined for Ellen to believe this was a simple joyride.

The realization shot cold dread through her. Kevin was waiting for her. Once he saw Tessa's gun pointed at her head, he'd do everything to deflect Tessa's intentions. Hadn't he already shown his willingness to protect her? Through this whole ordeal with the horses, the one person she could always count on to stand by her, for her, was Kevin. Ellen had no doubt Tessa wouldn't appreciate his attempt at heroics. As angry as Ellen was with him, she didn't want to see him dead. What chance did he have against a bullet?

By refusing his help, she'd put them both in danger. She had less than twenty minutes to come up with a solution.

Fatigue and stress took their toll. Ellen had to grip the steering wheel solidly with both hands and still the muscles twitched. Keeping her eyes focused was becoming harder and required much blinking. All she had to do was hold on until they got to the ranch. Bracing herself, she focused on the road—and on the horses.

"What's so special about RLP–045913Z?" Ellen asked. The mere mention of the code had shaken Tessa enough to bring out her gun and threaten murder. There had to be some clue there.

"Why couldn't you just let things be?" Tessa shook her head like a disappointed big sister.

Ellen shrugged. The move was jerky, betraying her anxiety. "The horses can't speak. Someone had to be their voice."

"If you'd just fed them the oats I sent, you could have avoided all of this."

"The feed? That's all it takes?" Was it really that simple?

"The feed maintains them—to a point."

"What's wrong with them?"

Tessa sighed, exasperation thick on the exhale. "It's a combination of things."

"Such as?"

"Why do you care?" Tessa's gaze narrowed as she pressed the gun's muzzle more firmly against Ellen's neck. Ellen flinched, wondering if the gun would accidentally go off. "They're not your horses. Tomorrow, I get them back."

"Because they're suffering and need someone to care for them."

"They're dead. Don't you get it?"

"How can I when I haven't got a clue what's going on?" Ellen bit back her anger. With a gun pressed to her neck and an unstable woman's finger on the trigger, now was not the time to lose her temper.

Lips pouting, Tessa seemed to consider, then relented. "Why not? They were bred for hardiness and speed. That gave us a good base to start from. The genetically engineered oats trigger certain genes. The problem is that we got a few unplanned side effects."

"Such as?"

"Anemia."

Kevin was right. They had known about the anemia and

tried to compensate for the symptoms. "Hence the feed blend with the high iron."

Tessa's eyebrows arched in surprise. "And high in B_{12} vitamin."

"But?" Ellen asked, keeping her tone light, yet dismayed by the unwanted waver.

"That works only short-term."

"Because…"

"Because eventually bone marrow production is affected, which leads to a form of leukemia."

"Leukemia!" Ellen wobbled the wheel. The tires hit the shoulder gravel. The truck lurched from side to side before Ellen could get it back under control.

Tessa thrust the gun's muzzle deeper under Ellen's jaw. "Keep the damn truck on the road!"

Ellen gulped and shifted slightly to ease the jab of the hard casing. "The horses have leukemia?"

"Which is why a painless death is much more charitable than your ill-advised zeal."

Ellen's mind buzzed as it tried to wrap itself around the information Tessa had given her. "How could this happen?"

Tessa dismissed her worries with a jerk of her shoulder. "Every new invention is bound to have a few glitches."

"The horses aren't expendable pieces of machinery. They're live beings."

"They're animals."

Ellen clamped back her retort, knowing it would get her nowhere. "So, is it the feed or the activated genes in the horses that causes the leukemia?"

Tessa seemed to relax a bit. She leaned back against the door, easing the gun's prod against Ellen's neck. "The chicken or the egg? That *is* the question."

"And what's the answer?" There had to be an answer. She had to help those horses.

"Triggering the extra growth also causes mutant cells to generate. These mutant cells invade the bone marrow. This disrupts the normal production of red blood cells and platelets. Next they invade organs and tissues, causing them to enlarge. From there it's all downhill."

"Surely, something can be done for them."

"Nothing that warrants the cost."

Ellen sneered. "That's what it comes down to for you, isn't it—money?"

Tessa leaned forward and spoke through gritted teeth. "That's where you're wrong. It's not the money. It's the payoff for the investment."

"How does RLP–045913Z fit into this?"

"Zeus is the next generation."

The powerful Zeus, master of the sky—master of Tessa's dreams? "Mutation free?"

"So far."

The horses weren't headed to the Double B, to a trainer's barn or to a slaughterhouse on the night of the storm. They were headed for Dr. Warner's clinic. How far would Tessa go to protect her project? Ellen licked her lips and took a calculated risk. "Why didn't you take Zeus back when you murdered the Warners?"

In the dim light of the truck's instrument panel, Tessa's smile had a sinister slant. "You think you're so smart."

Of course Zeus couldn't leave. That would call attention to Tessa, and hadn't Tessa said she didn't want that kind of attention. If Zeus was still there, then the murder-suicide scenario played realistically. Ellen pressed on. "Why did you destroy all the paperwork in Dr. Warner's office?"

"He did that all on his own." Tessa scoffed. "As if a

few pieces of paper could stop this project. Zeus guarantees it will survive.''

''How?'' Ellen's pulse tripped so fast she could hardly hear herself over the sound. They were nearing home and she still hadn't thought of a way to warn Kevin of the danger speeding toward him.

''He's the next two-year-old colt Texas Breeders' Cup champion.''

''Is that something special?''

''Don't play the innocent. It really doesn't suit you.''

Ellen shook her head. *Think, think, think.* ''I *don't* know a thing about racing.''

''It's the highest award possible for a Texas-bred Thoroughbred.''

She thinks she can buy respect, but she's usin' the wrong currency, Garth had said. Had Tessa switched from sex to racing to reach her goal? If she was desperate enough to kill Dr. Warner to win the championship, she'd do anything.

''The incident in the pasture the day before the judge's visit, that was you,'' Ellen said.

Tessa didn't answer. She reached inside her bag with one hand and drew out a remote. Aiming at the gate, she pressed the button. The gate swung open.

Ellen snapped her head Tessa's way. ''Where'd you get that?''

Tessa merely smiled. ''Watch where you're going.''

Suddenly too much became clear. ''The flood in the barn, you engineered that, too.''

''I needed the horses back,'' Tessa said matter-of-factly.

''And the judge foiled your perfect plan.''

''He's blind.''

''You were going to kill the horses,'' Ellen said. The

weight of the knowledge bled precious energy from her. "Why?"

"To protect Zeus." Tessa jabbed the gun's muzzle against Ellen's throat. "Park by the house."

Ellen slowed. She had to attract attention. Kevin and Blue would come running out. When Tessa was distracted by them, Ellen would jump her. There was no time for a more complicated plan.

Instead of reaching for the key to turn off the engine, Ellen leaned against the horn.

Tessa hit her over the head with the butt of the gun.

Ellen's vision filled with stars.

"WHAT IS WRONG with you people?" Brad Bancroft bellowed when Kevin charged into his office.

Pumped up on adrenaline and worry, Kevin didn't stop until he reached Bancroft's desk. He swept the paperwork off the surface and grabbed Bancroft's collar. "Where's Ellen?"

"How the hell should I know?" Face red, jowls quivering, Bancroft reached for the phone.

Kevin slapped his free hand over Bancroft's beefy one and squeezed. "Where's Ellen?"

"She was here, raised a fuss and left."

"Just like that?"

Bancroft narrowed his gaze. "What are you implyin'?"

"She came here to talk about the horses. Now she's missing."

"As I explained to Ms. Paxton, the horses are Tessa's project."

"You were the one barking to get them back."

Bancroft puffed out his chest. "Tessa thought the judge might be more apt to listen to a man."

The protocol. Tessa's desire for what? Success? Power? "Where's your wife now?"

"In bed where she belongs."

Bancroft pried Kevin's hand from his collar. "Do you mind? I've got work to do."

"When did Ellen leave?"

Scowling, Bancroft shuffled the scattered papers. "I heard the truck pull out about half an hour ago."

Slamming the door, Kevin left Bancroft's office. He took the fancy stairs two by two and checked every room on the second floor. All were empty.

He couldn't get the image of Ellen unconscious and bleeding out of his head. He hadn't been there to save her from Garth's manipulations sixteen years ago. And now Garth's quest for success had once again put her in the jaws of danger. He had to find her.

As he went through the front door, something caught his eye. He backed a step. On the dark wood of the door's frame, a bloody mark like a smeared fingerprint. Whose? Heart thundering in his chest, he rolled Nina's feather round and round his fingers to calm himself. He had to keep cool. *Ellen, where are you?*

An unpleasant tingling sensation bristled down his nape. Dr. Warner was dead. Tessa wasn't in bed where she belonged. Sick horses. Anemia hidden with high-iron feed. All that stood between Tessa and her secret was Ellen.

A sick feeling sank through him, dark and cold.

It all led back to the horses. And the horses were at Ellen's ranch.

If he'd kept his promise, he'd still be there.

WITH NO ONE AROUND to hear her but the wind, Tessa saw no reason to swallow her curses. She let them tear as she dragged the unconscious woman to the middle of the ring beside the barn and let her flop on the muddy ground.

Things had not exactly gone according to plan. Ellen wasn't supposed to show up at Dr. Warner's barn or at the house. That honor should have gone to her ranch hand— with the help of a prodding phone call at just the right time. The plan was to make him disappear as he had six-teen years ago. People expected others to follow perceived patterns, especially a sheriff still mired in emotions over his brother's cowardly dodge of responsibility. And dear Ellen was to have her physical weakness get the better of her. She couldn't handle the horses and was trampled by them.

But Tessa was used to thinking on the fly, and when opportunities presented themselves, she knew how to turn them to her advantage. That Ellen had apparently mistaken the Taser for a handgun had only helped Tessa's cause.

Now time was of the essence to pull off this accident. She'd stuffed the stunned attack dog in the tack room, but she had no idea when the hapless ranch hand would return. She had to be ready to greet him. He would drive her home and then both he and his truck would disappear.

She led the horses from the pasture to the ring. The gray gave her a bit of a hard time, but the lure of grain finally gained her cooperation. The Appaloosa and Apollo had followed her willingly. Those three should cause enough damage. She could count on Apollo to freak with the noise of the close-up function of the Electro-Muscular Disrup-tion weapon. If the sizzling sound didn't panic him enough, then she'd resort to a jolt of electricity on the rump. The remote function, she reserved for the ranch hand.

The ring was relatively small—not much room for three horses to maneuver. Once Apollo panicked, the others would follow. In their hysteria, they wouldn't see the woman in the ring.

An unfortunate accident. Sad, really.

But no one could make a connection to her. Brad, the maid, any and all of the Double B's help would swear to her presence at the homestead tonight. Fear truly was a good motivator for those facing the threat of deportation.

This time, the horses would come home and the project's integrity would be protected. The judge would have no reason to extend their stay at Ellen Paxton's rescue ranch.

Zeus would run—and win.

Tessa rubbed the gold locket at her neck, then flicked the oval open. Inside rested the picture of the blond, blue-eyed teenager who'd abandoned her on the steps of the St. Theresa Church thirty years ago.

"I'm almost there, Sheree, almost there." Soon Tessa would sit as an equal to her mother, the pale imitation of a husband at her side and the two sniveling sons tugging at her expensive skirt.

Tessa would get the respect she deserved—horsewoman to horsewoman; mother to daughter; blue blood to blue blood.

For good measure, she jammed a piece of wood through the gate's latch. It didn't hurt to play out all the possibilities. Then she took her post outside the corral fence and aimed the weapon at Apollo.

CLOUDS SHADOWED the moon, cloaking the ranch in a blanket of black. The ground beneath Kevin's feet seemed to sizzle with energy waiting to discharge. The breeze stirred the air with whiplike pops and snaps, snarling sand in his face.

Using peripheral vision, he saw the lumbering outline

of his truck. No light in the house or barn. No Blue to greet him. No chorus of night creatures. Other than the wind scouring the ranch, everything was too quiet—as if the world was holding its breath.

Squinting, he searched the darkness, willing his body to stay still. Rushing headlong into a situation he didn't understand would help no one. *Do something. Don't just stand there, do something. Help her.* The image of Ellen helpless and bleeding filled his mind. His calf muscles jittered. His fingers twitched. His pulse stampeded. He ground his teeth and fought the urge to run.

Ellen, where are you?

His gaze scanned the darkness, took in the house, the barn, the yard between. He stopped at the ring. Horses. Three darker shapes against the black of the barn. Out of place. His whole body tensed.

Ellen, where are you?

Movement. By the back side of the fence. A deeper, denser black. Smaller than a horse. Bigger than a dog. But not Ellen. He would know her anywhere.

He fought off terror as the punch of something evil hit him in the gut. The scent of it was heavy and acrid in the air. It clung to him in sticky cold strands. He opened his mouth to drag in breath. Tessa.

Crouching low, he hugged the edge of the yard, melting into the darker shadows, advancing noiselessly toward the barn. He'd promised Nina to make things right. He'd promised Chance to keep Ellen safe. He'd sworn to himself Ellen would have the dream of her ranch. He had to get this right. Tessa would not get away with whatever misdeed she plotted.

He rounded the corner of the barn. Heart beating a mad race, he carefully peered at the ring. Luci, C.C., Apollo milled around in restless agitation, tails wringing, ears flicking. What he saw next made his mouth go dry, his knees turn to jelly, his gut twist.

Ellen, no. Despair flooded him. *Not again. Please, God, no.*

Before he could move, the hair on the back of his neck prickled. Icy fingers of dread skimmed his skin.

The shadow moved. An arm detached from the form, rose.

A string of rapid-fire clicks rent the air. Crazed blue light arced from probe to probe against the black of night.

A terrified whinny curdled the air. From the barn came a choir of anxious answering calls. Horses stomped and snorted and raced, stirring inside the ring in frenzied confusion.

And in the middle of the thrashing hooves was Ellen's slumped body.

Chapter Fifteen

At first Ellen thought the pounding came from her head. Then she realized that two rhythms hammered at her. The even *thump thump* of her brain against her cranium and the wild drumming of horses' hooves in the dirt all around her. The scent of panic thickened the air. Clumps of mud pelted her sides. Horse tails whipped her face. Hooves nicked her back.

Instinctively she turtled on the ground, protecting her head. Dizzy, she blinked, trying to focus her eyes. Black. All she could see was black. Was she blind? What was happening? Why was she on the ground in the middle of petrified horses?

Tessa. The gun. The horses. The ranch. Kevin, ohmygod, Kevin. The blinding clarity of the answer also served to clear her vision. Why were the horses stampeding in the dark? Where was Tessa? Where was Kevin? If Ellen hadn't been so bent on punishing him, he'd have been with her, and together they could have dealt with Tessa before the situation got out of hand. Now she was alone, and if he was hurt, it was her fault.

Snorting and stomping, the horses slowly wound down. Then a loud *snap-crackle-click* fired the air, seemed to make it alive with electricity. Apollo trumpeted. C.C.

snorted. Luci whinnied. A horse cow-kicked. Another reared. The third made a mad dash away from the rip of electric air. Saucer hooves clipped her arm, her back, her leg. What was that noise? Where was Tessa? What was she doing?

"Whoa, whoa, whoa," Ellen said in the calmest voice she could muster, trying to ignore the bruising pain that seemed to cover every inch of her body. "Luci, Luci, Luci. It's me. Whoa. Please." Ellen frantically sought to orient herself through the manic stir of legs wildly seeking escape from the nerve-rattling noise. Shadows finally detached from one another, giving shape to the charged horses, the barn, the fence.

The gate. She had to get to the gate and let the horses out, get them away from the noise that was frightening them.

Talking in easy tones she stood up slowly in order not to panic the horses more than they already were. Apollo bumped against her, nearly sending her sprawling to the ground once more.

"Stay down!" Kevin shouted.

Kevin! He was all right. A surge of relief almost knocked her to her knees "The gate."

"I'll get it."

Forcing herself to block out her own mounting panic, she sought out Luci. But the horses' terror had her dodging blows and desperately struggling to stay on her feet amid rumps and shoulders and heads and feet milling madly.

"Luci, Luci, Luci," she croaked as calmly as she could. If she could calm Luci, the rest would follow.

Apollo rammed into her, knocking her off balance. She fell on all fours. C.C. hopped over her, clipping the side of her head with his back hoof. Rounding herself into as small a ball as she could, she peered through her arms.

Out of control. The horses were out of control. One stepped on her boot, pinching her big toe. A tail whipped her eyes.

She sensed Kevin crouching low to her right, heading for the gate. *Hurry, hurry, hurry.* Where was Tessa?

At that moment she felt movement to her left. Using the fence as a step, Tessa stood. Grim determination etched her face as she aimed the gun at Kevin.

"Watch out! She's got a gun."

The horses were going crazy. Agitated whinnies and snorts reeled beside her, above her, all around her. Hooves cut into her, faster, sharper, harder. She could feel her energy draining with each blow, couldn't help seeing herself trampled to death, fought to blink away the horrid picture.

Cursing violently, Kevin struggled to open the gate. "It's jammed."

Tessa fired. Two probes shot out, lighting the night in a deranged light. Like guided missiles they flew a true course. *Snap-crackle-click.* Kevin roared in pain, went rigid and dropped to the ground like a stiff corpse.

"Kevin!" Ellen's shout only served to stir the horses' terror. It was her nightmare come to life again, watching helplessly as the man she loved drowned and the rough water swelled over her. Unable to move any muscle, she was too weak to help him, help herself—help the horses. Stamps of frenzied hooves pounded all around her. "Kevin!"

"There's no getting out of this, sugar. You might as well just let the horses finish their job." The gun fired again—no flying probes, just the nerve-grating noise—sizzling the air with its charge.

Ellen had to get the horses out. She swallowed her panic and ordered herself to breathe, to think. Holding her breath, she rolled to the fence. A hoof caught the dial of her watch, ground it into the mud, pulverizing it. She snatched her arm away. The limp band fell from her wrist.

No time. No time. She cursed and fought the tears blurring her vision. And without Kevin, time wouldn't matter. Too late. Why did she have to discover the truth in her heart too late?

No, not too late. Never too late. She hadn't given up then. She couldn't give up now.

The gate was stuck. There was only one way to get out. Horses were flight animals. Instincts made them run from anything they feared. That left her no choice.

When Luci rushed by, Ellen grabbed her mane. Using all of her strength and will, she vaulted on. As her weight landed on Luci's back, the mare stopped dead and bobbed her head in her usual riding stupor. Rounding over the mare's neck to avoid becoming Tessa's target, she mimicked Kevin's hypnotic tones and murmured to the mare.

"There's no other way, Luci. We're going to have to jump. You can do it. You do it every morning."

Ellen gave Luci her cue to move and got no response but more insane head bobbing. Ellen's shaking legs weren't strong enough to bully Luci into action. She saw the whites of Apollo's crazed eyes as he collided with them, bumping them into C.C.'s path. C.C. kicked, landing a blow on her shin. Still Luci bobbed her head like a toy in a car window.

Ellen rubbed the sides of Luci's neck. "Luci, please, Luci. You've got to move."

Then she remembered Calliope and knew she had one hope left. At the top of her lungs she shouted, "Blue! Blue! Come, boy. Blue!"

Mad thumpings and muffled rusty attempts at barking were followed by the sound of shattering glass. The dog flew through the tack room's stuck window, scattering

C.C. and Apollo to the far end of the ring, adding to their maddened stirrings. Wood cracked but held. C.C. bucked. Apollo bugled as he skidded in the mud. Luci kept on bobbing her head.

"Herd, Blue, herd!" Was that the right command? How could she tell the dog what she needed?

Another zap of the gun arced at the weapon's muzzle. Blue shot toward Luci and nipped at her heels. The mare kicked out with one foot. Blue scooted out of the way. Luci lunged forward.

"That's it, Luci. That's it." Ellen hung on by sheer determination. Blue came at the mare again. "You can do it, Luci. Think of rolling in the mud. This is nothing for you. You can jump this fence in your sleep. Come on, Luci. That's it."

With Blue's help, using knees and weight shifts, Ellen maneuvered Luci to the long end of the pen. She'd get only one shot at this. Pointing Luci at the other end of the ring, she shouted to the dog, "Blue, herd!"

Leaning over Luci's neck, Ellen spoke soothing nothings into the mare's ears. "A roll in the mud, Luci." At Blue's nudging nip, Luci shot forward. "A roll in the mud." Ellen guided the horse straight to the fence. *Three, two, one,* she counted down. "Jump, Luci, jump!"

Ellen tightened her grip on Luci's mane, closed her eyes, held her breath. Her heart stopped as Luci gathered and sprung. Luci sailed over the fence and landed hard in the yard. The jar unbalanced Ellen.

She fell. Her back slammed into the ground, knocking the wind out of her.

MUSCLES CONTRACTING painfully Kevin fought the mental haze, the spinning disorientation of vertigo. Gritting his teeth, he willed his circuits back into order. Helplessly curled into a fetal position, he saw Ellen and Luci fly over the fence. C.C. followed suit. Apollo paced the fence, calling frantically, unable to jump with his hurt leg.

Ellen. He tried to shout but his vocal chords refused to respond. *Ellen.* It came out as a strangled groan. He'd seen her fall, and just as before, he couldn't do anything to help her.

Footsteps stalked, getting closer. Tessa. She stopped by him, kicked his leg and pulled out the probes still attached to the back of his shirt. Muscles shaking, struggling to control the sluggish neural transmissions, he focused all of his power and lashed out. With both hands he grabbed Tessa's ankle as she turned to head toward Ellen still slumped on the ground. With a growl he corkscrewed in a crocodile death roll and pulled Tessa down.

She aimed the heel of her boot at his face. He flopped down over her, trapping one of her legs beneath the weight of his body.

"You're not going to stop me," she growled, kicking. "Not now. I'm too close."

Scrambling, she maneuvered to use the gun's close-up stun feature. Pitching his still sluggish body at her arm, he turned the muzzle toward her and squeezed her hand. *Click-click-click.* Tessa stiffened and slumped.

On hands and knees, trying to shake the vertigo still tilting the world at a crazy angle, he scampered toward Ellen.

She moaned.

"Ellen."

She labored to a sitting position.

"Don't move," he said as he pushed her back down and patted her, looking for broken bones. Was that blood or mud?

"I'm all right," she said, and again tackled the task of sitting. "I got the wind knocked out of me, that's all."

Even in the darkness, her face seemed completely drained of color in between the dark streaks on her cheeks. Her eyes seemed to fill her face, silver in the dim light. But she was breathing. She was moving. She was talking. He took her in his arms, held her tightly, inhaled her scent and kissed her again and again. Her hair, her cheeks, her mouth. Then kissed her long and hard. He rested his forehead on hers and whispered thickly, "Don't ever scare me like that again."

"Trust me, it wasn't part of the plan," she said, sniffling and hanging on to him just as tightly. She dug her fingers into his shoulders. "You're all right? I saw you fall. Tessa. The horses. I thought I was losing everything all over again."

"It's okay. It's over. Tessa stunned herself with her own gun." His fingers scraped loose hair that had fallen across her cheek and came away wet. He sought the dark, shiny spot smearing the side of her face. "You're bleeding."

"I'm fine. Luci—"

"She and C.C. are grazing by the house. We need to get that cut seen to."

Ellen gave a semblance of a laugh through her tears. "They're probably eating my flowers."

"We'll plant more." His lips brushed the cut on her temple. If she could joke at a time like this, she was all right. She wouldn't fall into a coma. She would be fine. He chased the horror of seeing her slumped body on the ground out of his mind. She was okay. His heart filled with gratitude and his arms tightened around her.

There was so much he wanted to tell her, but Blue's low-throated growl reminded him there were still a few loose ends to tie up before he could raise the question of a future with her.

"Can you walk?" he asked, holding her away from him with two supporting hands on her arms.

"Of course." They stood. She wobbled a bit, then pushed him away.

Reluctantly he let her go. "Call the sheriff's office. I need to hog-tie Tessa before she's mobile again."

TWO HOURS LATER, the house, yard and barn blazed with light, giving the ranch the appearance of midday. The deputy had carted off Tessa into custody. Dr. Parnell had graciously come to examine and treat the horses and Blue after their ordeal. A semblance of normalcy returned with the horses safely settled for what remained of the night, munching on hay.

After assuring himself that Ellen was safe and sound and no more harm would come to her, Chance was heading back home. Kevin cornered him as he reached his cruiser. "Wait up."

Chance leaned against the cruiser, his face haggard. Tiredness rucked his forehead, bruised his eyes. Kevin knew his brother was itching to get back to his wife. He'd keep it short. But now that Kevin had the means and opportunity, he wasn't quite sure how to broach the subject that had brought him to Gabenburg in the first place. His hand dug into the pocket of his jeans and found the comfort of Nina's feather.

"I owe you an apology," Kevin said, kicking at the ground with the toe of his boot. "I've owed you one for sixteen years."

For a while Chance said nothing. Arms crossed beneath his chest, he just eyed his brother. "When I washed up in

Gabenburg, my mind was wiped clean. I couldn't remember who I was, what happened to me or why."

Kevin stiffened against the expected lecture on responsibility. "What did you do?"

"I started over. Angus and Lucille Conover took me in as their own. I'll be forever grateful to them."

"When...?" Kevin scowled at the toe of his boot.

"Did I remember?"

Kevin nodded.

"Last year."

"Last year!" Kevin's head snapped up. "That's fifteen years."

"That's how I found Ellen. By looking for myself."

Kevin was bleeding inside as the enormity of what he'd done hit him. He didn't know how to stop it. "I'm sorry, Chance. You'll never know how sorry I am for what happened."

Chance shook his head. "Don't be. I know you tried your best to save me. You left Ellen to come after me." He paused for a beat. "You were right."

"I was?" Kevin frowned. "About what?"

"You can't stop the river. That wild water carried us both to new lives." He placed a hand over his chest. "I've got everything I always wanted. Taryn, she's my world. And Shauna, she's my heart. There's nothing to forgive." Chance laughed roughly. "I should thank you, actually. Without that unexpected trip down the river, I would never have found them."

Kevin hunched his shoulders. "I still owe you an apology. I was angry. I didn't know." He blew out a long breath. "I loved Ellen so much, it hurt."

Chance nodded. "Anyone who'd seen you two together could tell you were a matched pair. I knew you'd work it out if I could just get out of the picture."

"You were trying to walk away and I didn't give you a chance. I thought... I thought..." Kevin shook his head, desperately searching for the words to explain the unexplainable. "I didn't know how to deal with it, how to tell her. I thought if I could make you understand, then she would, too."

"You took that ranch job and hoped to sort it out over the summer."

A thread of relief hissed out. Chance understood. "Yeah. Then that whole incident at the river changed everything. I never meant to hurt you. You're my brother..."

"I know." Awkwardly, Chance cuffed Kevin's shoulder. "We'll have plenty of time to catch up."

Time. How much did he really have? Once he'd seemed to have forever. Now time felt stopped in its tracks. Colorado held no appeal for him, but if nothing else, he always had Nina's ranch to return to.

"You're staying, aren't you?" Chance asked.

Kevin shrugged a shoulder. "It's not up to me."

Chance grinned. "I'll have Taryn put in a good word for you. She likes you."

"She does?"

"Stop by the house tomorrow. I'll buy you a beer."

Kevin nodded.

Chance eased into the cruiser and started the engine. "Kevin?"

Kevin slanted his brother a questioning glance.

"I'm glad you're here."

Kevin swallowed hard. Not knowing what to say, he nodded.

He watched the cruiser fade into the night, then headed toward the barn. He found Ellen crouched beside Blue, talking to Dr. Parnell. She smiled at him. His heart gave a funny little kick, then hummed.

"Dr. Parnell dressed the cuts on Blue." She scratched Blue behind the ear. The dog gazed up at her adoringly. The sight of the fresh bandage on Ellen's temple and around her wrist bruised Kevin deeply. She could have died under those frenzied hooves. "He's a real hero. I don't know how I would have gotten Luci to move if he hadn't jumped through the window."

"He's a good dog." If it came down to going away, Kevin would leave Blue here. She needed someone to look out for her.

"And guess what?"

He hadn't seen her so excited since he'd arrived, and he wanted nothing to dull that lovely light from her eyes. "What?"

"Dr. Parnell thinks he can help the horses, too."

"Now," Dr. Parnell said as he dug into his pants pocket and brought out a peppermint, "don't get your hopes up too high. I said it might work."

Luci stretched her neck over her stall door and lipped at the peppermint in Dr. Parnell's hand. With a twinkle in his eye he pretended distraction and let Luci nab the candy from his palm. She crunched it with appropriate delight, licked her lips like a kid, then searched for more.

"It's an experimental drug," Dr. Parnell continued, "but it's had good success in trials with humans who suffer from acute leukemia."

"No chemo. No radiation." She looked so pleased that Kevin wanted more than anything for this solution to work.

"Leukemia?" Kevin said. "That's what's wrong with the horses?"

Ellen nodded and gave a short snort. "Tessa knew it and wanted to hide the fact because she's got a newer model of racehorse she was planning to unveil soon. News of this genetic mutation would have ruined her chance at glory. Can you believe that?''

"I can believe just about anything," he said. They'd never know what drove Tessa, but he could understand that sometimes desperate people took desperate measures to get what they wanted. He was living proof.

"I'll see if I can hold of some STI–571 and let you know," Dr. Parnell said. He grabbed his bag. After shaking hands with Ellen and Kevin, he duckwalked out of the barn, twirling a piece of hay in his mouth.

"Isn't that good news?" Ellen said. She picked up a round massage brush from the caddie beside the door and walked into Luci's stall.

"Great," he said. "I hope it works."

As tension wound inside him, he grabbed a bar on Luci's stall. "Ellen?"

She didn't look up from her task. "Umm?"

He took in a long breath and let it out in a whoosh. "I'm sorry I lost my temper all those years ago. I never meant for what happened to happen. If I would have known..." He shook his head and stared at her stiff and very still form. "I'd take it all back if I could."

He silently cursed the crack in his voice. "I loved you, Ellen. I was crazy in love with you and it scared the hell out of me. What I did was stupid and unforgivable." Gripping the bar tighter, he rushed on. "I'm sorry, too, for lying to you. I never meant to hurt you. I only meant to protect you from more pain."

Slowly she turned. Slowly she dropped the brush in the caddie by the stall door. Slowly she raised her gaze to meet his own. Fear as he'd never known trampled through him, draining him of all strength. He'd rather meet a hundred Tessas armed with Tasers head-on than suffer the torture of trying to decipher what was going on behind Ellen's impassive face.

"I have no right to ask," he said, wishing for a tall glass of water for his desert-dry throat. His voice sounded hot and rushed to him—as frantic as the pulse galloping through his veins. "But I'd like another chance. I never stopped loving you, Ellen."

The gray-green of her eyes shone bright, but she said nothing.

"You have a right to be angry."

She said nothing for so long, Kevin thought she wouldn't.

"What happened wasn't your fault," Ellen finally said. "Garth called me from the burger joint. He told me where you'd be and came up with the suggestion to make you jealous. He thought I should pretend to come on to him. I chose to use Kent instead. Garth knew you'd get angry. He was counting on it."

And as always Kyle had played right into Garth's hand. He'd let his temper fly with disastrous results.

"I never blamed you," she said. "What Garth did, it wasn't your fault."

"I know, but it shouldn't have happened." He should have had the courage to tell her what was in his heart.

"He cost us a lot of good years together."

At the note of promise in her voice his heart skipped a beat. He dared to ask for his fondest wish. "Can we start over?"

A smile wavered on her lips. She pressed them tight, blinked madly and nodded.

A strange lightness filled him. "Okay." Whistling to Blue, he strode away, feeling reborn.

"Kevin?" Ellen stood by Luci's stall door, hanging on to the wood with a white-knuckled grip.

He shot out the barn door, counted to three, then turned around. He knocked on the barn door frame. "Hi, I'm Kevin Ransom. I hear you're looking for a ranch hand."

"You heard wrong," she said, walking toward him. Not once did she take her gaze from his. "I'm looking for a partner."

"Yeah?" He wrapped his arms around her waist and rejoiced at the purr of contentment filling him at the perfect fit of his hip to hers. "I did have a lifetime position in mind."

She quirked an eyebrow, slid her arms around his neck and smiled that glorious smile of hers. "Moving kind of fast, aren't you, mister?"

"I've got a lot of time to make up."

"That's good because this time I'm not letting you go." Her hands skimmed over the uneven skin of his face. Her expression grew serious. "I never forgot you, Kevin. Not one day went by that I didn't think of you. You and the horses, that's what kept me alive all those years." Her eyes gleamed. "I thought I'd never get the chance to tell you how much I love you."

He kissed her then, felt his heart settle, his body hum. He'd finally found his way home.

Epilogue

Fall colored the Colorado mountains all around him. Wind tinkled the golden aspen leaves at his back and reminded him of Nina's laughter. Kevin thumbed the bone feather in his jeans pocket.

The past few months had been the happiest in his life. The Thoroughbreds were slowly pulling through. C.C. and Pudge had found new loving homes. Two new boarders had joined their ragged band. He was getting to know his brother, his sister-in-law and his niece. Tessa was in jail awaiting trial. And life with Ellen was a constant feast of the unexpected. Every night when he came through the kitchen door she was waiting for him, a ready smile on her face.

Little by little he was learning to stop looking over his shoulder waiting for the other shoe to drop, for someone to steal away the peace he'd found. Not a day went by when he didn't give thanks for Nina's push to face his past.

Nina was right, he thought as he looked at the valley below. The day had come when he was ready to let the ranch go. There was just one last thing he had to do before he closed this chapter of his life.

The last time he was here he'd sung Nina's spirit home.

Horses, coats thickening against the coming winter, grazed contentedly. The noon grandfather star winked on the pond. Wind skipped through the grass. His heart suddenly grew warm, felt almost too big for his chest. In the steady rhythm of his heartbeat he sensed her and finally understood. She would be with him always. All she'd taught him lived on through him.

"I was afraid to love, Grandmother," he said to the memory of the woman who'd given him a second chance at life. "All those years, I was afraid. I'm sorry I never found the words to tell you how much you meant to me."

The wind teased at his hair.

"But you were right. By loving, fear and sadness disappear."

A pat of breeze caressed his cheek.

"I'm happy now. I'm in a good place."

Ellen walked up to him and wrapped an arm around his waist. "There you are."

"You shouldn't have walked this far."

She laughed. The sound always filled him with deep joy and immeasurable gratitude. "I'm pregnant, not an invalid."

He placed a hand over her still flat stomach. "Twins."

"You sound so sure of yourself." Her gray-green eyes shone with happiness.

"Nina told me. A boy and a girl." She'd been right about everything else.

Ellen's golden braid slid over her shoulder like liquid gold as her gaze circled the valley. "Does it make you sad to sell your land?"

He took in the mountains, the horses, the marker indicating Nina's grave. "No." Kneeling by the marker, he gently placed the bone feather at its base. *Goodbye, Grandmother. Thank you for everything.*

He rose, draped an arm around Ellen's shoulders and pressed a kiss against her temple. Leading her back to the small ranch house to sign the sale papers, he knew he'd made the right choice.

"Home is where the hum is." He smiled at her. "And you make me hum."

Nail-biting mystery…
Sensuous passion…
Heart-racing excitement…
And a touch of the unknown!

▼ Silhouette®
DREAMSCAPES...

four captivating paranormal romances promising all
of this—and more!

Take a walk on
the dark side with:

THE PIRATE AND
HIS LADY
by Margaret St. George

TWIST OF FATE
by Linda Randall Wisdom

THE RAVEN MASTER
by Diana Whitney

BURNING TIMES
by Evelyn Vaughn
Book 2 of The Circle

*Coming to a store near you
in June 2002.*

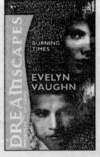

▼ Silhouette®
Where love comes alive™

Visit Silhouette at www.eHarlequin.com   RCDREAM7

A ROYAL MONARCH'S SEARCH FOR AN HEIR LEADS TO DANGER IN:

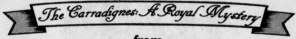

The Carradignes: A Royal Mystery

from

HARLEQUIN®

INTRIGUE®

Plain-Jane royal secretary Ellie Standish wanted one night to shine. But when she was mistaken for a princess and kidnapped by masked henchmen, this dressed-up Cinderella had only one man to turn to—one of her captors: a dispossessed duke who had his own agenda to protect her and who ignited a fire in her soul. Could Ellie trust this man with her life...and her heart?

Don't miss:
THE DUKE'S COVERT MISSION
JULIE MILLER   June 2002

And check out these other titles in the series

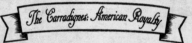

The Carradignes: American Royalty

available from HARLEQUIN AMERICAN ROMANCE:

THE IMPROPERLY PREGNANT PRINCESS
JACQUELINE DIAMOND   March 2002

THE UNLAWFULLY WEDDED PRINCESS
KARA LENNOX   April 2002

THE SIMPLY SCANDALOUS PRINCESS
MICHELE DUNAWAY   May 2002

And coming in November 2002:
THE INCONVENIENTLY ENGAGED PRINCE
MINDY NEFF

Available at your favorite retail outlet.

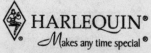

HARLEQUIN®

Makes any time special ®

Visit us at www.eHarlequin.com

HICR

TRUEBLOOD, TEXAS

Coming in May 2002…
RODEO DADDY
by
B.J. Daniels

Lost:
Her first and only love.
Chelsea Jensen discovers
ten years later that her father
had been to blame for
Jack Shane's disappearance
from her family's ranch.

Found:
A canceled check. Now Chelsea
knows why Jack left her. Had he ever loved her, or had she
been too young and too blind to see the truth?

**Chelsea is determined to track Jack down and find out.
And what a surprise she gets when she finds him!**

Finders Keepers: bringing families together